The Sink

To Stephen
W Messer
Kashe Lake
Aug. 1, 2004

THE
SINK
The Last Days of Driving

W. Messer

BRELLER BOOKS
GRAVENHURST, CANADA

Published by Breller Books
Box 789, Gravenhurst, Ontario P1P 1V1 Canada

NATIONAL LIBRARY OF CANADA
CATALOGUING IN PUBLICATION DATA

Messer, W. (Wendel), 1939-

The sink : the last days of driving
ISBN 0-9730094-0-3

I. Title.

PS8576.W765S5 2002   C813'.54   C2001-904273-6
PR9199.4.M47S5 2002

Design & typesetting by Fox Meadow Creations
Typeface is Elysium, by Michael Gill
Printed in Canada by Hignell Printing
First trade paper printing June 2002
PERMANENT PAPER

This book is dedicated to the memory of
my mother, Ida D. Messer (1908-2001),
and her father, Simon Butler, MBE

Contents

GLOSSARY

anti-confederate *Newfoundlander opposed to joining Canada in political union*

brin bag *burlap sack*

chummy *unnamed person; device, object, thing*

cracky *small dog; little person or thing*

croodle down *to hunker down*

cuddy *cabin at bow or stern of vessel for accommodation*

dishy *dishwatery; pale or sickly in complexion*

ditties *shivers*

dog rose *wild rose*

duckedy-mud *tan or brownish*

dumbledore *bumble-bee*

dung sink *drain or pit for garbage*

fess *1. bright, lively, alert; 2. odd, peculiar, unusual*

finnan haddie *smoked haddock*

fish an' brewis *dish made of cod, pork, and hardtack (pronounced: "fish an' bruise")*

fog man *supernatural creator of fog*

flapper *young, wild duck*

futter *lazy person*

gaffer *boy, young fellow*

gatcher *swaggerer, showoff*

glim *glow over a distant icefield, shimmer over ice*

harses' farts *puffballs*

jinker *person bringing bad luck (on a vessel)*

moocher *idler, loafer*

mummer *participant in Christmas tradition*
of going house to house disguised to
dance and entertain
nipper *a large mosquito*
pickle *brine, salt water*
pissabed *dandelion*
posey *any single flower; dandelion*
pucklin *boy*
ragged-arsed *tattered; disreputable*
scuff *social get-together for dancing*
shocking *very, extremely*
slew of yer eye *short time, moment*
snog *to hit*
sog along *walk slowly, sail slowly*
tallywack *rascal*
ticklesome *difficult*
tiddly *game: a short stick tapered at each end is placed*
on the ground and then struck with a longer stick;
while airborne, it is struck again.
tissy *angry, irritable*
totty *dandelion*
twite *to reproach, to taunt*
upalong *away from a person or locality;*
to or on mainland Canada or USA
whist *keep silence, hush*
yarry *quick, sharp, cunning*

Who stops being better
stops being good

Oliver Cromwell

THE PROFESSOR

As Pappy and I go outside, our next-door neighbour is busy getting grass-cutting credits. Having finished his own lawn, he's now doing ours. He's already raked up all the leaves and put them in bags. Don't, we told him years ago. Don't mow and don't do the leaves. And above all, when spring comes, don't touch our dandelions. But he wept and said he was only trying to help, so we gave our consent and told him to do whatever he had to. We also christened him "Jinkerdiddle." In Newfoundland a "jinker" is a pest.

Pappy is my dad and his real name is Albert Prince. He was born in Joe Batt's Arm, Newfoundland. At birth, a caul or membrane covered his head. The white witch said it was a sign of second sight. That was back when folk still believed cats' eyes dilated and contracted with moon and tide, and oxen knelt to pray. When he was young the fishing captains courted him for the luck he brought to their vessels, taking him on their schooners and paying him a fair share just for being aboard.

Jinkerdiddle, who's wearing his swamp-buggy shorts with flowers, mows like a fury when he sees us. I grin to put him at ease, so he won't run over the cord and electrocute himself on our lawn.

Then I move Sergeant McDuff's 2007 Ford Quasar 9 to the curb. We're all set to drive off in Pappy's 1951 Chevrolet, when the Sergeant comes running down Gascap Bend from his place. He comes to us to get his brakes done cheaply. I don't mind since I'm teaching his daughter, Julie, to drive. But right now his steely-eyed cop gaze is not turned on, and his moustache is drooping.

"Van's not ready," I tell him.

"Boys, they...they gave me a reprimand," McDuff says, putting his hand to his mouth and trying to speak low enough so Jinkerdiddle won't hear.

"We're going to visit the Professor. Hop in," I say, recognizing his need for some hand-holding.

McDuff loves riding in Chevy. She's a '51 two-door deluxe. Pappy and I spent years on her, bringing her back to life. Lots of plastic metal and fibreglass, filing and sanding. I can still feel it in my lungs. I swear never to do it again. But Chevy sure is a beaut. Pa needed a project like that, after he lost his job at MTO – the Ministry of Transportation. Best driving examiner they ever had, he was. They fired him because he never passed anyone. It's what comes of having high standards.

"Can't," says the Sergeant. "Gotta work. Wear these, you guys. It's work to rule." McDuff pulls some ribbons out of his pocket. "We got one hellava surprise for that idiot down in Queen's Park. Premier's gonna find five thousand cops on his lawn tomorrow morning. Imagine, having to file a report every time I shoot a goddarn sniper!"

"That's rough," I tell him. "You shouldn't need to do that, Duff. You're a good officer. They're trying to make it tough for you guys."

On the way to the Professor's we pick up Gloria. She's a mellow blonde, slightly past her prime, but she does have a nice figure, especially legs. I'm big on legs. She wears too much makeup and her bumpers are too large, but what the heck! Third time I picked her up she made me wait, came to the door in a silk gown I could see through. My kind of client. I told her she was wasting her money. She claims she just wants to pass the road test. Bad, bad sign.

In spite of my employer's prohibition on dating clients, I've been seeing Gloria for several weeks. Hell, some risks are worth taking.

"Hi, Dad." Gloria gives Pappy a big grin and climbs in behind the wheel. To me she sounds pushy.

Being not quite satisfied with Gloria's progress as a nascent driver, Pappy and I have decided to chance a ride

14

THE
SINK

with her, allowing her to drive us in Chevy to the Professor's. We hope Chevy will inspire her. But once we get going, Pappy rides in the back quiet as a mouse on Christmas Eve. I think he's worried. I think he has a presentiment of some impending evil.

Gloria does fine at first. We've plotted a good route to avoid trouble. But then we're passing some parked cars, and though we can't see between them, she hasn't slowed down, and so I'm asking her politely but urgently if she doesn't think she should consider it, when – a kid pops up in front of the car!

Poor Chevy's rubber burns as Gloria slams to a halt – what a way to treat Chevy! Fright-frozen, the kid escapes injury by a nanosecond, comes to life, gives us the Finger Sign, and flits.

My God!

"I told you, Gloria. I told you it's not their fault when they get hit. And that's what you almost did; you almost hit that little bugger." Gloria's in shock. She's trembling. That's why I can't help laying it on, while she's vulnerable. "Doesn't matter whether it's a cat, a dog, a raccoon, a duck, or a little brat, it's never their fault. Doesn't matter whether it's a street or the freeway ... !"

"Shuddup!"

If looks could kill, I'd be dead now. I try to think what she could be doing right. Try to find something to praise. Not a chicken peep out of Pappy. I know he's disgusted. And Chevy – there's a nervous flutter in her idle. If only Gloria had half the respect for me that Julie McDuff has! I want to say something good to her but I can't. As Pa says, her driving "can't smell no smeller."

We sit there in a long, strained silence. Is Gloria worth it, I wonder? Pappy gives a snort and a buzz; must have been asleep. It's tough for old guys to stay awake through moments like this. "You drive," Gloria sourly says at last, and we trade places. Hearing Pa stir, I suggest he tell Gloria how we met Doctor Radshak Abedni.

"Eh, what?" Pa rubs his eyes, clears his throat. "Well, girl, that was two years ago. Summer of 2008. We was polishin'

Chevy when up de street comes a great huge monster lurchin' hither and yon. A crowd of kids ran along behind. Snogged two cars on Gascap Bend, it did. They was a mess after gettin' hit by that ting. Then it went right up over Jinkerdiddle's lawn, completely destroyin' it. By then we was standin' next to Chevy hollerin' for it to stop, as we feared de worst. But it did stop all right when it smashed into Jinkerdiddle's verandah. Army personnel carrier, that's what it were. Anyways, out climbs this chummy in a turban. He were kind of duckedy-mud–brown skin, you know. Big grin on his face. First ting I seed was his teeth. He always got this big tooty grin. He did a bow to all de kids who was followin' him. Then, to us he says in an odd lilt, 'Dear me, I am unable to drive.' So we knowed he were uncommonly honest. Then he presents himself as de world's farmost expert on de human cereberellum."

"The human what?" says Gloria.

"De brain, girl. What some of us has in our skulls."

"Golly, Pappy, I just didn't hear what you said," Gloria replies, upset over Pappy's tone. Then she asks, "Where would this Abedni get an army vehicle anyway?"

"Camp Borden, that's where. Ever so often they has an auction. Now at this time de army was switchin' to de new hydrogen engines. De Doctor also got hisself a Harley. Know what that is, girl? A Harley motorbike? Lucky dog, those Harleys was still in de packin' crates. Never been used. From way back in de sixties they was. He come to us to put de bike togedder."

"Strange duck." Gloria's ruby lips are down in the corners. All that makeup's really ugly when she does that.

I can't see the grin on Pa's face but I know what he's thinking. Gloria is about to encounter the third most significant person in her life.

Doctor Abedni lives in a usually quiet old area just north of Bloor Street. Edwardian houses in outrageous colours, small lawns, huge oaks with branches cut as a penalty for interference. But tonight party sounds invest the street. The Professor himself lets us in.

"A thousand welcomes, gentlemen!" he gushes, giving us a toothy grin that reminds me of Peter Sellers. In fact, the Pro-

16

THE

SINK

fessor looks a lot like him. "Undoubtedly this charming lady is Miss Gloria?" Two cats, one black and the other white, take a cue from the master and rub themselves against our legs. "Come in, my dear friends, come in and be welcome. Live it up as they say. Ha-ha!"

Doctor Abedni and Gloria scuffle over her coat. She has no intention of being helped. The Doctor contents himself with passing her the hanger. Place is packed. Really jumping. There's a motor bike in the middle of the room, the Doctor's Harley. It's the most beautiful bike in the entire world. Shines like a god in the middle of this shabby room. It's an awful presence, ten times its street size. Clearly, it's never been on the road. It's immaculate.

There's a goonball sitting in the saddle and he's got Gloria's attention. Her eyes are all over him. A skinny, scruffy type in sweatshirt and jeans, dirty blond hair to his shoulders. Oh-oh! He notices Gloria, their eyes meet. She casts a wary glance at me, don't think I don't see it, and to cover she says to the Professor, "What's the bike doing in here, Doctor Abedni? Don't you want to ride it? It's so beautiful."

"Dear me, I do ride her, Miss Gloria." Professor's eating her up with those languid eyes of his. "At least I sit on her every day, just like Mister Jake is doing."

Gloria gives me a wry smirk and circulates. I know she's headed for Mister Jake, only her route is slyly devious. Sure enough, Jake doesn't miss this gesture of independence. He slides off the bike and slithers up to her. They dance. Can't help thinking of my sandals. Jake's got some really nice leathers. Just get a load of the way she's lapping up his words. Kitten at the cream.

"Crank 'er up," Jake says, after the dance. "Come on, Professor, buddy, let's take this hog around the block."

Doctor Abedni laughs nervously, says his bike is a show bike, not for dirty streets.

"Oh yeah? Really? Get some chrome and show her off then, buddy. Take her to the bike show. You don't have to ride her, you know."

"Golly, Jake was almost killed this morning," says Gloria. "On the 401."

"Oh no, what happened?" a broad with a ring through her

nose asks. "Did you fall off your bike?" A crowd gathers round Jake to hear what happened.

"Pugh!" says the biker, as though that is something that would never happen. "I'm on my bike, see, flyin' along, jes' flyin'. I see an overpass and I think, what if a sniper's up there? Well, you never know, eh? Anyway, as I get closer, I look up. There's a car parked there, and I see this dude silhouetted against the light. Can't make out no details or nothin'. I'm not worried. Most of them only strike at night, sonsofbitches. That's what I'm tellin' myself when I hear this crack. Somethin' whizzes by on my right real close. Christamighty!"

"A sniper!" somebody cries. All the women are oohing and ahing, especially Gloria.

Jake grins with his skinny lips. "Nah, it wasn't. It was a brake cylinder pod come off the truck in front of me. Shit, was I lucky! Didn't know what the hell it was till I read about it in *The Star*. Sonofabitch missed me. But it had somebody's number. Lady in the car behind took it right in the face. I heard the impact. Paper says it took her head clean off. Shit!"

Moans and grimaces.

Gloria sidles up to the Doctor. "Jake saw you at the Children's Safety Village, Professor. You were showing the tots how to drive in those little electric cars? My, I think that's a lovely idea."

"Indeed, my dear. Those little cars are such fun. You can drive like crazy and — and they are perfectly safe. I am — ah — a consultant, you know. But I take it upon myself to sew the seed of discontent. Small minds are impressionable, malleable. That's where our revolution begins."

I can see Gloria has a question in her mind about that last statement. She's just about to ask it when that skinny biker butts in again: "You're chicken, Doctor buddy, admit it. You got this great hog, but you're scared stiff of the road."

Abedni chuckles unconvincingly. "Got me there, young fellow. Dear me, I admit it. I am afraid. I am terrified, in fact. It is not safe, you know, not at all. You yourself almost paid your dues this morning."

"Hey, buddy, life is risk, man." The biker winks at Gloria.

"Listen, buddy, I just won a safe-driving contest. The one in the paper."

Pa and I are supposed to be impressed? "We know about that one," I can't help saying. "How to extricate yourself from five situations you should not be dumb enough to get into to begin with. Sponsored by a beer company and blessed by some guru of racing. Everybody answers correctly and the winner's drawn from a hat."

"Hey, buddy, who is this guy?"

Gloria gives me a bad face; she's good at that. I fade into the landscape but still can't help hearing that skinny biker: "Let her feel the road, sir, buddy. It's the least you can do for her. You'll get to know her. You'll find out a lot about yourself. Believe me, good buddy, amazing things could happen. Shit!"

Sure, the Doctor could have a sudden fatal encounter with kinetic energy. What a bold braggadocio this biker is! What a brain!

Pa and I are very grateful when the Professor leads a retreat into the kitchen. "Gentlemen, my plans are going to shock you," he tells us. He gives us a spicy vegetarian sandwich. We ask if his brain-scan experiments, which we read about in the paper, are about to commence.

"In due time, gentlemen, dear me. But right now I am investigating certain molecules. I suspect they act as an on-off switch for the genes controlling brain chemistry. Once we know about those molecules, no driver ever again need enter his vehicle with his brain turned off."

"A pill to turn your brain on?" I say. "That's revolutionary, Professor. Think what it will mean. No collisions. No little innocents getting killed and maimed for nothing. No more squirrels pressed into the pavement. No insurance ... "

The Professor loves to be stroked. The limpid brown eyes are deep wells of intelligent thought. This is a man who is eternally young and whose age cannot be guessed.

"Well, Mr. Rufus, of course one cannot be helped if one does not have a brain to start with, heh-heh. But as you know, even those who do have brains appear to have little use for them. Which only makes them more susceptible in old age to various degenerative dementias. At any rate, when they get in their cars, their brains are off, that is one thing for certain. They think, 'I do not need my darn brain for walking. I just walk, I just do it. I do not need my darn brain for eating. I just eat. So I will not need it for driving either. I will just get in the car and go, tra-la.' And regrettably, we see the awful result of this fallacy in the news every day."

It's Pappy's kind of talk, and he's delighted to hear it. "Right on, Professor. De minds've been sucked clean out of their little skulls."

Abedni gives Pa an odd, perhaps puzzled, look and goes on: "The crimes they commit while in this brainless state are quite bizarre. Babies crushed in their strollers, toddlers flattened in their own driveways, pedestrians dragged for blocks, or even from one city to another. Last summer a man dragged his victim all the way to Florida and back again. The remains were only discovered when he went to the local pit stop for an oil change. And the last few years, all these terrible highway vendettas, shootings, bombings—God only knows where it will all end. Something very basic is missing here, gentlemen. Something is terribly wrong with the mass of humanity."

"We call them Triffids," I say proudly.

"Triffids?"

"That's what we calls 'em," says Pa. "Well, we has to call 'em someting, don't we? Triffid's a clinical term. It be neutral. Now 'idiot' woulda done fine, had not de Triffids taken it over long ago. To de Triffids, anyone in their way's an idiot. And so, Professor, we had to have a word not in common parlance."

Abedni, whose keen eyes have been going over Pappy's plain, honest features like a microscope hot on the trail of some elusive new bug, begins to snicker in a way we have not noticed before, deep down in his gorge. "Please," he begs, "Let us not talk about Triffids."

I explain nonetheless that we get our cues from two classic movies. The term itself is from a movie about people-eating plants, *The Day of the Triffids.* But the metaphor we use takes its inspiration from another great flick, *Invasion of the Body*

Snatchers, in which human beings are replicated in giant seed pods. The mindless copies replace the originals. Everyone looks the same as before; people even do the same things they did before; but mind, soul and brain are gone.

More deep-throated snickering on the part of Abedni. His eyes are kind of wide and strange. Then he says, "Yes, I do remember those films. My goodness, they lose their humanity, do they not? They all become the same. They exist only to serve some strange and incomprehensible purpose."

"That's it," cries Pappy, eyes afire. "You got it, Professor."

"Dear me, and the *Body Snatchers* had that magnificent conclusion, Albert. The last real person in town escapes to the highway, screaming, *Stop! Please listen! You are next!* But of course nobody will stop or listen, ha-ha. They all think he is nuts. Just another idiot. And those who have already lost their minds say, *Leave him alone, no one will believe him.* And nobody does."

"That's it, that's it. There's a lesson in that movie for de tree of us. But I hopes we all concurs in recognizin' that someting in de air causes de brains of these folk to infuse, like tea bags in hot water. I tinks I knows what it is, Professor. There's a vortex up in de Bradford triangle. I seed a saucer up in Holland Marsh. It come skitterin' over de rooftops, bold and brazen as ye please, and it slowed right down to have a gander at me. Dogs was barkin' all over. Chevy was shockin' terrified. She shuddered and died on me. Radio went, lights went. When it passed over me, there were an eerie stillness, as if every livin' ting had ceased to breath. And me, I had no weight. I was all airy and without substance, like a spirit. It were not an earthly ting. Not of dis earth at all. Yep, I tinks they're de ones be messin' around wit' folks' brains."

I give Pappy a nudge, but it's too late. Whatever the Professor has inside him, now bubbles up from the depths of his soul. At first it's only a giggle, but it soon turns into violent guffaws, like some kind of animal cries – hyenas, perhaps. Abedni runs to the bathroom and tries to muffle his attack in a towel. He's there so long that we feel justified in helping ourselves to another sandwich from the fridge.

Abedni apologizes when it's over, saying he had something in his system all day. I notice he bites his lip and tries not to look at Pappy.

"Why do people drive like such pricks?" I ask, to help the Professor focus again.

Abedni regards me kindly from the depths of his being. "My goodness, they are indeed terrible little pricks. That is why I do not drive. It has been shown, Mr. Rufus, that there is a direct relationship between collision involvement and social or personal maladjustment. Oh, yes. There are far too many maladjusted people out there. Far too many. But we should not be surprised, since the founding principle of our civilization is buy-and-sell. It would appear these wounded people are trying to satisfy a whole range of lower-cortex needs – excitement, risk, power, status – all the things that were so important to us way back when we emerged from the swamp. They may not be aware of the process at all. Sometimes driver motivations are so hidden they only show up in dreams, or under hypnosis. That is why there is a big gap between what they profess and what they practise."

"Jekyll and Hyde, Professor. When they get in their vehicles, Hyde takes over."

"Yes, Mr. Rufus, you can say that. Yet, I am convinced their driving tells us something very significant about the way they live. The connection is undeniable."

From there, Professor Abedni moves on to a consideration of evil, and whether proof of extraterrestrial life would have any effect on the way we, as practitioners of evil, regard ourselves. "It will soon come to light," he says, "whether evil thrives among the stars, or whether it is a purely human preserve. The answer could have fundamental import for our relations with E.T. Indeed, for the way we will be regarded – or disregarded – out in the galaxy."

Encouraged by our admiration, Abedni launches into a general indictment of humankind, with particular emphasis on the human predilection for sexual titillation and perversion, which in the days ahead we would come to see as a steady fixation of the Professor's marvellous mind.

"Half of all males are prepared to rape if they can be certain of getting away with it, heh-heh-heh. Dear me, oh yes. Nasty little animal we are. We are prepared to do violence to our fellows. Indeed we are. All we need is a little help. The darkness of night, a lapse in civil authority, a crowd, a riot, a sports event…"

"Whoa there, not in Newfoundland!" Pappy's gaze is infinite and toward the east.

Abedni smiles and looks at him kindly. I imagine he looks like that when he has a couple of bugs under his microscope having sex.

"Albert, I appreciate that you come from a very special place on earth. There are such places where the dirt is not as thick. But speaking generally, we are a filthy animal. Indeed, we are *the* filthy animal. There are no others, ha-ha. Perhaps not in the whole galaxy. Just look at your daily paper. Look at what you read. Medical doctor uses threats to get sex. United Nations force cited in child-sex trade. Sexual harassment in the army and navy. Christian brothers being sued. 401 Bomber blows up 150 children. It goes on and on. It never stops. We are all tormentors at heart. Indeed, yes."

"My God!" says Pa, his dander up. "That's takin' a wide view, sir. Ya has us all in a leaky dory, pumpin' to keep out de pickle."

What the Doctor then says, I hold to be highly significant, both as a clue to his thought and to his intentions: "My good friends… philosophers and revolutionaries must always take wide views, if ever they are to have followers. And that is what we must do."

I like the sound of that. I take it as a promise that we three will find a common destiny in the heroic overthrow of the tyranny of the vacuous. Surely we will plot together and have stormy times ahead. Surely the world is ripe again for ideology. Surely a force will be born to stir the hearts and minds of stalwart men and women.

And so we talk into the morning, and the party noises subside. And from time to time I hear Gloria's laugh, and wonder if it isn't the laugh of a stranger.

But the Professor, who has imbibed but a single beer, grows oddly and alarmingly personal. He astounds me by clutching my sleeve and imploring me urgently, "Never, Mr. Rufus, never ever leave me alone with Miss Gloria. Promise me you will never do that. She is such a charming, exciting young lady – I cannot be trusted, you know."

I tell him I'm shocked. I can't imagine what he means. Pappy is shaking his head sadly.

"No, it is true, I am not to be trusted. I am a bad driver and a bad gentleman too. As I have pointed out, there is a definite connection. I blame my upbringing – dear me, do not we all? But my circumstances were particular. There were no girls, you know. At least, you could not see them. I could only see their eyes. Bright beautiful eyes, encompassing a world of delight and mystery. Sometimes I could smell the females. I would get as close as I dared and sniff. Sometimes they were sweating under the arms or in other places. Sometimes a girl would risk stoning and put some very mild perfume on her body. I knew the ones that did. I would walk behind them all through the village, sniffing sweat and perfume. It was so exciting!

"But then one day I realized it was not enough to smell them. I had to touch them. Do you understand how important it is just to be able to touch a female? Well, I did it. I touched a female. I touched quite a few females, heh-heh. And to my great surprise, they let me.

"But after a while it was not enough, you see. It occurred to me that I needed to squeeze them. I had to feel what they were made of. So I bought a bicycle and I would run into the village girls on my bike. Yes, that is correct, I would knock them down and fall on them, ha-ha. Amazing how wonderful it felt! Exhilarating! Sometimes I hurt them. They cried. That was wonderful too. They always thought it was an accident, ha-ha. I would apologize and beg their forgiveness. They were only too willing to forgive. They would look right into my eyes, telling me with their eyes that they enjoyed it too. My, how the blood raced! I developed hypertension as a result of it…"

There is a heavy silence. Why does such a luminary have to have so gross a flaw? But at least he's not hiding it, I suppose. The kitchen door opens and a blond head intrudes. It's scruffy Jake, the biker, invading our precinct like an angel of mercy to say good night. I wonder if Gloria is getting ready to leave with him. Good riddance, then!

"Hey buddy," Jake says to Abedni, "you can get that baby customized at Hogtown, the chopper shop. A chopped hog is what you want, sir. A chopped hog."

"I just want to ride it east or west," Abedni tells us when Jake is gone. "I want to ride that bike clear across the country. If only it were safe out there, that is where I would be. On my beautiful bike."

I give Gloria and the goonball biker time to clear the premises. Abedni seems to sense this, as he offers us coffee. And so we continue our inquiry far into the night, passing good and evil, and this mundane world; seeking out the crushing mysteries of the cosmos, and plotting a future realm of reason, as far as three good brains unaided can.

At last we decide to conclude, but not before a parting exhortation from the Doctor. "Be good, gentlemen, and endeavour to control the noise."

I give him a quizzical look.

"The static of disparate impulses, gentlemen. The debris that competes for the space in our skulls. Beware of it. May the great peace come over you. Form through peace. Content through form. No form, no spirit. No spirit, no content. People without form are all the same. They have no spirit, and so they are like your Triffids, Mister Pappy. They serve no purpose but to hold gas and water. They are walking gas-and-water bags. Beware of the gas-and-water-bag culture."

"Right on," I say and yawn. Where the devil is he heading? Pappy is scratching himself behind the ear, like a dog waiting for something more interesting to develop.

"Silence – that, my friends, is what the world needs. A grand, roaring silence, as thundering as Niagara. To flush out the mind. To give it some breathing space. So it can resist the culture of formlessness. The monks and hermits of old well understood this. Silence is more than golden. Without it the brain does very little ... "

"I don't like pop music neider," says Pappy.

Surely it is singular stuff for the ears of an old Newfie.

Especially when the Professor quits stickhandling and lets fly with a slapshot right into the unguarded net: "I should very much like to introduce you, dear friends, to the incomparable rewards of yogic flying."

His proposal is delivered with astounding ingenuousness. Yogic flying? Sure, we know about that. A bunch of dumb weirdos jerk their butts around on mattresses. If they try hard, they're supposed to levitate. Leave the padding and fly away. Fat chance! In my mind's eye I see Abedni with a whole troop of turbanned flyers, bouncing like frogs at night on a road through a marsh.

It's not something a man from Joe Batt's Arm can handle. So now it's Pa's turn to suffer hysterics. What makes it worse is that he's not able to laugh without getting the hiccups. Poor Pa, he needs half an hour in the bathroom to cure his condition.

Doctor Abedni wisely spends the remaining time in smalltalk.

What a surprise when a bedraggled Gloria appears in the kitchen doorway! My surmise has been unjust. She's apparently been asleep in the living room. She gives me a kiss and I give her one back.

"Up the revolution!" the Professor cries as we climb into Chevy.

"Death to the Triffids!" I call back.

2

DRIVING TO A STANDARD

I've got Sergeant McDuff's daughter for a lesson. She has
dark, compelling eyes and long, dark hair, and she's a great
student. I like her. She tells me Joey Slimeball Snookums, a
creep who goes to Hillcrest High, has been following her
home from school in his pink Mustang. Wants to take her to
the drag race at Blind Summit. But then as we get into traffic
I shut up. You can't really talk and drive at the same time.

We're approaching a major intersection. Left turn coming
up. Julie signals and fades left. Good so far.

We're in the turn lane, we're on our diagonal, we enter the
intersection, we straighten in line with the oncoming turn
lane, in which a wide truck is waiting to turn left. We're one
metre farther left than the guy behind. This time, however,
it's not enough. We can't see. We don't make the turn. We
wait.

We're not moving. Trucker on the other side can't make his
left, we can't make ours. We wait and we wait. Julie lets the
car creep. I have my own brake but almost never use it. I ask
her if she can see.

"No."

"Then stay on it."

There's a truck behind us too, and now he's rumbling and
revving, rocking and snorting. All that racing he did on the
401 to save a minute, it's all gone now. So he shows his
muscle and kills the space between us. We're only a ladybug
in the path of mobilotyrannosaurus. I picture the operator
looking down on us from his cab in the clouds. I see a cave
man. His name is Ally Oop.

27

*Last Days
of Driving*

Buuuaaaaahhhhh!

Just what I feared – the hairy hand on the horn. The raging trumpet of this mastodon has rent the world and shortened Julie's life and mine. Can I blame her for doubting? For thinking that maybe, if she doesn't move, this monster behind is going to ram us? After all, it happens every day. So can I fault her for coming off the brake a bit and letting the car roll again?

"Stay on it," I say.

Light turns amber.

The great bull behind bellows again. We shudder. Take a chance, he's telling us. Get moving. But as we still can't see, we don't. And then – an oncoming 2008 Thunderbird races through blind at the end of amber! It's the one that had our number. It's the one that would have creamed us. It's the dork destiny trained to kill us.

But Ally Oop does not understand.

Light turns red, we still have seconds, we creep into the turn, see the way is clear, and get out of the intersection. We take the first right, into a little side alley, to purge ourselves of poison, and to be rid of Ally Oop. (I have his number in my little black "Doomsday Roster.")

"Now, Julie, suppose you'd made the turn blind. We collide with the Thunderbird, get ourselves crushed and broken, pressed together with torn and mangled steel, shattered glass. We're wet with our own blood. The pain of squashed and riven bone is unbearable. We barely apprehend the busy sounds around us. We hear the ambulance. But we're already sliding into silence eternal. We just want to die. The paramedics won't reach us in time.

"And so we die, Julie. We draw the losing ticket. But our noble trucker, he prides himself on getting it right for the police: 'She screwed up but good, officer. She couldn't see that Thunderbird comin'. Instructor she had was one helluvan idiot.'

"And then, Julie, the media arrive to capture our mistake and our last moments of agony. It's news and people need to know about it. Close-ups of the blood, our blood. Questions to the police, who only say, 'Tragic,' and shake their heads, meaning we should've known better. And the papers all say,

Tragic. And so does the priest at our funerals. But the trucker, he goes to the line dance and has a good time."

"I hate to think of it," Julie replies, heaving a sigh and running the fingers of one hand through her long, dark hair. "All those killers out there who get away with it. People like that truck driver. Nobody ever knows the carnage they leave behind."

"You're right. Nobody does."

I drop Julie off, certain that from now on all her left turns will be good ones. When I get home, I discover she forgot her workbook under the passenger seat. Oh well, slide it under her door tomorrow.

While Pappy and I are just finishing a supper of pickled herring and boiled potatoes plus sour cream – with beer it's great – Professor Abedni calls. I hear Pa say, "Everyone tinks only a small minority be jinkers. Yep, dey tink about ten percent. 'Tis always this mythical 'udder guy'."

I make it to the upstairs phone in time to hear Abedni say: "Definitely. I would say so. Yes, as high as ninety percent. Give or take a few. We agree on that then, Albert. Dear me, if we can prove it, they will not find it so convenient to blame some phantom."

"That's a big 'if'," I interject.

"Oh, there you are, Mr. Rufus. Not to worry. I have access to all the tools we need. U of T, ha-ha-ha – I am an invaluable adjunct to their international image. The University gives me a free hand to do just as I please."

"Yeah, we knows yer a good man," says Pa.

"Thank you, Albert. But now let us get down to brass tacks, shall we? I am planning a – well, a convention – at Convocation Hall – yes, at the University. We must all be there ... "

The Doctor cackles convulsively. When he continues he does not sound like himself. I surmise he's placed a towel over his face, or even stuffed it into his mouth. He fires off some mumbo-jumbo and hangs up.

It appears he was trying to say, "Leave your Triffids at home."

As it's a shocking fine fall evening, we agree to help

Sergeant McDuff with his latest car problem. His Quasar 9 is vibrating like a jumbo jet on the shortest way down. "Sure we'll take a look," I say. We love Quasar 9s. Last Ford vehicle powered by an internal-combustion engine. And next to the smells of good cooking, there's nothing better we like than the sweet, familiar odours of oil, grease, and gasoline. It's just not the same with the new technologies.

"Devilmajig of a doohickety-jigglewick!" That's Pa's comment as he finishes his inspection down under and slides into view again. He climbs in behind the wheel and turns the key. Engine still spits and rattles furiously, as if trying to self-destruct. Coughs, chokes, dies.

"Well, byes, we got us a mystery!"

"Shoulda taken it to Canadian Tire," McDuff grumbles.

Pappy pays no heed. He wouldn't let the van go now anyway. He retires to Chevy to think. He turns on the radio:

I—I just went nuts—When it hit, I went nuts. First thing through my mind was—my kids! Where are they? My family?

"Turn that up!" cries McDuff. "A sniper just shot somebody!"

If I'm gone what are they gonna do? I thought they might fire again and this time they'd get me… It ricocheted off the hood, tore a chunk out of the fibreglass, hit the windshield. Jesus, was I lucky!

"De revolt against de Triffids has begun," Pappy solemnly announces from Chevy.

I can see McDuff's still in the dark about Triffids. He thinks "Triffid" is another Newfoundland word; I can tell by the look on his face. Ever since we gave him a Newfoundland biscuit to chew on and he broke a tooth—I found the biscuit later in our garbage can—he's pretty well turned off anything from down there.

Pappy's wrong. The freeway snipers are Triffids suffering from full-blown road rage. But because McDuff is present, I keep it to myself. I don't want to talk about Triffids in front of just anyone.

Sergeant McDuff, who's been shifting his weight strangely and giving us odd glances, now stiffens. His moustache bristles. "Have to ask a few questions," he declares.

I look him right in the eye. Now what?

"Questions?" says Pa from Chevy.

"Now don't get your dander up, Albert. Just a few routine questions."

Pa slithers out of Chevy, like a snake investigating bad news. "Questions?"

Duff takes a couple of steps back as Pa approaches. For a cop he sure is timid. "Now, guys," McDuff says, "chief told me to ask you some questions, that's all. It's not my fault. We have this – ah – this profile. There are a few points of concordance..." McDuff is sweating and shifting his weight from foot to foot. Looks like a rookie practising his first arrest.

"Nunny-fudger!" Pa calls him. "Bet you paid big bucks for that profile. Made in de U.S.A., idinit?"

"Now listen, Albert –"

"You listen. I'll tell ye what it says. Eccentric, unemployed, paranoid weapons freaks wit siege mentality, big chip on their shoulders. Got a debt to settle wit all udder drivers. Wadaya tink of that, fuzzfunk?"

"Jeez, Albert, not bad!"

Pa gives me a look, and I know what he means. Cops wasted their money on this one. "Don't bother askin' where I been either. I can't recall nuttin' further back than de night before."

"Same here," I tell him.

Duff seems relieved he got that far unscathed. "Well, I know you guys are okay. I knew you wouldn't mind. Well, I – I'll go phone for a tow."

Pa ignores that. He climbs back in the van and starts to tinker and mutter. Duff tries some small talk. When we don't respond to that, he tries to butter us up.

"Got to hand it to you guys at Galaxy Drivers," McDuff says. "I thought it was all malarkey at first. Kids in my day didn't need to bother with lessons. My dad took me out to the country, showed me how to use the pedals, and away I went. Never had no trouble. Well, few scrapes and bumps – who doesn't have those, eh? But Julie, she thinks she can do better than that. She swears most of us could drive collision-free forever, if we had a mind to. Yep, you sure got her attention."

I tell McDuff he'd do well to study her progress, if he hopes to grow old.

"Yeah, right. Some things take a lot of getting used to though. All that space she leaves when we stop for a light. I can't help telling her to move up. But she won't. Doesn't listen to her dad anymore. And when I'm driving – you should hear her! All she does is find fault. She's always telling me how Rufus would do it. Must be gratifying when kids take you so seriously. My opinions are worth nothing. Absolutely nothing."

"Right, McDuff, your opinions on driving are worth nothing. And yes, I am gratified. It's the progress of kids like Julie that keeps me going. I think I've given her what she needs to be free. She'll never be just another braying lamb in the fold. She'll never run with the wolf pack. Think of what it means. She'll rise to the full stature of our race. There are very few like that. Very few."

"Well, if you say so, Rufus. Some things are tough to understand, though. Take last Sunday. Julie and I are on this busy four-lane street. Julie stops for a light. She's way back of the guy in front – just a huge space. She says to me, 'If a few cars come up behind, my rear's protected, so I might move up. But not all the way up, because I don't want to be boxed in either.' That's what she said. Son of a gun, eh?

"Yep, I always thought it was just a matter of driving up close enough to the guy ahead so you could smell his gas. Julie says, 'Uh-uh, that will make you impotent.' Christ, I never thought of that."

Pappy's standing on a chair, and his head is under the hood. He still hasn't done anything – just hovers there looking, waiting for the right cue, like a hound dog.

"So we're at this light, Rufus, and the car's just slowed down to a stop. There's a gas station on our right and this gentleman is exiting from the pumps. He moves out over the sidewalk right where we are. He sees all this space we got in front of us. He thinks we're going to move up so he can get in behind us – because there's one helluva string of cars behind.

"He goes 'honk-honk!' Now me, I would've moved up. Jeez, it's only courtesy, isn't it? Besides, he might be armed. Let's face it, these days anything can happen. So I say, 'What are ya gonna do if he jumps out and starts firing at us?'

"'Well, in the first place,' she says, 'It's not courtesy. I'm driving to a standard. How can I do that if I'm compromising it to do every jerk a favour? If he jumps out with a weapon, I'm ready. If we were boxed in, we'd have to get out and run, and he'd mow us down. But see, with all the space I have, I can move up over the curb and take off around the corner. Don't worry, Rufus showed me a thing or two.' Can you beat that? Then she says, if my generation had taken a stand instead of being so cowardly, we wouldn't be in the mess we're in today.

"I tell her she's being unreasonable. She says, 'Daddy, I need this space. I'm not giving it up.'

"Well, by now this gentleman blows his rad cap. His hand's on the horn and he's got his arm out the window giving us the Finger Salute. Then he gets out of the car and comes over to tell us off. When we don't roll down the window, he starts pounding on it. I've just persuaded myself that I need to intervene when the light turns and we take off. We had a good laugh over that. Julie stayed on the brake through it all. Did not budge. She was right to do it, wasn't she?"

I tell him whatever's not safe is stupid. I tell him space is life insurance. I tell him space is sacred, and a good driver surrounds himself with it. I tell him, if you don't have space, you don't have time either. Even Einstein, quite average when it came to driving, understood that.

I congratulate him on the progress of his thinking and invite him to our meeting at Convocation Hall. At that precise moment, Pappy cries, "Ouch!" Either he hurt himself or I have erred in extending this invitation to McDuff.

"Let me phone for a tow," McDuff says. "I appreciate the effort…"

"Quiet!" I command, giving McDuff my elbow. I can see Pa is about to triumph by the way he glows. Yep, definitely. Now he's starting to sing:

My dear, I'm bound for Canada;
Love Sally, we must part.
I'm forced to leave me blue-eyed girl,
All wit an achin' heart;
To face cold-hearted strangers,
All in some foreign land...

Pappy, who has been caressing the distributor cap, now feverishly unscrews it. He's found the trouble, all right. Even McDuff can see him glow now. Like a magician, Pa fetches a clean white cloth out of nowhere, gives it a triumphal flourish, wipes the inside of the cap, which he then screws back, and declares the operation a success.

"Is that all?" says McDuff, dubious.

"That's all. Gi lang wid ye now, McDuff."

McDuff climbs in the van, turns the key. The motor runs like butter and oil. Pa tells him to get some coolant and come back tomorrow for a gasket. Duff starts to back out, stops. "What the devil was wrong, Albert? What was making it vibrate?"

"Coolant in de distributor, Nunnyfuzz."

"Oh?"

"One more thing, Duff," I tell him. "Next time, back in. Good drivers back in."

"Yeah, sure."

"Oh, and don't forget the meeting."

"Son of a gun, what's it all about anyways?"

"Trouble. Just be there."

McDuff eases out into the roadway. Sometimes he's not as dumb as he lets on.

3

THE HOLD-UP

Traffic is sparse as we ride the back roads through woods and
fields that are mauve, crimson, and gold. Small birds flit
among the ranks of dried-out cornstalks, and geese gather at
ponds to persuade themselves to migrate. Horses frolic
where hay stands in great wheels ready to roll on the yet-
green grass. Chevy, dust-defying, purrs all the way. Chevy
loves a dirt road. Last year Pappy threatened to replace the
engine, but Chevy talked him out of it and has been keen to
perform ever since.

As we turn into the orchard, the smiling, red-faced apple
farmer comes to greet us with a jug of cider. "Gut ta see ya,"
he says.

We drink a sample in small white paper cups and ask how
the crop is. What we'd really like to know is how much
money he makes. He doesn't tell us. No more than he did last
year. The more he grins, the more we see him depositing at
the bank.

"Great cider!" I say. "Got any apples left?"

"Oh, *ja*."

"You must be making money," I try.

"Oh, *ja*!" He laughs, surveys the apple trees. "*Ja, ja*."

"Well, see ya."

"Two hundred apples on this one," Pa says, when we're
deep among the trees eating apples. "Fifty trees per row.
We'll count de rows after."

We pay Mr. Appleseed five bucks for our bag. "Oh, *ja*, small
crop but really gut apples. Lousy spring. Rain too much. No
darn bees."

We leave him grinning and laughing, as if he's keeping from us something really big. Can't be because he makes his cider from the apples that fall on the ground?

Gloria's waiting with pie shells, brown sugar, cinnamon, and cloves. I ask her to skip the cloves, but we make some with and some without; they're all delicious. Gloria looks so good with her blonde hair tied in a ponytail that I have to sneak a few hugs. She's very mature in her ways, very much at ease with Pappy. I really must cock a snook at Galaxy Drivers for expecting me not to have a relationship with her just because she's their client.

Pappy's still wary of her, though. In his eyes she has yet to prove herself. And it's quite true, we just don't know how she'll turn out. Her driving stinks. And I really wish she'd go easy on the perfume, powder, and lipstick. I keep telling her, a little goes a long way.

It's Halloween. In my time the older kids used to set piles of leaves on fire and drop cannon crackers into door letter-openings. If there was a second door, the blast was particularly devastating. It was stupid and mindless, but they were too old to go house to house with bags. The magic had gone, and they didn't know it was time to quit. What they did know was, it wasn't fun any more. A smart kid will do this kind of thing once or twice and then give it up. Kids will always do something that's in relation to the images in their skulls. If I were a kid today, I wouldn't bother with fire-crackers. I'd be putting dynamite in their porches.

Pa's writing a book. He's been writing it for twenty years. It's supposed to be a book on manners, but you'd never know it. Tonight there's a chapter spread out on the dining-room table. It's entitled, "Contemporary Irreverences," and I see it has to do with Halloween:

Nothing can gratify the expectations of kids today. On Halloween night they go out with a pumpkin, symbol of the celebration. But when they're finished with it, symbol immediately transforms to mere used commodity. As commodities have no sanctity, they destroy it. Many kids are not up to the challenge of having to take home a pumpkin that will be in tomorrow's garbage anyway. In this, as in everything, they take their cues from the parents. (Triffids!)

I have to tell Pappy that this stuff is a bit off the mark for a book on manners. And what has it got to do with Triffids? But it's no use. He claims to have a wide mandate. Says it's all about making connections.

Gerdie, who lives just a couple of houses down on Gascap Bend, comes over for the usual Halloween colcannon, which is a hash of cabbage, potato, and turnip, sometimes with pork or rabbit in it. Might smack of Dogpatch to folks around here, but the truth is, people like what they're used to. You're supposed to eat it till you burst, or at least till someone finds the button hidden in it. Gerdie's an old maid about Pa's age, originally from St. John's – Toronto's crawling with Newfies. She never found the button, which is why she never married. The young men don't want to find it, as it dooms them to bachelorhood forever. When my mother was living we used to have pumpkin pie and colcannon at midnight on Hallo-ween. That's the custom, can't remember why. Guess it's why things change, because we don't remember.

When Gerdie was a little girl, there was an old lady living in the woods who had a tribe of cats. The locals, believing her to be a witch of the blackest kind, dressed up as mummers and killed her, and every cat they could lay their hands on too. The villagers managed to keep it to themselves. It's the reason Gerdie gives for rooting out the dandelions as soon as they appear. She's always been afraid of offending the neigh-bours. But since the era of rage began back in the late nineties, her fears have intensified.

"You be right, old girl," says Pa. "'Tis hard to keep a single posey. They hates 'em wit a vengeance in this city. Jinker-diddle cuts down ourn, as we won't do it ourselves. Nuttin' prettier than a lawn full of totties, I says. They makes good wine, totties does. And young, tender totty greens, I loves 'em. Spring tonic. Wish I had a plateful now wit butter and vinegar. 'Winegar' dey used to say down in old Lunenburg, remember Rufus? Yep, Rufus and me, we be positively foolish for totties."

My lesson with Julie has to be cancelled. Practically the whole of Hillcrest High is going to the funeral of two girls killed while making a left turn. I will not attend, since I didn't know the two deceased. Some students of mine, who did know them, assure me they have been trying hard to get friends and parents to drive safely. I tell them, good for you. But Pappy and I know they're wasting their time.

"How does we separate those poor kids from de greatest corruptin' influence in their lives – mom and dad? That's what you got to do, Rufus bye."

Hell, I'm already pushing the limits. Just last week Lenard Klutz' father phoned Galaxy Drivers to complain about me. Said I talked too much and wouldn't let the kid drive. Said I was trying to turn the boy against him. It was an incredible story, and of course nobody at Galaxy believed it. (Or if some of them did, they didn't let on.)

Since Julie is attending the funeral, I fit Lenard Klutz into the spot. As his driving is such an abomination, I've been concentrating on his mind. Last lesson I told him to forget his old man, who is a rotten influence. I suggested he might consider leaving home.

"Klutz," I told him, "Your old man put you at a real disadvantage. Pack your bags and get out of there. You're in more danger driving around with him than you would be kicking around the streets of Toronto."

He resisted. So I had to bring him down a peg or two. I had to show him how far he was from his self-image. Time he learned he's not Number One.

"Now listen up, Klutz. Here's what you've accomplished so far. You allocate all your attentional capacities to the driving task – the mechanics. The result is, you miss everything else. You don't know how to distribute your attention adaptively. Got that, little worm?"

Boy, wouldn't they love to hear that at Galaxy? Wouldn't they love the hamburgers I give him? Way too much meat, they'd say. Where the hell's the bun? Meaning my hamburgers are all criticism, no praise. Too much beef, they'd cry. It's way over his head. Too much hot sauce. It's pure abuse.

"In other words, Klutz, your visual fixation patterns are a big hinder. Your dependence on peripheral clues is absolute.

Your perceptual judgements are non-existent. You miss relevant variables. Your failure to adapt from one speed zone to another is abysmal. Time and space, Klutz, they're key concepts in creation. Distance and velocity and acceleration — they're all related to time and space. Do you know any of that, chum? Do you know you can't drive like a human being without having mastered this stuff? I'd rather take a chimpanzee to the road test than you."

Klutz gave me such a beaten look. "I—I thought all you had to do was use the pedals and steer," he whined. "I guess my dad's right. Everything I do stinks. I—I'm just a little turd with mousy hair and glasses. No wonder the girls don't like me!"

"Right on, Klutz. Glad to hear you say it. You have to really know what you're worth if I'm going to help you. We agree, then. You're not Number One. You're just a stinking little turd and everything you do smells. Is that right?"

"Yes, sir."

So I took him to the remotest part of the mall and let him practise curb parking. I gave him a burger with lots of bun, hardly any meat, so he'd go home with a positive charge on his brain.

That was last week.

This week he takes me by surprise. I think he's had his grey matter to the laundry during REM sleep. Amazing things can happen in the rapid-eye-movement phase of slumber. The proof is, he's refused to take any more lessons from his dad. Progress at last!

"Well, Lenard, you're on the moral highroad. But I want you to humour your old man for a while, short of getting in the car with him, of course. That will throw him completely off his guard."

He calls me a genius and he's all keyed up. He gives me his "crime of the week," which he's cut out of *The Star*, about a man who backs up in his driveway over his two-year-old son. Perfect. A real classic. Nobody ever checks those blind areas. Nobody ever thinks to back in, so when they leave the house, they're coming front-first down the driveway. They'd rather make it a lottery. Somebody, sometime, has to draw the losing ticket. Too bad it has to be the little guy.

I praise him and he takes from his workbook a mess of other clippings. He's been clipping all week. It occurs to me he may be hoping to do the entire lesson at curbside. Can't have the old man phoning the school again. I'm not supposed to work on the brain.

"Just one more now, Lenard."

He selects a favourite, and I give it a glance. *Run-away car hits Good Samaritan. Hit again by three more vehicles — none stops. Quote from one of the drivers: "I thought it was garbage."*

"So, young man, what is to be learned from this?"

"Easy, Rufus. You stop to help one Triff, you get killed by another. Never stop to help anyone. The age of chivalry is gone forever."

Well, I am astounded. Klutz has all the answers. "Bravo, young man! Bravo! Your progress has been amazing. I never quite expected you to go this far. Super performance."

Klutz can't stop now. He's a little worm hungry for a kind word: "Some of the nicest people are Triffids. Dads who tuck in the babies at night. Kindly grandmothers. You just never know. Triffids are everywhere. Disguised as real people. They're just waiting to get us. So the word is, never trust. Always be suspicious. Never turn your back. Never take anything for granted. Never —"

"Top marks for that, my boy. You're ready for something special now, aren't you, Lenard? Supposing I were to ask you to recite the Litany?"

Other times Klutz shrank from doing the Litany, but now he goes for it like a cub scout eager to reel off the Promise: "There are no accidents. There are no acts of God. There are no terrible tragedies. There are only Triffids and the crimes they commit. No Triffid is ever blameless, even when obeying the limit. Good drivers do not have collisions unless hit by an earthquake, a tornado, a stellar body, a missile, airplane toilet ice, or a sniper. I therefore promise never to blame the weather, especially not the snow and ice of True North. Nor will I blame the road or anything on it. I will take full responsibility for my driving. Amen."

I praise him lavishly for this. All bun and garnish, none of the meat. I begin to believe in the possibility of his ultimate redemption, even in the redemption of many Triffids. Klutz is on a roll and I intend to make it work for him. We forego the drive for today altogether. (Fireworks when Daddy Klutz finds out.) Tonight, as he sleeps under the rising moon, Klutz will come to terms with himself and his destiny as a real person. It is my earnest hope that the Triffid in him will die.

"Before we part, Lenard, sign of the Triffid?"

"Stupidity."

"And?"

"Conformity. They love to be as dumb as everyone else. Their voice is the Horn, their flag is the Finger."

"Well done, my boy, well done."

In the full of the moon, while Klutz struggles with the Triffid inside him, I get out of bed and drive to a convenience store, where I buy a girlie mag and a carton of cream. The mag is one I've noticed before, though I've never thought of buying it, nor have I even looked inside the cover.

On the way there, I'm aware of my bare foot on the pedal — I like it. I'm also aware it's cold. I wonder why I'm not wearing a coat. I feel loose and free. I can do whatever I want. It's not every night one goes to the store in a red scarf and pyjamas.

I get there in jig time, missing stop signs and even a red light. The store broad looks surprised and frightened. She puts her hand to her mouth when she spies me (I like that). My eyes are wide open. But I see only what I want to see. I'm in a trance, somewhere between dreaming and waking.

In effect, I have become a Triffid.

Only once before have I somnambulated. I thought I was at Uncle Jed's cottage on Moon River. But it was the backyard at Gascap Bend. I went out and peed on the dandelions. And yet, I remember having the presence of mind to check the Jinkerdiddles' for any sign of activity.

The store girl's fear turns me on. I'm in the Stone Age. I wave my Glock at her, I think it's my Glock. I rarely go out without it these days. Her scream is terribly thrilling. Torture, it's in my blood. Make her suffer. She throws cash on the counter. I walk out with the cream, the mag and the cash. I think the cream is to make shrimp soup from a recipe in the paper.

On the way home an idiot gives me trouble. He follows me, banging on his horn and flashing his high beams. Very dangerous game. Maybe I'm a hit man. Maybe I'm a sniper. What the hell does he want anyway? An apology for the way I drive? A bullet in the brain?

At a stop sign he's right on top of me, so I leap out and stick my Glock in his face. Oh boy, what a thrill! I always thought this kind of thing was crap in the movies. But when it's real it's super. No animal likes to be tormented. If you torment me, I bite back. Boy do I bite this guy!

I poke the Glock in his ear, take the car keys. What a rush! Talk about power! Thought you had the jump on me in that Mercedes, eh? Well, here's the equalizer. Know who I am, bud? – I'm Number One. That's who I am.

I make him get out and sit on the curb. He's trembling and whimpering. Hey, what happened to the big man? I love it. I feel the way I did in grade school when I had an invincible chestnut on a string. It was vinegar-soaked, oven-dried, and hard as granite. I destroyed five champion chestnuts without mine taking a scratch. We had no knives or guns in those days, but we were tough little buggers just the same.

I pour my cream over the idiot as he sits there shivering, then I make him walk. My wheels spin, rubber burns, pebbles fly. And I'm gone.

Come morning I remember it quite well, awakening with a vague feeling of accomplishment. Pappy learns of it over bacon and eggs.

"Great to give 'em tit for tat, idinit?"

"Yeah, Pa. Guess the urge was in me. Just been tormented too many times. Maybe we all kinda hate each other at heart. Maybe that's what it's come to. Maybe all this rage is just folks being honest with one another. I'll return the loot."

"Long's we don't hate each udder, Rufus. Better croodle down and lay low till de blow be over."

"Yeah, Pa, that's what I'm gonna do. Croodle down and lay low."

PARTY SLOGANS

Hamburger and coffee at Bea's. It's chili I want, but the new manager screwed that up. He's fresh from their training session, "Bea's Burger Mind Bend," and all souped up. Last time, he had my chili coming even before I got in from the parking lot. That was after I'd ordered chili three days in a row. I guess he thought I'd go on ordering it forever.

Today is the day I burst that little bubble.

"Cancel chili!" he barks. "One burger!" The Mind Bend smile reappears. "No problem, sir. Absolutely no problem."

"No relish," I tell him without smiling.

I feel like drawing my Glock and letting him have it. Especially when they turn the music up. What the hell, they shoot people for less on the highway. Guess I'm suffering from burger-joint rage.

Lately, I carry my handgun everywhere, because you can't be too careful. I keep it in a deep pocket. Stroking it reassures me. "Go forth unafraid," my trusty Glock says to me. "Drive through the darkest alleys whilst fearing not to obey the rules of the road, for I will protect thee from the asphalt savages."

I like the washroom. It's the first consideration for anyone involved in defensive living. Bea's washroom has a door I can open in and out with a touch of my foot. My one firm rule is, never let bare skin touch anything. That includes faucets and doorknobs. Nine out of ten washroom users either don't wash, or else they get their hands all over the taps. Third world standards. They go unwashed from toilet to salad bar, and hover there along with the fruit flies.

I can't help them. Triffids do not take enlightenment easy.
They want more bun and less beef in their burgers.

Oh-oh, I'm halfway through my hamburger when an ugly
spectre invades my mind, a filthy beast, the shadow of E.
coli 0157:H7, alias haemolytic uraemic syndrome. Yes, otherwise
known as hamburger disease. Can I really trust those guys in
the kitchen? What do they know about E. coli?

Place is crowded. See how they all munch and chatter away,
as if there were not a care in the world. Their lives depend on
those guys in the kitchen. I glance at the new manager, busy
taking orders and smiling. I roll up the rest of my burger in
a serviette and dump it in the bin. Sandwiches for lunch
from now on.

What will the new manager think when I don't show up
tomorrow? Will he rack his brains trying to figure what he
did wrong? Will he try to smile harder? Will he double-
check the burgers?

In the parking lot I encounter McDuff on his way in. I tell
him Julie's overdue for a lesson. I can't seem to reach her. He
gives me that neutral, steely-eyed look that cops cultivate.
You either want to tell the truth or run.

"Thought *you* might know the answer to that," he says.

Talk about deadpan!

I head for my wheels, but turn and call out, "Don't touch
anything!"

Lenard Klutz continues to progress. His lesson is entirely
uneventful. So I have him return home early, to test his mind
for the great strides I have anticipated in REM sleep.

He does a beautiful curb park. "Now, Klutz, before you get
out of the car, before you open that door, what are you going
to do?"

"Check behind," comes the answer, quick as the crack of a
whip. Success is really making him sharp. "Might be somebody there. A bike, a skater, a roller-boarder, a runner, a
scooter, car, truck, bus – or even a carjacker."

"Thank you, Lenard. Oh, look at the pedestrian over there,
the one passing between the two parked cars! See?"

Klutz squints, adjusts his glasses. "What? Yeah, I see him. Wait a minute, there's a driver in one of those cars. Good way to lose your legs. Never trust. Never rely. Maybe they've got an old manual trans, maybe they're in a hurry, maybe they just can't drive. Presto, no legs."

"Hey Lenard, you're hot."

"Maybe they're on drugs, maybe they didn't get any sleep, maybe—"

"That will do, Lenard."

"Yes, sir. Oh, another one. I see another one."

Sure enough. It's a young lady tucking in her baby, ignoring the chaos around her as if it were unimportant, as if it had nothing to do with her and her baby. As if anyone ever can ignore the world and its burgeoning population of dorks and still be secure! She's like a bird on a back fence in a yard full of cats. Worse, because she can't fly away.

"She's asking for it, isn't she, sir? Anything can happen. She's thinking, I'm safe on the sidewalk. I'm safe because people are sane. I'm safe because people are in control. I'm safe because there are laws. I'm safe because the sun is shining—"

"Yes, thank you, Lenard. Is she right to think that way?"

"Are you kidding, sir? She's dreaming. All those people around her, they're not real. They're Triffids. Do they care about her and her baby? No, they don't care. Look at her, all she sees is her little bundle in the bunny suit. Silly twit."

Now at last Klutz is using the word "Triffid" with reverence and conviction. His grip is tight on the wheel, as if he has some Triffid bastard by the throat.

I have one last question: "That guy waiting for the bus, the guy in the shelter—good place to be?"

"Gimme a break, sir. It's a trap. You know it's a trap. The Triffids want everything to result in occasional death. He's trapped in a glass cage. It's suicide."

"Astounding, my boy, truly astounding." This is my hamburger for Lenard Klutz.

As I arrive home, I spot Gloria's bicycle in the driveway; she will be doing her lesson from my place. Pappy is at the living-room table clacking out the final words of a chapter called, "Practical Body Kinetics for Street and Sidewalk: the Defensive Walker and Cyclist."

I wish the lady with the baby carriage could read it, so she'd wheel her bunny-suited baby with eyes wide open.

Gloria, wearing oven mitts, has been baking buns for the conference at Convocation Hall, in case our tummies grumble. We have, in fact, invited her to the meeting even though she's not a Party member.

"What party?" she reasonably asks.

I tell her with head held high. "The CDA, of course. Cerebral Drivers Alliance."

She cocks her head, looks as if I'm putting her on. "Get out!"

"Seriously, Gloria. It's an organization of good drivers. To belong, you have to have a perfect record from day one. Day one must have been at least twenty years ago."

"Huh!" Gloria looks sceptical.

"Yes, and you also have to be able to give some assurance that your perfect record is not the result of simple hazard, which is to say, normal operation of the laws of chance."

"Oh dear! It must be a hard party to join."

I tell her it is. It has to be. Its goals are revolutionary. I don't bother to mention that Pa and I are the only members. So far, the Party is one way of keeping our spirits up, rather than anything real. I have not told her either that we want her to say a few words at our meeting, since we are short on speakers.

Pappy, I notice, has put up some slogans on the dining-room walls. There are cardboard letters taped in place and scrawls in acrylic or crayon – really quite a mess:

Prime Directive: never trust
Remember: tainted blood, fornicating bishops,
  lusting school principals
Never rely on the other guy
Never assume anything but the worst
Never assume the other guy is rational
Never assume the other guy is in control

Never assume the other guy is aware
Never assume the other guy is conscious
Never assume the other guy is unarmed
Never assume the other guy is sane
Never take your eyes off them
Never turn your back

On one wall Pappy has pasted headlines from *The Star* under the title "Defensive Pedestrianship," which he has scribbled in red ink:

Bus shelter massacre
Car kills man in barber chair
Three officers hit investigating same accident
Gas jockey incinerated
Backs over whole family: "I thought they were seed potatoes."

Way to go, Pa! These are the nightmares that possess us by day and by night—every time we fire up our wheels. These are the deeds. Deeds of every day, every hour. Deeds that are bloody, obscene, imbecilic. Deeds that cry out for justice and vengeance.

Gloria is unimpressed.

"Slovenly," she says, her red mouth down in the corners. Then Pa berates her again for coming here on her bicycle.

"Helmet won't save ya," he tells her. "Ya only got a ten-percent chance de guy behind's competent. Tink of it. Ten percent. This is de guy ya turn yer back to. Ya wouldn't walk in front of him, would ye? Why cycle there, then?"

"I dunno," Gloria replies.

Too bad! That response is typically Triffid. It does not endear her to Pappy. Newfoundlanders are the most honest and forthright folk in the country. They have little patience with evasion. Newfoundland is one of those rare places where Triffids least desire to be. Even though Pa has not been back to Newfiejohn since the first traffic light went up, he has remained true to his heritage.

And he's still the world authority on Triffids.

"So tink about it, darlin'. Only a ten-percent chance of de

guy behind havin' a brain that really works. A Vulcan, like Spock of *Star Trek* fame. A Pappy Prince or a Rufus. You'll know when we're there, girl, because de Triffs behind us'll be skittish. They'll honk like trumpeter swans spyin' a stranger. In their minds de space we leaves is wasted. They wants us to be sniffin' de rear of de guy in front. Udderwise, they'll gnash their teeth, pick their noses and chew de wheel."

Gloria yawns and checks her finger nails.

Pappy never apologizes for his "explications." Pa holds out little hope for her, pointing out she was weaned on afternoon soaps, loud music, theme parks, animal shows, and Niagara Falls.

I tell him lots of people worship at the altar of popular taste without being necessarily evil or less worthy. But these doubts don't augur well for any future relationship with Gloria.

Gloria's lesson for today goes tolerably well at first. But then her brow wrinkles, she grows older, lines of apprehension appear around the blue eyes and the ruby mouth. She bites her lip till it starts to bleed. Yet, I've said nothing.

"What's wrong, Gloria?"

"They hate me," she says. "You can see they hate me. They don't like anything I do. See how they stare and honk? The two behind – they're laughing at me!"

"But, Gloria, they're Triffids. When Triffids laugh at you, it's a sure sign of progress."

I get her out of the traffic and let her do curb- and stall-parks, as well as back-ins, for the rest of the lesson, to take her mind off the dinglewits. Then I give her a big hamburger. Large bun of praise with a dime-thin, minuscule patty of critique. Sweet relish, no mustard.

"Don't worry, Gloria, all us good drivers have to put up with a certain amount of harassment from the mindless – till further notice, anyway. Goes with the territory. These are the jerks that drive around like jet-propelled turds in a sewer. They know there are bad drivers out there, but they haven't a clue who they are. They suspect *we* are the troublemakers, because we don't drive the way they do."

"Golly, how childish!"

"You said it, babe. It's where the rubber meets the road."

To terminate the lesson, I ask Gloria if she'd like to recite the Credo. She gives me her Mona Lisa smile, takes a deep breath and gets right into it: "I believe in the mindlessness of the other guy. I believe these other guys have surrendered their brains to–" Here she can't suppress a giggle–"to the Triffids. I believe–I believe–Golly!"

"That the Triffids intend–"

"That the Triffids intend to have every last–every single mind on earth. I believe they are engaged, on a cosmic scale, in eradicating the dignity and worth of every intelligent creature. I believe they do this by annihilating good sense and good judgement, making folk into–into rude parodies of what they might have been, turning lives of destiny into might-have-been shadows. I believe they cripple and crimp us, so we no longer stand straight in the presence of the Spirit of Living Things. Amen."

"Excellent, Gloria! Now, doesn't that make you feel better? Tell me how we can protect ourselves and fight back."

Big smile. I love Gloria's smile when she's not wearing too much lipstick.

"The Party."

"Yes, the Party."

I sigh deeply, as I have seen Captain Jean-Luc Picard of the Starship *Enterprise* do, when some great satisfaction comes his way. A warm smile envelops me as I look into the blue vastness of her eyes and see there a universe of promise.

5

To Serve Man

Pappy and I motor up to the Bradford Triangle, stopping at the UFO Conference in Aurora, where we learn more about the Triangle as a port of entry for cosmic travellers, who apparently reach Earth via a vortex from a parallel universe.

I'm sceptical. I can't see how anyone can know that. But Pappy is more open-minded, and he has his powers.

Got a real good telescope from the Scope Shop on Dundas Street. We follow the back roads. Fewer lights. Also more space. Classic cars, like great architecture, need space around them. Night's clear, chilly. Great hosts of spangling stars.

"Small nippers, about de size o' Munchkins," Pa says, getting in the mood after we have droned up Warden Avenue for a good stretch in silence. "Look a bit like bugs."

"I've been calculating, Pa. The figures say nobody can travel that far – no earthling, at any rate. Nearest star is forty trillion kilometres. In Chevy, at present speed, it would take us ten million years to get there. At the speed of light we could do it in five."

"Yeah, Rufus, if we can get Chevy to go dat fast."

In the north a shooting star streaks, giving me the feeling we will not be disappointed in challenging the mystery of the cosmos.

Suppose we did get there at the speed of light. We'd still be in our own backyard, cosmically speaking. And when we returned to Earth, every person and every thing we knew, perhaps the human race itself, would be long gone because of relativity. "Robots," I say. "Only robots can travel those distances."

"Truth is, Rufus, we don't know. But eternity, de absolute night of space-time, is filled wit life-givin' suns. If there's nobody smart out there, what would be de point?"

North of Newmarket we take Yonge Street for a bit, then branch off onto the dark, steep road that goes down into the hollow toward Holland Landing. At the bottom we follow a dirt road to a canal, and there we find a good quiet spot to set up our post.

I ask Pa if he has any reason to believe this particular night will be a good one. He just shrugs. I know he goes by some secret internal clock that tells him when the time is right.

"Has it anything to do with the Triffids?" I ask, without really expecting an answer. "Or with their inveterate foes, the Tau Cetians?"

"Maybe. Just maybe." Pa has a knack for maintaining an air of mystery.

Wish I could see a UFO. So far, haven't been that lucky. Odds are against it. Yet, even Aunt Beulah, up on a visit from Newfoundland, once stumbled upon something not far from this very place. It rattled her placid Newfie wits. "What?" everyone was asking her as she came staggering toward the car like a newly risen zombie. She'd been in the bushes to answer nature's call. She gave us a blank look. Then finally she gasped, "A thing. A bright thing. It come up from the cowbelly." She meant the swamp. But we couldn't get her to be really coherent. She went home to Joe Batt's Arm quick as she could, married a man from Blow Me Down, and never again left her native island.

"Swamp gas," Pappy declared at the time, to explain Aunt Beulah's apparition. But that was before he spotted a UFO of his own. It was also before the vision of the all-conquering Triffid loomed into his fertile consciousness, which was late one starry night on the Don Valley Parkway, as he wended home with his brain in overdrive. When he returned that night, he showed me the Triffid Sign, the finger that points toward home.

A dog's bark brings me back to the canal. Otherwise, nothing breaks the utter quiet of the place as Pappy and I take turns at the telescope. A cloud draws over the moon and the canal slips into near-total darkness.

Pa must either be nervous or impatient, as he talks to himself: "Bet they'd come and get me if they knowed what I was doin'. Sure they would. Kill me and dump me in de pickle." I suggest we look for another place while waiting for the cloud to pass over, one with fewer trees. But Pappy doesn't answer, just keeps scanning the dark on all sides. Must be onto something.

All I can see is a faint glimmer on the water. There's a smell of putrefaction from the canal. An owl hoots. Pa gives me a nudge and directs my attention to where I know the road is, and I see a strange reddish glow, about the size of an orange. But I have no idea how far away it is. We communicate in whispers, while the object makes odd evolutions and pulsates red and green and orange alternately.

"Can't be a bike. No bike light glows like that."

"Oh, it ain't," says Pappy, in a tone that makes me shiver.

I feel I have to say something now, before things get out of hand. "Pa – Pa, remember the summer of – "

"Whist!" he says, to shut me up.

That dog somewhere – sure is going crazy.

"Pa, let's watch from the car."

"Nuttin' doin'. This be rarer than a lunar rainbow."

"But – "

"A shipful o' tiny aliens, same size as garden mites. Maybe a foo fighter – they's not been seed since de dogfights durin' de war – "

"Pa, listen – "

"Or it may be an intergalactic egg. Maybe ready to hatch. Or maybe a naked mass o' alien protoplasm, an interstellar jellyfish that grows by sluckin' people up. Remember *De Blob*?"

"Pa!"

Pa darts into the shadows, leaving me alone. I grope my way to the car, keeping an eye on the mysterious object. It looks just like the pulsating cobra head of the Martian death ray in *The War of the Worlds*. I make it to the car and stand beside it with my hand on the door handle. I can't help thinking of the summer of 1978. I don't want to make that mistake again. Definitely not.

During the summer of 1978 Pa and I were reading UFO books. We checked out everything at the library. We really psyched ourselves up. I guess we were paranoid. We didn't sleep, because we knew a lot of strange things were going on out there. We were learning all about close encounters of the first, second, and third kind. Scary, real scary. We knew what the ufonauts looked like. There had been reports from all over the world. Air force personnel, pilots of passenger planes, the army and the police: these witnesses were believable. And sometimes there were simultaneous, independent sightings over wide areas. Collusion was not possible.

True, there was no hard evidence. Nothing you could touch or examine under a microscope. No bodies or hardware, unless the authorities were hiding it. Still, whatever was going on was serious enough to come under investigation by the U.S. Air Force. It was not a hoax but a genuine mystery. Pa and I could not get it out of our minds.

Oh yes, they were out there all right.

I remember how keyed up we were after seeing the *Twilight Zone* episode entitled "To Serve Man." Aliens had come to our planet proposing peace and friendship. They were taking Earth folk away to visit their home star. People were lining up to go there. They just couldn't wait. The aliens had a plan for these friendly intentions. The plan had a name: "To Serve Man."

Finally, the aliens' chief contact on Earth is about to make the trip himself. He's on his way up the boarding ramp with the rest of the crowd when he hears a friend call frantically from the sidelines. *It's a cookbook,* the friend cries. *"To Serve Man" is a cookbook!*

Panic on the ramp. The bovines are loading for the slaughter house. They slide and shove and try to turn. They all want to escape. But it's too late.

We don't want to be collared, tethered, caged, and eaten. It may be what we've done to our fellow creatures on sorry old Earth, but we don't want it done to us.

I think after that episode we lost our judgement completely. At night we lay on our backs in the dandelions,
looking up into the star-spangled void, persuaded that visi-
tations were immanent. We followed Venus or traced the
course of aircraft, fully persuaded we were on to something
very suspicious. Now and then, in the late-night stillness of
Gascap Bend, resonated an odd, eerie hum, which we knew to
be the inertial dampers of a starship, oscillating down into
our world from the parallel universe.

The haunting hum of those dampers kept us awake and
watching many a fitful night as the stars made their primor-
dial trek across the cold dark void. Noises in the alleyway
frightened us. We remembered Betty and Barney Hill, the
New Hampshire couple who were carried off by bug-eyed
aliens with long arms to have their cavities probed.

One particular night, the drone became a rumble, interrupted by a whistle. It hit me like a slap in the face. UFO's
were not making that noise. If I hadn't been so psyched up, I
would have understood this long ago. It was plain, ordinary
railyard acoustics. Friction between track and train wheel.
On hot and humid nights the vibrations resonated eerily.
That was what we were listening to.

Hallelujah, my brain was on again!

Our fixation did not evaporate immediately under the
force of this revelation. But it was a beginning. It did not
destroy our interest in UFO's, but it did tell us we'd been
cruising with our brains off.

That's why Pappy so rashly attacks the mysterious glowing
object at Bradford. He knows hesitation will bring us face to
face with our fears again. He's too proud for that.

I wait by the car and bite my nails. The object I have my
eye on turns from green to red, describes a short arc, and disappears.

"Pa, are you there?" I keep my hand on the car door.

Voices! Shouts from the dark and rustling in the bushes. I
shine my light there. I see Pappy emerge on the other side of
the road. I'm shocked to discover – Gordon McDuff! Pa has
him by the collar; looks like he just gaffed himself a fresh
codling for the pot. McDuff, in a sweater and bluejeans, peers

sheepishly into my beam of light. His own light, I observe, is one of those gimmicky things you could send away for back in the nineties for two bucks and a couple of tops from cornflakes boxes.

"This crappy flashlight is what mystified us?"

"Yeah, but I snogged 'im," says Pa.

I notice McDuff is feeling his jaw. Guess Pa slugged him all right. He's lucky we didn't bring our brass knuckles. He hems and haws but can't find anything smart to say. He won't admit to spying. "Just had nothing better to do, boys. Thought I'd see what you were up to, that's all."

"Devilment and diversion, that's what 'tis, McDuff."

The Sergeant invites us to donuts and coffee in Bradford. But I tell him no. "You're one dumb cop, sir. You can't buy self-respect with a few cheap donuts. We know you can't take the beef, McDuff, so you always go for the dough."

We make him take us to a place where the hamburgers are old-fashioned meaty, not overpowered by the bun. Prime Canajun beef. Raw onion, hot mustard, and dill pickle.

After I relate this adventure to Dr. Abedni over the phone, he says, "But, my dear friends, you cannot expect to see any-thing real in a single night, or even in a thousand nights. My goodness, no."

Has he ever seen anything himself, we ask? But we lose the gist of his answer, as he drowns it in a flood of abstruse spec-ulation. Something about the universe being only half as big as generally believed, together with the expansion rates of near and far galaxies. He tells us near galaxies, in his lifetime, have travelled farther away from our own by about 1.2 tril-lion miles, while far galaxies have gotten farther away by about 118.2 trillion miles. I ask him what this has to do with UFO's, but by now he seems to be in dialogue only with him-self, and is muttering powers of this and powers of that.

So I hang up.

The Incredible Meeting
at Convocation Hall

I'm surprised to see so many people at Convocation Hall. Almost a hundred. Pappy and the Doctor linger for a while at the entrance to help with any disputes – this is one meeting we don't want to let just anyone attend.

Gloria and McDuff are certainly nervous and feeling out of place. McDuff figures he owes us one for the fiasco at Bradford. Gloria came because she loves me. I hope we didn't make a mistake by inviting them.

Surveying the audience from the stage, I nervously spy a variety of expressions, and I have to wonder if any good can come of such an assembly. I refuse to be nervous. I take a deep breath and signal for the lights. My points of interest all come up perfectly on the screen:

Man loses head in slide under tractor-trailer
Woman run over by own car
Backs into sushi bar, kills world-class chef
Stabs taunting driver
Runs over grandmother in crosswalk for being too slow
Car drags pedestrian 25 kilometres
Boy killed by runaway horse trailer
Cyclist left in ditch bleeds to death
Boy critical after being hit at crosswalk
Father finds son dead on sidewalk after hit-and-run
Girl, mom die cycling to work
Officer jailed for deadly crash
Gun duels continue on 401; snipers still at large

"Well," I begin, "don't look too hard. All of us have seen these headlines in the paper. That's where I got them. Nothing new here. These are all daily occurrences, and have been fairly common for the last thirty years or so.

"Let's look more closely at a few. Take the cyclist left to bleed to death. The driver who hit him kept right on going. This in itself is not noteworthy. It seems to be the rule that when you hit somebody, you run."

I see disapproval on the faces out in front of me.

"The dead man's father said, and I quote, *All the driver had to do was phone—let somebody know my son was in the ditch.* That's what he said. Don't you marvel at the self-control of this poor man? Don't you wonder why he doesn't say, 'Find the bastard and crucify him'? Friends, this is not hyperbole."

I'm gratified by the round of applause I get.

"Now, friends, consider this poor boy killed in a crosswalk while walking his bike. No one ever told him it's a good place to die. The impact of the collision imbedded the bike in the front of the car. The boy's head hit the windshield and was crushed like a coconut under a sledgehammer. Heavy rain was falling. The driver claimed he didn't see anything.

"Now, I know what you're thinking. Heavy rain, dark day, driver saw nothing. Clearly, it's one of those tragic concatenations of events that we read about every day. An unforeseeable act of God. That's probably why no charges were laid."

Boy, have I got them squirming! Some are grunting, some growling. Some of them are crying, "No!" or "Wrong!" A young man in the third row yells, "Damn driver! He had eyes, didn't he?" Someone else bellows, "He had a brain, didn't he?"

"Bravo!" I roar, "Bravo!"—mainly to regain control. "Good questions. Excellent questions. Did he have eyes? Did he have a brain? Those are certainly key questions.

"Now, good people, you and I know he was driving blind—it's done every day by countless drivers. This driver excused himself by citing reduced visibility—as if that were a mitigating circumstance, rather than a condemnation of his judgement. This guy would have had some credibility if he'd said, 'I gambled and lost.' Or better yet, 'Blame those who gave me a licence.' Now those are real arguments.

"But now we must move on. A mother and daughter were mowed down while cycling to work—"

I want Gloria to take special note of this one. But in the corner of my eye I glimpse her going nervously over her notes and biting her nails.

"Early morning it was. They were always very careful. They were determined not to be caught out by any of the creeps on our roads. So they rode on the oncoming side. Not that there was any traffic at that early hour. They had their helmets on.

"But no precautions could have saved them, once fate had this moron coming up behind them over the crest of a hill and on the wrong side of the road. He killed them. The papers and the police said it was a terrible tragedy—"

"It's a bloody crime!" yells a lady in the front row. And I think, good, I'm plucking sensitive cords here.

"Now this one, good folk, is a classic. *Car drags pedestrian 25 kilometres.* How is it possible? Can anyone tell me that? You'd really want a chimpanzee behind the wheel, wouldn't you?

"Let me tell you what this guy said, once they got him stopped. He said, *How am I supposed to know?* That's what he said. Those are his words. Does he have a point? Is there any way to know when there's a body under the car? Is there really any surefire way of knowing that? I don't think so."

The audience moans. Some laugh derisively.

"Friends, you know what all such drivers say: I didn't know, I didn't see, I couldn't help it, I don't remember, I thought it was a sack of oranges."

More moans and jibes.

"Now, good people, to conclude this introduction, I wish to say a few words about something very sacred to all of us gathered here. There is a great want of it on our roads. A dearth. They vie for it, they kill for it. And yet the universe is full of it. Space. You knew what I meant, didn't you? Space. Without it there could be no universe. There is nothing more plentiful. But these criminals can't see it. To them it's mere nothingness. Something to stick their snouts into."

"You can't sink any lower!" a listener yells.

"The odd thing is," I tell them, "these persons come from all walks of life. Only a few of them can claim deprivation or abuse in childhood. (Here I glimpse Dr. Abedni nodding in agreement.) Only a few of them drive cement trucks or pizza cars or taxis. Hardly any of them are involved in off-the-road criminality.

"Yes, my friends, there are philosophers, psychologists, aesthetes, teachers, police, judges, lawyers, and nuns among them. People who meditate, people who pray, people who preach calm, tranquillity, and enlightenment. Authors and professors of know-thyself. Experts on self-control. Folk who know how to relate. But it doesn't matter how good they are or how much they know. Once they get behind the wheel of a car, they all regress. Their brains become travellers in time. They're all suddenly equally dumb.

"If they were to walk as they drive, they'd always be at the heels of the person ahead, sniffing for any gas, periodically making rude noises and signs so the world doesn't forget how seriously they take themselves.

"These are the same duds who follow us into parking lots so closely that we can't back into a stall. Chances are, they'll go front first into the stall we've chosen while we're slipping into reverse. Our signals mean nothing to them."

Boy, the audience is growing ugly! I hear cries of "Hopeless!" and "What can we do?" It's time for me to conclude. I feel I've done a great job in bringing out the latent hostility of this small convocation of good drivers. Guess the Professor knew what he was doing when he asked me to speak first.

Poor McDuff, when it's his turn he gets up and mouths the usual platitudes. At first, the folks are really impressed when I introduce him as a member of the Toronto Street Violence Unit. At last, they think, a cop who's on our side. But then he comes on with the usual stuff about safety elephants, RIDE campaigns and the like, all the smokescreen ploys the Triffids promote.

My fault. I should have warned him.

Toward the end though, he does say something meaningful. He says, "I blame the pace of life. We want fast food, fast banking, fast everything. We even talk faster than we used to. With some people, if you're not fast enough, your life is at risk. That's one reason why you have to be wide awake when you're driving these days. People just don't have the patience to drive safely. But if your mind is somewhere else, not on your driving, you're asking for trouble."

McDuff gets polite applause and seems to be happy with that. It wasn't brilliant, but he didn't screw up either.

Gloria's turn. She's nervous as she comes to the mike. Looks too leggy in her short red dress. Too much lipstick; I told her to tone it down. I detest bright cherry red on a pale complexion. But the crowd likes her. Whistles and murmurs of appreciation as she moves to the lectern. She starts hesitantly but soon warms to the many signs of approval from those present.

"When I was a little girl, I never used a crosswalk," she bashfully begins. "Cars frightened me. It was really nothing compared to today. Back then they never ran you down if you had a green light. And you didn't get shot just for being in the way. We still had some, to use an old-fashioned term, law and order. But just the same, I was always scared to death to cross the street.

"My dad taught me how to do a rolling stop when I was three. He always used to say he felt badly doing a full stop because he was holding people up. Well, truth is, he never really said anything, but I was taking it all in, nevertheless. What you do is, you slow down and roll past the sign, unless someone else has beaten you to the intersection, in which case you may need to stop, but not necessarily. I could tell Daddy knew all about it."

Smiles and chuckles everywhere in the crowd. They love her. She's off the mark but she's sexy. Abedni is grinning like one of his pampered cats. But Pappy is shaking his head sadly.

"Lighten up, Pa," I tell him. "The folk out there need that. This is heavy stuff we're into. They need a break. They think

she's great. After we're done with her, she will be great."
Gloria's really at ease now, really turning on the charm.
"Well," she continues, "it's good of you to clap. I know Daddy
was wrong, but I love him anyway. I want you to know that
in spite of all dear daddy's lessons, all my stops are regula-
tion ones ... "

The applause Gloria gets for this modest admission is
astounding. When she's done, she curtsies and blows kisses,
and we begin to think she'll never sit down.

Doctor Abedni has traded in the usual baggy pants and
dishevelled look he cultivates for a sharp crease in his pants,
and tie and shirt. ("Professor Curry-Funk!" Pa whispers, as
the Doctor preens himself.)

Abedni sizes up the crowd over the rim of his glasses.
"Now, ah, ahem. First let me say a few words about 'the guy
behind.' You have all heard of this fellow, heh-heh – fellow or
gal, let that be understood. I am talking about the idiot who
loves to neutralize our brakes. I am afraid I have some really
bad news ... "

Groans all around. "Bring back the blonde!" somebody in
the first aisle shouts.

"Heh-heh-heh. Bless you, she was good, I grant you that,
heh-heh. Of course, I cannot compete with lush ... with
attractive young ladies. But – ah – I do promise you brevity.

"Now, where was I? Yes. Safety devices are not working.
We have known that for about ten years. Anti-lock brakes,
air bags, side-impact reinforcement – that kind of thing. The
news is bad. People with these devices are driving their cars
harder than before – pushing them to the limit. You must all
have noticed, when these things were first introduced, how
they began coming up faster and stopping closer to our rear
ends. Our ends and our necks have been in great peril ever
since. My research shows that drivers with ABS accelerate
faster than they used to, maintaining higher speeds and
braking later than they did before."

There are cries of "Fools!" "Idiots!" "What a way to treat a
car!"

"Yes, dear auditors, they are fools. They are idiots. They are
a pack of impotent little bark balls, heh-heh-heh. Think

about it. We wizards of science and technology give them some slack – to save lives, mind you. And what do they do? They screw their recklessness up a notch to compensate.

"That is why you and I have had to make an adjustment the last nine or ten years in our behaviour upon approaching a stop sign or a light. We have had to apply our brakes even earlier than what we were used to. Because if we don't get 'the guy behind' slowed down, then we cannot make a safe and legal stop ourselves. So we must continue forcing them to decelerate early. In my humble opinion, the sooner they see our brake lights, the better."

"They don't like that early braking!" a gentleman in the audience shouts.

Another one yells, "Yeah, they hate us already. Some of them are ramming drivers that come to a full stop at stop signs."

"You said it, they have a short fuse as it is," says a lady in the third row. "Many of them are armed. They're blaming us for what goes on out there. Most of them are so dumb they really believe it."

Boy, is he ever flying high, that Abedni! See how thrilled he is with himself as an orator! But I guess professors gotta be good at it.

"Dear me, you are so right, ladies and gentlemen. It is not in human nature to love those who are in one's way. Unfortunately, there are so many of us now on this planet of apes, it cannot be helped. And you are quite right. They hate us with a vengeance. Believe you me, they hate us. But we hate them even more, and for good reason. What is more, we are smarter than they are by several light years. But rest assured, before this night is over, I will have a remedy to put to you. However, let me conclude for now by saying there is little reason for optimism. The motor car as we have known it is nearing its demise. Yes, yes, well may you have long faces. The car is so dear to us all. But we all know, the pleasures of motoring are long gone – it partly explains the viciousness you see out there. It is no fun to drive anymore. The good old internal-combustion engine is being phased out. Soon you will not be able to fire one up without a penalty. And the future is not promising. I believe science and technology is about to save average drivers from themselves by enclosing them in impenetrable cocoons, which will be foolproof and crashproof. But if you think it will be fun, or anything like driving, think again. I thank you."

Wow, what a speech! In spite of his pessimism, Professor Abedni receives tremendous applause.

And now it's Pappy's turn.

Wait a minute, what does he think he's doing? He no sooner launches into his address than he's dropping terms like "interstellar connection," "Bradford vortex," and "parallel universe." I warned him not to do that.

What a disaster!

Folks are shifting nervously in their seats. Nobody laughing. Probably wondering, how did this kook get in here?

"No human beings," Pa is saying, "could really be as dumb and as rude as de cokeheads in cars these days. I wants ya to hypotetize that these devils be from somewhere else. Tink now, if a sinister and insidious force, totally alien to de human spirit, well-travelled in de galaxy ... "

What a hush has come over the hall! You can hear their thoughts scramble. They don't know what to make of this old guy with the accent.

"Alien, I say. Profoundly alien. A fearful, ugly, evil force. Shocking evil. A force that's already taken de hearts and minds of ninety percent of us. Nine parsons out of ten — gone. Be on yer guard, some of these aliens is here wit us tonight."

Pa looks round at us, no doubt to see if Gloria and McDuff squirm, or otherwise betray themselves. And sure enough, Gloria is picking her nails, not even listening. Duff and Abedni are snickering and trying not to look at each other.

"Vapour-like, they invades de human mind by osmosis. I speculates we's dealin' wit an ethereal protoplasm, more loosely structured than gas. They possibly arrives at de cranium by way of de body's orifices. Reachin' de brain, they eider invests it through osmotic infusion, or else they attacks de cerebrospinal fluid, thus altering de pressure on this organ. Common sense is dead at this point.

"So you see, comrades, most brains today are like tea bags in hot water. Alien protoplasm sucks from them de very essence of—"

Pappy is interrupted by some frightful screams on the part of Doctor Abedni, who falls off his chair and slams into the platform floor with a dull, resounding thud. Everyone is shocked to see the Professor struck ill and in the throes of a terrible fit.

But they soon comprehend that he suffers from uncontrolled mirth, and that the noises he makes while rolling and thrashing about should in fact be interpreted as laughter. So everyone present begins to smirk and snicker and then roar.

Pappy is dumbfounded. I amble over to him as he hangs on the lectern, feeling little and betrayed. "They're not laughing at you," I tell him. "Now lay off talking about Triffids."

He says all right, and I head over to Abedni who is pounding the floor with his fists. "Better get up and behave, sir. Professor, did you hear me?"

The crowd's going nuts at these antics. My words have no effect on the Doctor, so I yell at him and even resort to a kick in the shins, an act which all but brings the roof down. How the hell is anyone going to take us seriously now, I wonder.

I kick him again, harder this time. He winces, his fit intensifies, he writhes and wriggles toward the back of the stage, pulling himself along by the elbows like some strange, wounded bird, till he crawls under the curtain and disappears. His cries echo for a moment, a door slams, and we hear him no more. I believe he's gone out into the night to howl at the stars.

In the hall, the mood of mirth and merriment subsides. They've had their fun, and now they cough and run their fingers through their hair, and look at their neighbours and smirk; and they look at Pappy, thinking he might be ready to resume.

"Well—ah—er," says Pa, trying to pick up the thread of his thought. I am amazed he does not follow my advice but immediately begins to talk about Triffids.

"I was talkin' about aliens. Well, call 'em what ye wants, I calls 'em 'Triffids.' It's just a name. But a name is needed.

Udderwise, we just don't know what we's talkin' about. De Triffids constitutes ninety percent of any population. My colleague, Professor Abedni, intends to prove this empirically.

"All right then, nine out of ten parsons can't drive for beans. Tink what that means. Well, for one ting, it means nine out of ten police constables can't drive worth a hoot. We see that in de papers all de time. Thus, they has no moral autority when it comes to highway enforcement. Same goes for judges, lawmakers, educators. Don't bother callin' on any of them to fix tings. Wherever you turn, de odds are nine to one de parson you want help from is corrupt. A Triffid, if ye will.

"Oh, I grant you, they may very well, most likely will, rant and roar against drunk drivers and de like. They loves drunk drivers. But they knows nuttin' will change. And it's just what they wants.

"These same people you might call upon for reform— they're de ones who blames their own poor dog when it gets run over. 'Poor old Bones,' they'll say, 'He shouldn't have run out in de road like dat.' If they hits your dog or mine, will they stop and do their duty? No, they will not. These are de same pumpkin heads who's on your back and mine, fumin' and tootin' while we're slowin' down 'cause we see de cues they misses. They're de ones who tears de guts outta their own cars, while they treats you and me wit hostility because we lacks de leadfoot touch. They're de pie brains who expects us to sacrifice our Sacred Space for de sake of their convenience, risk our skins so they can gain a millisecond or half a metre. Why on earth should we call on them?

"You know de answer. No use at all. They's not goin' to help us. We's de enemy. They wants you and me to be as dumb and empty as themselves. They wants us wit our drawers full of jumpin' beans and our skulls full of pap, so we be just like them. That's what they wants.

"Never forget, kind folk, this be a Triffid world we live in. They's de ones in charge. So please, always be on guard. Mind what ye say, and to whom ye says it. Be good and keep yer chins up, till that glorious day when we finds a way to keep Triffids from sniffin' up our behinds. Tank you."

Wowie, what a speech! Pa gets great applause. They thought he was quaint, but they loved that Triffid figure of speech.

Professor Abedni, who had returned to his place looking demure as a dung beetle contemplating a fresh load, now comes bounding forward to the lectern to say a few more words. It's obvious he's given himself a good dusting off, and has taken himself by the scruff of the neck and resolved to do better. He does not look at Pappy but keeps his horn-rimmed face buried in his notes.

"Let me bring to your attention," Abedni gravely begins, "an article which appeared in the paper on June 21 of this year. I quote: *Ontario will promote safe driving with a TV ad showing panicked family members and frantic hospital workers in the aftermath of an accident. 'We want to reach their hearts,' the Transportation Minister said today at Queen's Park. 'We have tried reaching their brains but it doesn't work. Sure, the ads are hard. These people need to be hit hard. Every three minutes in this province there is an injury – 480 injuries every day. We can't go on like this. We just can't!'"*

This reading is met with cackles and curses. "Hang the Minister!" someone cries. "Crucify the bitch!"

"Well, dear me! More money down the drain. These stupid ads will eat up fully a third of the budget for highway safety. And who, pray tell, is the target of this sham campaign? Right on, it is our ubiquitous troublemaker, 'the other guy.' But when you have a message to deliver to this 'other guy,' this Scarlet Pimpernel of the road, he is nowhere to be found. The plain truth is, the Minister, in Mr. Pappy's terminology, is, heh-heh-heh, a Triffid. She does not want anything to change. Now, I suggest to you that the Minister knows full well that, even if anyone were persuaded to a critical examination of his or her behaviour, the wretch would not have a clue as to how to do better. The infrastructure is missing. Opportunities to learn and be tested – missing. Proper enforcement – missing."

Way to go, Professor! I swear he's got them mesmerized, the way they sit on the edge of their seats and hang on his every word. Pa, the Professor, and I must be three of the most cunning demagogues that ever led crowd to crucible.

Pa's worried though. He says to me, "Professor Curry-Funk's bold pushin'. Bet there's a fox eye round de moon tonight."

I tell him to relax. It's just what we want—to get them all stirred up.

McDuff is yawning. Bet he wishes he were home in front of the box watching some cheap whodunit. Gloria keeps checking her watch. You can sure tell who doesn't belong here.

Then the roof falls in. The Professor tosses a bomb and blows us away, me and Pa. It's a real Molotov cocktail. It's completely unexpected. He just looks back at us under the hornrims with a mischievous grin, and then messianically addresses the assembly. "Revolution!" he cries, waving his fist at the faces in the first row.

"Friends, the message is sacred," Abedni roars. "The cause is just. Rebellion is our duty. Dear hearts, I propose that we unanimously declare this present concourse a full and duly constituted plenum for the purpose of founding—a political party! Our party. I further propose that the aim of this party be nothing less than the overthrow of—of Triffiddom! Revolution! Freedom! Down with the Triffids! We are not going to take it any more!"

Well, they're all out of their seats, raising their arms, clenching their fists, shouting, "Death to the Triffids!" Dr. Abedni has to plead with them to let him finish. Eventually they do.

"Thank you, dear hearts. I understand your impatience. We nurse a lifetime of injury. We thirst for justice. We crave revenge. Think of the fun we are going to have! We will plot and scheme, throw bombs and go to jail. How grand it will be to have a cause! Give structure to this meaningless existence. Wake up in the morning like a god. Have something real to do instead of the mundane money-grubbing of the masses.

"And when at last our star does rise, as rise it must, the

star of Reason – when that glad day is come, good folk, you and I will truly be in the driver's seat. And the ride we give those evil, pesky gadflies will be something to behold.

"My goodness, I am so giddy! We will have our Lenin and Trotsky, our Danton and Robespierre. The heroes of tomorrow may be here tonight – young men and women who will be feared for their attachment to principle. Their deeds will speak. The tyranny of the vacuous will come to a speedy end, I promise you!

"Heads will roll, be certain of that. Blood will run. We will have our people's justice. We will have our Terror. We will outdo all the storms of yesteryear. A show of hands now for Revolution!"

A sea of hands, then the hall dissolves in chaos. People leap from their seats or crawl over them to embrace and debate with their neighbours.

Pa and I are also electrified, though not for the same reason. Pappy is furious with Abedni. "A low-lifted fellow of de first water," he calls him. Then he tells him, "You have no authority. We's de Party, Rufus and me. We don't need to call for anudder one, you – you mystical turkey!"

To me, Abedni looks more like the cat that has all the mice by their tails. "Now, now, calm yourselves," he mews. "You two shall have all due credit and honour. You cannot keep a party to yourselves, you know, unless you just want to dream?"

He certainly has a point, and it's one I put quite plainly to Pa. Do we want to dream, or do we want to get the Triffids and make our mark in history? Besides, I say, we have to go along with this rising tide or it's a putsch and we lose the Party.

"Well?" Abedni is polishing his spectacles with his tie. "Well, Mr. Prince from Joe Batt's Arm, sir? Will you make your mark, or will you be swallowed by time's great tide without leaving so much as a ripple? What do you say? Shall we bring those Triffids down?"

There's a faint glow around Pappy's forehead. He looks Abedni in the eye and grins. "Wit a bastard like you in de Party, we can't fail. Yes, I accept, for great glory's sake, and because I hate de Triffids. Yep, de wind's beginnin' to haul. All hands on deck!"

And so it is done. The CDA is truly born. The Cerebral Drivers Alliance. And the course is set for the millennium.

But we accomplish little this night, as we sing and dance and are jubilant, because we know the day of reckoning is at hand. And we feel we are born again.

Still, on the way home this night, Pappy bewails his speech, saying it is too early to talk about Triffids. "There's a risk they won't understand," he worries. "Then they'll call us de dulce and dogberry faction from Joe Batt's Arm."

We tell him they weren't laughing at him or his Triffids but at that clown Abedni.

"Imagine, interrupting your speech to hee-haw like that!" says Gloria. "Obviously, the man is unbalanced."

"He be that all right, high-learnt wonder o' de East. Anyway, we got us our Party. That sure do change de water on de beans."

PUFFED-UP TURD BALLS

Pa never experiences writer's block. What he needs for a day's work comes to him quite handily in sleep, though it may not be apparent till pen touches paper just what his inner self expects him to write.

In the beginning is the word, he has written. *The idea comes after, and also the form. The first word is* space. *This means we should have room to move and breathe, room to manoeuvre, room to be alone, room to feel safe, room to think, and room to hide.*

Pappy loves philosophy. But then, what folk is accustomed to wide open spaces, if not Newfoundlanders? They certainly do not feel compelled to breathe down the necks of their neighbours, nor to sniff up behind them. Heck, they didn't even have roads before they were tricked into joining up with Canada.

One evening while we're eating scallops, I challenge him on definitions. "The word 'Triffid,' Pa, it's not our own private expletive, you know. You say only Triffids leave cigarette butts in the sand at Wasaga Beach."

Pa gulps down the remaining scallops, wielding his fork like a cod gaff. "Had de right smack, didinim?" he says, his nose glowing from hard thinking. "Rufus bye, there be a common thread o' stupidity unitin' all mankind. Triffidus has to be more than lousy drivin'. Much more. I used to tink you and I could never be great tinkers 'cause we got no science. But a man like de Professor has his head full of clutter — atomic valences, tables, formulas. You and me, we got more room in our skulls for real idiers."

"Sure, Pa. So what?"

"Hark now, this here be central to me thought. A common thread of stupidity holds de human race togedder, transcendin' all our petty differences. So don't you tell me these cretins in their cars ain't busy spinnin' webs of evil in everyting they does. They has much bigger schemes afoot than plantin' butts in de sand at Wasaga. Sure they does."

"But Pa, you don't want *Triffid* to wind up like the word *idiot*. When they're all calling each other Triffids, then what use is the word to us? You said you wanted a clinical term, without all those venomous associations."

"Well, maybe I am a bit crusty," he admits. "Remember when they had those yearly drivin' tests for folks over 80? At MTO they used to say, 'Here comes old Newfiejohn. He used to be an examiner here, would ye believe it?' At that they all would have a good laugh. Maybe I'm sufferin' from old age rage, do ye tink? Maybe that's why they laugh. Who was it who said: 'Hell is all de udders'? Lord help me, I longs for that far-off future time when folks may join de dog and de harse again in guileless being. De circle will close again one day, me bye. To make sense, it has to."

Pappy and I are looking at *The Thing from Another World*, original black-and-white version. It's a classic to blow you away, in which bad acting is part of the charm. It's the message that counts. And the message is central to the fears of our race. As the great enslavers of this planet, we fear that far-off race who will come here to put tethers and harnesses on us, make us eat in stalls, and keep us fat for the alien table.

Be watchful. Scan those skies. Any day they may be coming. Who knows what they'll look like or what they'll want? Who knows what horrors Bitch Nature may have forged on Mars?

But now we're in the next century and we no longer fear the Red Planet. The neighbourhood is safe. Relax, breathe easy.

Not quite, if Pa is right. We're in real big trouble. The Triffid threat comes from far out in the galaxy. Light years beyond our sun. Specific origin unknown. Purpose can only be inferred from observing effect; apparently, it is to subdue and use humankind by turning the race's baser inclinations against itself. Method is to invade minds in stealth, a cell and a synapse at a time. Victims notice nothing, but they finish as base, shadowy copies of their forebears. Much harder to fight than the Martian death ray. Much harder.

No use to ask Pappy how he knows all this. Once when I asked, he replied, "Chevy." Just that one word. Other times he put a finger into the weather, as though making the sign of the Triffids. But in all likelihood he was indicating the star Tau Ceti, meaning it was the Tauans who had enlightened him.

He was born with a caul in Joe Batt's Arm and he has seen the Far Travellers. He also sailed for many years on the old *Bluenose*. And he's the son of Simon Prince, MBE, who, though he was Deputy Registrar of the Supreme Court of New-foundland, never put his boots on till he got to town. With these distinctions Pappy has a right to a certain amount of mystery.

Julie McDuff phones toward the end of the movie. She's lucky I answer, as few are the times I've missed the electro-cution of the carrot man just to answer the phone.

I'm gruff at first, but I finish by listening patiently. I remind myself that she's been scarce lately; besides, she sounds anxious and plaintive, like a forlorn kitten mewing for some kindness.

"I've let you down," she says. "Can I see you right now?"

Nuts, I can hear Pa cheering; they got the carrot man. It's all over.

"See you in ten minutes," I tell her.

Coffee and brownies when I arrive. She looks pretty in a black pinafore and white blouse, hair tied behind. Faint per-fume, like the lingering of some rare blossom. Sure wish Gloria knew something about plain and subtle.

Brownies are perfect, chocolaty and chewy. They're packed with walnuts too. By then she's telling me she's sorry for what happened. I'm looking into those deep brown eyes of hers, wondering what it's all about.

Apparently, somebody found Julie's workbook, which I had

shoved partway under her door. Whoever it was, left a rude message in it. I can't believe she thought I did it. But that's what she's telling me.

"Well, it did look like your writing," she tells me defensively. "I guess that was the intention. Anyway, I didn't really think you wrote it. I mean, I didn't know what to think."

Christ! If I'd known that the past few days, I'd have felt pretty crumby. "So that's why you've been kind of scarce lately."

"You did tell me not to trust anyone," she says.

"Forget it, Julie. It's the climate of fear we live in. It's the Triffids. People are dazed and on their guard. That sometimes makes them behave stupidly. Got any more brownies?"

Sometimes Pappy and I reminisce about the pre-Triffid dawn of motoring, when I was only a tot, and we travelled on the winding little roads of Nova Scotia. There were marvels then beyond every bend in the road. There were so few cars that folk would greet each other with a honk when they met – in those days a honk was a cheery sound, a glad hello. It said, "Hi comrade! How are you? Enjoy your journey." Imagine that. We had kin up from Newfoundland who'd never heard a car honk, nor even seen a car, except in the movies.

When we tell McDuff, he says, "Geegosh, that musta been fun. Bet you were able to look at the trees and the cows in the fields and still drive safe."

"Sure," I tell him. "Those were the days when all roads were slow and crooked, because they followed the land. The Yellow Brick Road that Dorothy follows in *The Wizard of Oz* is just such a road. It's a road that really goes somewhere, because you do a lot more on it than just pass time. Yessiree. The cows were fat as butter. You could see the dee-dees dreaming in the dog rose. Chickadees," I explain. "We didn't know it then, but we were nearing the end of the Middle Ages."

In all innocence, McDuff asks, "Whatever made us the way we are? How come we turned into puffed-up little turd balls always in a rush? Why do all the roads have to be straight?

Why do we have to drive so fast we can't see anything? Why do we have to carry a phone wherever we go? Why — ?"

Amazing comments coming from a fuzz face like McDuff. "Why indeed," says Pa. "When I were a lad, I'd lie in a hay pook and wonder why seals were slippery and polar bears white. But then Fadder give me Darwin to read. After that I knowed, or thought I knowed, all de answers.

"Even so, McDuff, I could not answer those very questions you pose, till de theory of de Triffids dawned on me one glorious night on that ribbon of infamy, de Don Valley Parkway. There being no barnacle aback of me for such a while, Chevy began to hum oddly — I thought it were a hum, but in retrospect I tink Chevy had someting to say. I went home that night and prayed to Tau. In de marnin' 'twas clear as an ice crystal. I knowed then where all de evil come from. Triffids."

When I tell Doctor Abedni on the phone what Pappy said about his glorious ride on the Don Valley Parkway, the academic apparently falls to the floor in a vicious fit of laughter. After listening to his cries for an unconscionably long time, I hang up in disgust.

In spite of such silliness, Pappy presses the Doctor to recognize the Triffid hypothesis and the term "Triffid" itself.

"I wholeheartedly concur in the value of this name," says Abedni upon our next visit. "What is named is known, as they say. I have not found anything better. Triffid, the human vegetable, heh-heh. Very cunningly conceived, sir." He gives us a toothy smile. "Yes, you may have this honour, Mr. Pappy. And why not? You are probably the best and the safest driver in the Milky Way. And to think that I, a genius in neurology, and spectroscopy, and mathematics; a wizard and wonder in physics, a master of yoga, a serious student of the stars, et cetera — to think that I cannot drive for a bag of garbanzo beans! Genius works in wondrous ways, Mr. MTO-man."

"You know about my career at de Ministry of Transportation?" Pappy asks.

"Ha-ha, are you kidding me, Mister Pappy? You are the bugger who failed me on four road tests. You do not remember me. I was just one of those turban bastards, ha-ha-ha. I know about your little rule of thumb at MTO. Turban equals cannot drive, equals fail two or three times. Do not deny it. They warned me, the other turbans did. 'Better hope you do not get that old bugger,' they said. Of course I did get you, and I did not pass, not on four tries. By the fifth attempt I was broke. The lessons cost me $2000. It was fat city for the driving school. But you probably saved my life, sir."

I give the Professor full marks for recognizing his limitations. We try to overlook his eccentricities, as we hope he will overlook ours, recognizing that oddness is part of being special, and of having uncommon insight. According to Pa, it is precisely our quirky imaginations that have saved us from Triffid infusion.

"But what about my hypothesis?" Pa asks, taking the bull by the horns. "Ye's willin' to adopt de term 'Triffid.' Do ye also accept de theory behind it?"

"Theory? What theory? What hypothesis? The invasion of the Body Snatchers?" Then Abedni's face cracks and he falls to the floor making more noise than a rabid hyena. We stand around for a while in case he needs help. He tries to smother his fit in the carpet, then picks himself up and staggers to the washroom. We hear bubbling sounds. I picture him with his head in the toilet.

"Mystical dickie-bird!" says Pa.

TRIAL OF A MINDLESS WOMAN

All my nighttime dreams are crystal-clear and have the logic of prophecy. I record each one in my bedside journal upon awakening. Lately, I'm dreaming of the future, a time when justice reigns. Thus the mind prepares us for things it knows will come.

I see her cringe again as they bring her in, especially when her eyes rise to the bench and she spies me in my black robe of office. I'm sitting there like Grandpa Simon Prince. He never put his boots on till he got to town, but they made him deputy registrar just the same.

I begin at once, reminding the defendant that she is wrong in thinking the parked cars had to do with the death of her little boy. Bethinking me of the irrationality of her thought, I consider it a wonder she hasn't blamed the poor tiny tot who is dead, her only child, who was killed by a taxi.

The woman rants and cries, and well she should.

"The cabby!" she moans. "The parked cars!" And yet again, "The cabby! The parked cars!"

A voice booms from on high and echoes in the courtroom. "The Court will not be influenced by your crocodile tears." It is my voice. I wish to establish a tone. "The Court reminds the defendant that the cab driver has been absolved."

This I say hoping to goad her into the desired line of thought.

It works. She savagely attacks the cabbie, who ought to have shown more care, she says, since the view of the curb was blocked by a line of parked cars.

"And that's what you would have done, had you been the cabbie?"

"Certainly."

"The taxi was only doing the limit," I remind her.

Her voice rises hysterically, causing a flutter of imitative cries in the courtroom. "But he killed my baby!"

Jeers all around.

"Madam, the street in question is quite busy?" I ask, when order is restored.

"Yonge Street is always busy, Your Honour."

"Ah, Yonge Street. In your estimation, how fast is the traffic at the place in question? Normally?"

"Sixty to seventy kilometres. The limit's fifty, but everyone goes through there at sixty or seventy."

"Including you?"

"Of course."

I point out again that the cab driver was obeying the limit. "He was only doing fifty. That's ten to twenty kilometres slower than what you do yourself through there. You never have a thought that you might strike a child, or a dog, or a cat?"

"Well, yes, but ... I'm a careful driver."

Such a foolish remark the Court has not heard in a long time. The dog jurors on the east side of the courtroom are barking and growling, some snarling and showing their wolf fangs, causing the defendant to shudder. The cat jurors on the west side have all got their backs up, hair on end, and are hissing and spitting like hockey stars in the box after a brawl.

I use my gavel. The court falls silent. I lean forward and ask the defendant kindly, "What would have been a safe speed, do you think, right at this particular spot, on the day of the — incident?"

"With all due respect, Your Honour, how am I supposed to know?"

I adjust my robes, just as I imagine Grandpa Simon Prince used to do. I experience a ventral growl. My brain accepts a wandering thought on lunch. Perhaps I should give the defendant time to think. She may be having trouble getting her brain to turn over.

"When you can't see," she finally squeaks, "you should slow down."

Some of the onlookers and jurors cheer at this response. Others howl or hiss, thinking this is merely the lingering recollection of something she read a long time ago in *The Driver's Handbook*, or some other equally notorious and misleading publication.

I let these shows of spleen run their course. Then I gravely say, "Madam, I suggest that the cabbie in question did, in fact, slow down. He was not exceeding the limit; that has been established. But we know he could not have been obeying the law all the way up Yonge – that would be contrary to cabbie nature. Ergo, he must have slowed down."

"Damn you!" she cries, beside herself with rage. "He killed my baby!" She buries her face in her hands, her body heaving with great, wrenching sobs.

The cats and the dogs grumble at such a brazen tongue. Imagine, addressing the Grand Doomer in such a tone! But the Court is merciful; I choose to overlook this rudeness.

"Madam," I proceed gently, "you maintain that this 'other guy,' the cabbie, should have slowed down more than he did. Could you give the Court some ballpark speed? What about twenty-five kilometres? Would that be safe? Twenty? Fifteen? Ten? Five? Two? One?"

She wipes away the tears, looking very haggard, and gives the Court a defiant look. "How the hell should I know? Sau ... sorry, Your Honour, Grand Doomer, sir. You – ah – you have to do whatever is necessary to – ah – to drive safely. Everybody has that obligation, I seem to remember."

Raised eyebrows all around at such apparent percipience.

"Yes, Madam, everyone does have that obligation."

The dogs and cats are becoming restless with the proceedings – so much so that I warn them to show restraint, especially the Dobermans and Pit Bulls, who appear ready to pounce, though the Great Danes are not much better.

"Madam defendant, no doubt if you had been the cabbie, you would have done the right thing, wouldn't you? You would have slowed down enough, to whatever speed was safe under the circumstances. Isn't that so?"

"Yes. Well I – I mean, sometimes there are cars parked at the curb and you can't see. If you see something going on, or maybe even if you don't, you slow down. Yes, that's right. You slow down and you – you have your foot on the brake – you're ready to stop. But as for stating a speed, nobody can say exactly what speed is safe because – because it depends on what's happening and – whether you can see. Of course, sometimes we're in a hurry; you know, late for an appointment or something. And we can't hold up traffic for fears of fancy..."

The men and women of the jury shake their heads at this. But the canines and felines just want to be done with it all. The dogs are grumbling and whimpering. The Beagles plead with their big brown eyes, except a few who have dozed off. Most of the cats are snaking their tails out of boredom. The Siamese are vindictively sharpening their claws on the wood of the jury bench.

Poor soul! The whole court knows she doomed herself with those last two remarks.

It well behooves my high office to commiserate with the accused. I lean forward and say to the defendant confidingly, "You know, madam, your son was probably too small to be seen coming out from between those cars. It's a pity."

She heaves a great sigh. "Yes, he was very small. I suppose it's too much to expect that folk will take care for creatures they cannot see. They can't reasonably be expected to, can they? He just ran when I let go of him. He was chasing a feather. A tiny little feather..."

She starts to sob again. I get the picture perfectly. "A most fateful feather indeed, madam. The most profound consequences are often born on the wings of innocence, while truth and revelation love the cloak of tragedy. Little boys are themselves small feathers, flighty and unpredictable. That is why we need to hold on to them."

Now she's calm as she wipes her nose and eyes, red with agony. I do feel sorry for her.

"Knowing what you now know, madam, if someone were to press you to state a safe speed for this stretch of road, under the same conditions as obtained when your little boy died, what would you say?"

She looks up at me with forlorn, beseeching eyes. I believe those eyes have reconciled themselves with guilt, and with the harsh doom awaiting her.

"I – Your Honour – considering the parked cars, no speed is safe, is it? Really, no speed. Why do they have a speed limit if it isn't safe? Nobody obeys it anyway. I'm afraid it's all beyond me. Beyond the power of this brain. He was only two!"

There it is, then: an admission of brainlessness. I pull the black mask down over my eyes. A grave and solemn hush falls over the courtroom. At that, the poor doomed soul loses all self-control and begins to rage and lash out like a devil from hell.

Thus, in due accord with the first law of dreams, which requires a return to the waking world when the most painful part is reached, I open my eyes, grope for the table lamp, begin to scribble. No dream is to be ignored or wasted, but is sign and symbol of things to come.

Pappy and I discuss my revelation over a breakfast of boiled eggs and toast. "'Tis hard," Pa says, "when de victim's not a Triff but some little innocent. A cat, a dog, or a little bye."

"True, Pappy. That court though, pretty scary place! My dreams are all blood and thunder."

"Well ya see, Rufus, dreams and revolutions has their own logic. But they ain't no less true for that. They'll unfold in ways to spite us. Good for you, bye! We both hears de tramp of destiny." He lops off the top of another egg, neat and clean, as if it's the guillotine coming down on the head of a Triffid. "When it be time to dream again, Rufus, when you get to be Grand Doomer once more, see if you can nail de cabbie who mowed down that little guy. No point at all in lettin' that bastard go free."

SACRED SPACE

One of Sergeant McDuff's colleagues is killed in a rainstorm while driving south on Yonge Street. Her picture is in the paper. Just joined the force. I have to come back to it several times. Damn, it makes me mad to see it.

They betrayed her. Got her all psyched up at police college to serve and protect. Pumped her full of slogans. But they didn't give her what she needed to stay alive. They didn't show her how to drive. Just sent her out with the Triffid still in her. Gave her a licence to kill, and she wound up killing herself. Even good guys have to respect the water on the road. They didn't tell her that, and now she's gone. Gone too a lifetime of deeds that would have spoken well for her, and would have honoured the police family she came from.

She was hit broadside after skidding, or aquaplaning, into the oncoming lane. No charges were laid.

Bad weather, the paper says. *Torrential downpour. Dark as night.* The police report is similar: *Bad weather. Road flooded with water. Terrible, perhaps unavoidable, accident.*

Pa and I are suspicious. Too many cops crashing. According to *The Star*, Constable Jane Ricci is the fifth Toronto officer to die this year in off-duty collisions; five other officers have been killed in their patrol cars while on duty. I also read:

> *Staff Sergeant Barry Stonewall, when asked what hours Constable Ricci had been working before her death, said, "I don't have that information and I'm not getting it for you." When asked if Constable Ricci had had any driver training, he said, "What do you think?"*

Earlier in the week, a dedicated Toronto police officer and family man, John Bailiwick, was killed when his Camaro was rear-ended on the 400. Bailiwick was thrown out by the force of the impact and was crushed by his own car. He was not wearing a seatbelt.

Ironically, Bailiwick's accident occurred the day before police were to launch a national crackdown on motorists who don't buckle up.

We've just learned McDuff has recently had his second collision in a year. No physical injury incurred. Perhaps I've been too easy on him because he's Julie's father.

Today I catch up with him at Donut Delight. He's sitting behind a couple of glazed donuts plus coffee. Looks up at me from within a fog of doughy rumination.

"Oh yeah?" he says, when I tell him he sped by me the other day with his brain in reverse. "What of it? I'm just a cop. Hey, look at me, I'm human." He's smacking his donut and slurping his coffee.

He's preoccupied, so I leave him alone. No use to deny it. He's a Triffid. A poor player on the ice. Not real at all. Just one of the many who've had their brains neutralized. That's why he's always in a fog. It was that police college crisp-as-fresh-lettuce look that threw me off. That studied, frank expression the Triffids drilled into him, so he could fool those of us who are still sane. That Sergeant-Renfrew-of-the-Northwest-Mounted look. Easy to take him for a super-decent guy. Too easy. No wonder Pa calls him names. Guess Pa hit the nail right on the head when he said they fix them all up at police college with their Mr. Decent personae. Makes me shiver!

Before leaving, I ask him if he will attend the funerals of Ricci and Bailiwick. Affirmative. I tell him there's going to be trouble at Hillcrest High. Says, "Yep." Boy, talk about self-absorption – he's putting the napkin into his mouth along with the chocolate donut.

As I climb into my car, something clicks in my head. I'll have to dream about this guy. Yes, I think McDuff's turn has come.

Sure enough, several nights later I have my visitation. I find myself under a grand dome. I hear sounds of celebration. A new age is dawning. The sane rule on earth in the name of Reason. But here in this grandiose space a heavy silence reigns. The awaited one enters and takes his place on high.

Heaven help me, I am he, the one to whom all defer. Yes, the Keeper of Reason, Grand Doomer of the Age of Aquarius. The eleventh hour has struck and the court is risen.

Lo! See who stands head-hung before and below me. This sorry piece of fuzz, the policeman McDuff. The charge: conspiracy to subvert the True Spirit of Humankind.

He pleads not guilty of course, as all felons from time immemorial have done. His so-called defence is nothing but the usual mish-mash of Triffid unreason.

"I'm just your average all-round idiot, Your Honour," he stupidly tells the Court, as if it were a fine excuse to be exactly like everyone else. "I always go with the flow. I never hold up traffic."

He wears his uniform, as though it might help exonerate him. The Court pays little note as he babbles on, trying to show he's no different from millions of others, and therefore no more deserving of punishment—the favourite defence of the tormentor.

"I'm only one in a crowd, Your Honour. I'm just as negligent and inattentive as the next guy. I drive impaired all the time, as my brain is always somewhere else. I keep my windows grungy. Got no respect for the car I'm driving. Don't know the rules of the road any better than anyone else... Hey, I have a stressful occupation. I uphold the law. I could die at any time, because I'm no better prepared than anyone else..."

The jury have been yawning through all of this. Their faces look familiar. Wait a minute, they're my colleagues at Galaxy. There's Big Bob the trucker, Hing the mechanic, Severo, Justin, Sheila, Debbie, Donald, and Ray.

Pappy's here too, but in what capacity I can't recall. Small billy-goat horns protrude above his ears. "Ask de prisoner about manners," he demands.

"Manners? Sure, I know all about manners," McDuff says. "I always salute when the other guy lets me go first—you know, when the right of way is anybody's guess? And when making a turn, I take care not to clip a pedestrian's heels, especially if he's walking his dog ... "

I wink at the jury and notice Pa is drooling, the way he did once when he came home with some hardtack and a package of cod tongues.

McDuff goes on and on, thinking no doubt he's making an impression. And so he is. "Sometimes on a rainy day I miss the puddles and the pedestrian goes home dry. Nobody's perfect. I'm not rude, just in a hurry. Who isn't, eh? Maybe I'm impulsive, but that's not a crime. 'Screw You and Scurry on,' that's my motto. Sometimes I may appear to be out of control. Well, we've all got some bad habits ... "

"Ask him if he ever heard of Reason," Debbie shrieks, putting down her knitting. Then she cackles like a witch on her way to the Sabbat.

"Ask him if he ever heard of Sacred Space," Big Bob growls, as he takes a huge slice out of the jury dock with a carving knife.

Thunder in the courtroom. It's my voice again, the sound of retribution. "Defendant, are you aware that a void is Sacred Space, into which nothing material is permitted to intrude? Are you aware the universe is founded upon this principle? Are you aware that good drivers observe it religiously?"

McDuff swallows hard and glances uneasily around the court. The shadow of doubt descends upon his face like a poisonous veil, causing him to choke and to whiten.

I laugh, and then the whole court laughs. "For shame!" I say, without much gravity; like God, tired of pretending to take the Earth pricks seriously.

Everyone cries, "Shame!" Big Bob makes thrusting gestures with his carving knife. Justin rattles a bag of nails.

McDuff tries one last defence. He resorts to the maxim of natural science which proclaims that Nature abhors a vacuum. "Your Honour, Grand Doomer, sir, the great universal void is filled with stars and their planets, and the satellites of these planets, and also with asteroids, meteors, space dust, hydrogen, and other gases. Here on Sol III, if you pull out any weed on your lawn, it immediately grows back. And so fierce is this natural competition that grass will even find a way through the molecules of driveway asphalt.

"So when I'm driving, Your Honour, what could be more natural than to claim every turn of space I can, and move up to the ass end of the guy ahead? And even when I stop in traffic, I do the same, because then the guy ahead is less ahead than if I were farther back, and also I'm a few metres closer to home."

Snickers all around the court at these remarks.

"The rear-end emissions don't trouble you?" I ask.

"No, sir. I'm rather fond of them. The fact is, I was raised on fart and love a good stink."

My brows arch. The whole court cocks a brow. Then laughter erupts. A festive mood breaks out among the jury. Big Bob wields his knife, Justin shakes his bag of nails, Debbie is checking her needle points, Severo and Hing are playing with hammers.

I pull the black mask down over my eyes, and in ponderous tones address the defendant: "Gordon McDuff, you profess to imitate Nature. Such a vile practice must be excused in a rat, a lemming, a sheep or a wolf, and countless other spawn of Bitch Nature. They have no choice. But we, as the bastard offspring of Nature and Reason, ought to know better. The human life form is expected to rise, not descend into the sink with the rest. Reason has given us a high, holy purpose, that we may not slough off without endangering the galaxy. Rats and lemmings, sheep, and wolves are not accountable, and so they live their lives with noses in the dirt. But we humans are star gazers, made to stand erect and contemplate tomorrow. What a poor pastime you gave yourself, Gordon McDuff, when you started dragging others back into the primal slime. Jurors, how find ye?"

"Guilty!" the jurors all roar with one voice. Then they do a dance in single file with Big Bob in the lead, all brandishing their instruments.

And so I direct my final words to the prisoner: "Sergeant McDuff, you have been found guilty of sustained petty harassment, a most grave offence. Together with numerous 'other guys,' you have caused untold, perhaps irreparable, damage to the tone and temper of life in this city. And so you have put yourself in that class of criminals whose business it is to prey upon the innocent, to corrupt the stupid and vulnerable, causing them to imitate you, and to surrender their souls to Triffidus, the universal enemy.

"Gordon McDuff, this Court has found you guilty as charged. The law entails but one penalty for these crimes, and that is death upon cross-and-wheel. So shall you be nailed, affixed, and raised in the Valley of the Don, between the river and the parkway of that name. And there in the breeze you shall remain until dead, yea till the crows and ravens pick thee clean, and thy bones blanch in the sun. And from thy neck shall hang a gas pedal and a brake, symbols of your life of errancy. May your soul come to a merciful haven. Take the bastard away!"

McDuff is dragged off to the nailing, and those who are going down to see it hurry off after the prisoner.

Unfortunately, just as I'm thinking I'll go down to the Don and drive a nail into the traitor McDuff myself, I wake up, roused from my errand of justice by Jinkerdiddle's Dobermans, which just then decide to bay at the moon. I plug my ears with toilet paper and try hard to regain the shady kingdom of prophecy. To no avail.

I begin to scribble in my diary of dreams. I hold this dream to be a sign of things to come.

A RULE OF THUMB FOR THE DUMB

A beam of light is decomposed by a prism. The opposite reaches of my spectrum of students are Julie of great promise and plodder Klutz.

I say to Julie, "You're at the movies. A fire has broken out. Screams, shouts, panic, the herd stampeding—all the usual symptoms of dementia and regression. Everybody going one way. A frantic, mindless crush, like spooked bovines in a western.

"Except—except a few. One in ten. A few are different. They don't run with the crowd. Their first instinct is to get away from it. And while they're separating themselves from the others, they're evaluating their options."

Julie raises an ironic brow. "Come on, Rufus, I know all that."

"Good girl. I thought you did." It occurs to me that something is not right. I ask her if she feels okay to drive. I take the car up the road and park.

"It's that stupid note somebody scribbled in my workbook," she tells me. "My boyfriend thinks he has to even the score. At school they're all taking sides. They got guns and knives. I can't believe what's happening."

She starts to snivel lightly. Hell, I'm not a social worker, so I say the obvious. It's what most people want to hear anyway. I tell her to talk to this Ennio guy, her boyfriend.

"Tell him to smarten up or else," I say.

"Or else what?" she sobs.

"You're through with him, of course."

"Oh no, I couldn't do that."

We cancel the lesson because of indisposition. Boy, the schools are going right down the tube.

Poor Lenard Klutz. He needs shock therapy to get his grey matter free. About 30 million volts' worth. He ran over a mouse while out driving with his mother.

"So what's your excuse?" I inquire, taking on the role of advocate for all rodentia.

"Didn't see it in time."

That's what he says. But there's an undertone of bravado in his voice. I'd be inclined to think he ran over the mouse on purpose, if it didn't seem unlikely that Klutz could aim for and hit something so small.

"Watch it, Klutz. They take a dim view of that out in the galaxy."

"I'm not afraid of the Tau Cetians, sir. My mother says you're nuts."

So now it's the mother, eh? What makes him think she's any better than the old man? Old mother Klutz, eh? I picture Lenard as a little boy sitting between daddy and mummy Klutz in a succession of family cars. I picture them teaching him the Finger Sign, and how to say to say "idiot!" with a maximum discharge of bile. Sure, they're both to blame.

Boy's still got the Triffid in him. I can see that. They baptized and confirmed him in the name of Word and Sign. All those years in the family car. Just doesn't show it when he's with me – that would be to fling dung at knight and steed whilst girding up to fight the fire-breathing dragon. Nay, fie upon such villainy!

"No!" I tell him right in the middle of the lesson. "No! No! No! They are *not* all idiots! Remember what I said?"

"Yeah."

"Tell me."

He screws up his face. "One person in ten can drive, absolute max. People like you, Great Master."

"And … ?"

"The rest are scum. Malignant lumps. The cancer of human-kind. They only pretend to drive. The world is full of pre-tenders. People like my dad."

"That's it, son. I hope you sincerely believe it. When you can say that with a straight face, I'll be proud to be your instructor. Just remember, before you start calling people names, you've got to know what you're talking about. You have to be able to tell good from bad. It's really basic. Repeat after me: good from bad."

"Good from bad..."

"Try that on again, lad. Go on: good from bad."

"Good from bad. Good from bad."

"Attaboy, Lenard. Now, let me give you a little rule of thumb to guide you. Until you're sure you know what driv-ing is all about, always, always, always assume that 'the other guy' is a friend of yours, or even one of your heroes. Definitely somebody you like and respect."

"Somebody I like." Klutz scratches his short, wiry hair. "I like Madonna. I like Hulk Hogan. Could it be one of them?"

"You bet it could. Okay, Lenard, Hulk and Madonna it is, then. From now on, when another driver does something bad to you, know what I want you to do? I want you to say to yourself, 'That's Hulk in that car.' Or if it's a gal you can say, 'That's Madonna in that car.' Got that?"

"That's Hulk in that car. That's Madonna."

"Perfect. Now, I want you to practise that at home. Use toy cars if you want to. Imagine what you're going to say. Once you pronounce the magic word, though – Hulk or Madonna – you're not gonna want to bang down on your horn. You won't even think of yelling 'Idiot!' And you'll keep your fingers on the wheel. It won't be hard to do, because you're thinking what a cool chick that Madonna is. If she did some-thing stupid, you know she didn't mean it. Just remember, they're heroes, like Superman or war vets. Then you know how wrong it would be to call them names."

"Yes, sir, that figures."

"Now, son, I want you to take that one step further. When you meet 'the other guy,' you guard yourself as if he were a dork. Understand? As if he were champion idiot of all time.

And he just might be. There is no way to know. But no matter what he does, you treat him like a hero. Because you don't know, do you? You can't know. It may really be a dork, or it may be Hulk or Madonna. You just can't take that chance."

"Oh man, that's weird!"

"Just keep telling yourself: I'm not going to make an ass of myself in front of Hulk and Madonna. I'm not going to insult people I like."

I tell him some of the soundest principles are weird at first thought. "But once you master this one, Lenard, you're free to concentrate on the real dangers and worries; and, in the truest sense, you're way ahead of the crowd."

WINDOW OF ESCAPE

Pappy and I are invited to Dr. Abedni's for tea.

Usual types encountered on the way. Just a bit worse because the moon is full. The dung flies sniffing our tail are several centimetres closer than normal. They're drawn to the space we command as though by a magnet. They earnestly wish to stick their snouts into it. They wish to hell we weren't in the way. In the rearview I glimpse them bobbing like worried ostriches in a cage. All the cares of the world have focused at this one point to torment them. So their brows buzz with primal thoughts, like the first stir of life in the Frankenstein monster's brain. The Word is ready on their lips, the Sign is in their eyes. The Word is "idiot!" and the Sign is "finger." A little devil calls from the brain stem of each of them: "Get up a car! – Get up a car! – Get up a car!"

"Pickle's risin' on de kraut," says Pa. "It's de moon goddess, Silene. She pricks up de libido."

"Sure, Pa."

We turn off Bloor. The Professor's street is gloomy in the lamplight. It's one of those passageways obscured forever in the shades of time, the shadows of ancient, overpowering trees, heavy with secrets.

Pa finds a place at the curb. Abedni opens. The two cats, one black and one white, slide by us with plaintive, calculated mews. The Professor's unready appearance leads us to believe he's forgotten having invited us. Still, he's all smiles as he ushers us into the curried interior.

"Mr. Pappy and Mr. Rufus, so delighted that you popped in. Yes indeed I am. We have to stick together, do we not? To fight those Triffids, ha-ha-ha."

"Pyew!" says Pa, overpowered, but covers with a cough. He then has a fit of the hiccups, which don't go away till he's held his breath for half a minute and drunk two glasses of water.

"Dear me, is that nasty attack over? Amazing, isn't it, what a glass of good old water will do! Did I promise you tea and curry? Well the curry is on, as your noses have no doubt told you. I was just about to add some raisins and almonds. How about a nice glass of spiced buttermilk before we dine?"

"Fake it," I whisper to Pappy, as we follow our host into the kitchen. Pa can't stand curry. Makes his gorge rise. "Threaten him with blueberry wine or spruce beer," I advise.

Pappy settles for a brown ale and I enjoy spiced buttermilk. Dr. Abedni adjusts the gas so as not to burn the spices, and we all go into the living room, which is a mess of scattered books, papers, clippings, and photographs.

"Life is too short to spend on trifles," the Professor says, guessing my thought. "Triffids and truffles, they are okay, heh-heh. Some people like to do chores, depend on them, even. Not me. Why else did we invent specialization, if not to free us brainy types from the daily drudge?

"I am quite unsuited for housework. I am, you see, what they call – ah – spaced out. Head in the clouds sort of thing. Single-minded when it comes to science, but otherwise rather incompetent. Well, you saw me drive, so you know what I mean. I mismatch my socks, like Einstein, but – ah – I do it on purpose. So U of T does not forget who I am. The more disorganized I am, the more they think I am worth, heh-heh. If I look like a laundry basket, then it stands to reason my head must be occupied with something really big, like the unified theory. But you have to be a star to get away with it, heh-heh."

"Get on wit ye. Ten old maids at a mug-up, that's what ye sounds like."

Radshak comes back with a jibe of his own. "Tell me, Mister Pappy, is it true the road signs in Newfoundland say, 'Speeders have small dicks'?"

Pa sputters like a Model A about to quit.

"Your Newfoundland is a curious place – an exciting place. Do you think I would get on down there, or would the sight of me shock them? I am a restless soul, never content. I am a driven man. Demons hound me night and day. And it is all because the girls back home were covered up. You know, gentlemen, I believe when one reaches a certain age, one must have a solid memory of an undetermined minimum of satisfying sexual encounters. Otherwise, one winds up like me. Unhappy, out-of-joint, a desperate seeker ... But I doubt that you follow me ... "

"Not so," says Pa. "I has powers beyond your reach. And they be rarer than de white deer's pelt. Scarcer than de lunar rainbow. I would not trade this insight for all de esoteric claptrap in ten professors' brains. And so I knows you was about to take us into de darkest bays of de mind, where anyting might happen. You be itchin' to titillate us wit yer tender-hearted, puerile reminiscences, and yer frail failin's. Shame on ye."

That's taking the icing off the Doctor's professorial cake! Radshak droops visibly under this withering assault from the forces of superstition and creeps off to the kitchen to fetch more ale and buttermilk. Returning, he says, "So you have powers, Mr. Examiner-man."

"Pa can also remove the sorrow of one crow, and is good at all kinds of white witchcraft," I proudly inform the Professor.

"Dear me, the sorrow of one crow? White witchcraft?" Professor Abedni gives us a fragile look. We can't tell what's coming next. He looks at us warily over the rim of his but-termilk glass, as though weighing these new and perturbing facts.

"Well then, make it short," Pa says. "Out wit it. Let's get it over wit. Whatever misery be on yer mind, sir, let's have it."

Abedni gives a very childish pout. "I thought you already knew that, Mr. Allseeing Examiner-man. Look into your crystal ball and tell me what I am thinking, please."

"It's not that simple," I say.

"Only when de stars are right does I have this power. And never in de dark of de moon."

"Pa was pretty sure what you had in mind, after all the clues you gave him."

"Dear me, Mr. Rufus, you are right. I did give clues." Rad-shak brightens, apparently having persuaded himself that Pa's demonstration of foreknowledge was a hoax after all. "Dear me. Well, gentlemen, I – I wanted to warn you. You see, I have experienced a paucity of gratifying encounters. My primal urges have grown ravenous because of it. They are like a pack of starved wolves. The Mesozoic in me is just waiting to take over. It is always goading me to do this or that – things civilized folk ought not to do. If it were not for the calm and harmonic vibrations of yoga, I do not know how I would cope. We are all perverts and felons at heart, you know."

"Hmph!" says Pa, who has little sympathy for complicated lives.

I thank the Doctor for confiding in us. Full marks for being frank and open. "But you said you want to warn us, Doctor. Surely you didn't mean –?"

"Truly, Mr. Rufus, I blush to have to say this again – I was thinking of Miss Gloria. I have been thinking of her more than I ought. Cannot get her out of my head, to be truthful. She – she gave me a certain look when she was here, quite innocent I am sure, but it came straight from the bottom of her brain stem."

I shrug. "You're too sensitive, Doctor. You're not the first one to react to Gloria that way. I'm sure you pay her a compliment."

"Just the same, Mr. Rufus, I want you to be careful." The Professor smirks self-consciously. "If you bring her here again – she is most welcome – I want you to take her by the hand and guard her with your life."

"Professor, I'm not afraid you'll pounce on her."

"Please, do as I say. Tell her what I said and be on guard. We must always be on guard. I do not wish to sound dramatic. In all likelihood I am causing unnecessary alarm. I beg you not to hold these – ah – revelations against me."

"Won't be easy," Pa says.

To get off the subject I point to some large-format photos that are propped against one wall. "What are they?" I ask.

Boy, what a collection of ugly mugs and maws! I can feel Pappy's energy as he tries to connect with Tau to divine their purpose.

"Triffids," replies the Doctor, without any sign of a grin or a snicker. "All caught in their parkway angst." The Doctor reflects for a moment, then remarks, "The key to our Triffid, gentlemen, is indeed the brain. My research points to only three possible explanations for the way they behave. To wit: no brain; little use of brain; use confined to infundibula. Messages are not getting through or are being ignored, or both. I am not certain yet whether the difficulty is to be found in the neurons or in the synapses ... "

"Radshak, this research never ends," Pa says. "What about my theory of osmotic infusion? It postulates a general envelopment of de brain by alien ether, which our science cannot detect. Such a brain is like a tea bag in water. De essence is all gone out."

Abedni gives us a blank look, then begins to snicker in fits and starts. And as creeks and rills, brooks and streams run together to make one great flood, so do the Doctor's upheavals become one great, wide-open, full-throated, head-thrown-back laugh from the belly. "Haw-haw-haw, hark-hark-hark," he goes. He snorts and then hee-haws again. He's so foolish, I have to give with a few yuk-yuks myself. And I can't help thinking there may be something out of whack with Pappy's proposals after all.

Pa, of course, is mortified.

That silly academic rolls off his chair to convulse on the carpet, which appears to have never known the suck of a vacuum. Pa and I back away coughing and sneezing. Abedni turns over onto his stomach, pounding the floor with his fists, thus raising more pulver. Rolls again and collides with his motorcycle.

We hurry to retrieve our jackets from the hall closet – Pa would do anything to escape that curry – and we don't put them on till we're out on the sidewalk.

"Fresh air! Pig's trotters, that's what I wants. Or seal fin and pease puddin'. Let's get Chevy to take us to de Newfie store. Finnan haddie, fish and brewis ... "

I can't wait for Abedni to do his brain-scan experiments. Certainly should prove something. Odd though, that a man of science should carry on the way he does. So I understand when Pa disparages him, calling him a "dabbler" and a "mystical dickie-bird."

One night, at Abedni's, the eternal questions come up, even though we know their futility and suspect we might be better off home in bed. It's all about how we humans found science and set out forever on the road to tomorrow.

We agree that rational argument, unaided, could never have discovered anything about ultimate realities. Same goes for our senses.

But before science, we had only reason, our senses, and religion. All our arguments sprang from them. We were trapped in a finite bubble, in which all voyages of the mind returned us to the same coordinates. Jean-Luc Picard of the starship *Enterprise* had such an experience when lured into a spatial bubble by a creature named Na-*ghi*-lam. From the outside, the bubble appeared finite. But once inside, no matter how fast or how far the starship travelled, it could not breach the confines. From time to time, illusory windows of escape appeared, only to vanish when a course was set for them.

That was how we were before science. We had no means of escape, only our windows of illusion. We might have gone on hoping and imagining without significant result till the end of solar time.

Instead, we stumbled upon science, the one true window of escape. And now, at warp speed, we distance ourselves from cruel Na-ghi-lam, having traded our bubble for the universe.

This seems to be the consensus in Radshak's kitchen.

The universe, we agree, is a program that runs itself, with pain and evil duly encoded in the plan, though we do make allowance for interventions by intelligent beings.

Pa makes a case for the devil's being Triffidus, and no one is inclined to argue. But whereas Pappy's devil is an external agent, an alien, the Doctor stubbornly insists the devil is within – not necessarily programmed in from the beginning, but at any rate a chance development.

"Oh, what does it matter!" I protest, after much argument. "The main thing is we know it's there and that it causes great woe in the world." And so, for the sake of harmony in the Party, we agree to leave it at that.

Pappy and I begin to lose interest when Abedni starts on about God. It's more difficult to posit an Agent who was not made than it is to argue matter or a universe that did not need to be made, but just always was.

"*Something* had to always have been, hadn't it?" I ask, "since something cannot arise out of nothing." To me it seems like a starting point and a stumbling block at the same time.

"Limitation of the human mind," says the Doctor. "The dilemma is probably only apparent, since as we have noted, if the brain were sufficient to comprehend reality unaided, then we would not have needed science to rescue us from our minds. But, heh-heh, nothing can elude us forever. Not now, when we are out of the goddarn bubble. Not quantum gravity. Not the unified theory. Not even God."

The Professor lowers his voice, leaning over the table to be nearer, and tells us in a confidential tone, "I believe, ultimately, we shall meet the Godhead – and tweak his beak!"

"No!" says Pa, less scandalized than incredulous. But what else can a man from Terra Nova say?

"Dear me, it is all hubris," Radshak argues. "Everything we do. It is all a slap in the face to the Deity. I think we humans were meant to crawl around in the dirt like everything else, and be toyed with. We were never expected to stand up straight and gaze at the stars. Oh yes, we will tweak his beak."

"You think of the Deity as some kind of fowl?" I humbly ask.

"Sometimes I do. A great, sad, amorphous, indecisive question mark of a bird. When I do yoga, I feel he is near. And I have this sense that the Ultimate Force is not so far beyond our reach as we may suppose."

"Air in yer breeches," Pa says, acerbically.

"Yes, gentlemen, one day we shall touch God. But when we do, will God still be God? Or will we say to the Deity, with irresistible logic and crushing authority, 'Move over and let *us* do the job'?"

"Well," I say, "I hope you geniuses get it right, because there are a lot of people depending on you. I still have some doubt myself. How do you know we haven't just escaped from one bubble into another, larger one? How do you know we've seen the last of Na-ghi-lam?"

"Gracious me, there are no guarantees, Mr. Rufus."

"That will do now," says Pa. "That's enough spectaculation. Just tink, me poor old pappy used to walk barefoot to town, afore he'd put his boots on. Nowadays, it seems we straddles all creation in these seven-leaguers. We sure come on aways since I were a lad and sailed to Chiner on de *Bluenose*.

"Wish ya coulda seed her, Radshak. The *Bluenose*—what a vessel! There wasn't none faster anywhere. Beat de best de Yanks come up wit. 'Twas said there had to be some odd quirk in de design to make her skitter over de magic blue ahead of all de udders. But later, when they built a second vessel to de same plan, hopin' to have a new champion, they was disappointed. Maybe it was someting in de very hands o' de men who built her, de Lunenburgers; someting that died wit 'em. They calls it a great mystery.

"Yep. Old Captain Walters, he knowed me reputation. Never sailed witout me. But then I left de sea for good. Went badly for de *Bluenose* after that. She went under durin' a storm down in Cribby. Great loss it were. Terrible loss."

The Professor gives him a pitying look. "A salty yarn. Bless me, I can taste the brine and smell the herring. What an exciting tale! Perhaps I should call you 'Captain'? But that is what all three of us are—captains of men. Captains courageous!"

Pa's looking not too pleased. I suspect some uncomplimentary thought has passed through the guru's mind. Something like: Silly old salt, bet you blame the thunder when your milk goes sour.

Pa's probably thinking, what a turkey! And it's no wonder.

No sensible Newfoundlander would ever waste a thought on anything so bizarre as a grown person squatting and bouncing around on mattresses in the vain expectation of ultimately rising and flying away.

Professor Abedni, who loves to hear himself talk, soon starts in again on his own areas of expertise: "Look how stubborn the universe is, my friends, at the other end, at the level of the microcosm. We have it under our cyclotronic thumb, so to speak, accelerating ions to produce particles of energy right up to a limit set by the relativistic mass change, as the particles approach the speed of light. And yet, something eludes us. It's very clever, whatever is going on there. But I think I know what it is…"

Pappy and I do not wait around to find out where these speculations might be heading. And in any case, the Doctor becomes quickly incoherent and obviously unaware of our presence, so we feel like eavesdroppers at his own private, as Pappy might say, "confabulations."

Pa looks a bit wizened of late. One night, I get home to find him all spruced up and wearing combat boots. Boots are black with a shine to see your face in.

"Out for a scuff," Pa says, noticing my interest.

"A dance? With Gerdie? In those boots?"

Looks me right in the eye. "Been out gettin' plate numbers."

"Oh. Trucks?"

"Ever seen de roke that comes from 'em, black as night, foul and thick? Half of those rigs is fallin' apart. Pieces comin' off on de road all de time. Drivers ain't no better. Sleep-deprived, most of 'em. 'Tis sad to know nobody's watchin' over us. Real sad."

I wonder if that's all Pa is doing out there. I hope it isn't something stupid. I look into his tired old eyes and they seem to say: Ain't got much time, ain't gonna live forever, gotta get my work done.

"We've spent too much time smelling posies, Pa. That's why your book's not done. That's why people laugh at the

Party and call us names. But we'll triumph in the end, Pa. The good guys always do. You're not gonna spoil it, are you?"

"You mean by dyin'? If it's dyin' ya mean, ain't got much say over that. I ain't givin' up, if that's what yer talkin' about. They can send fer me if they wants, but I ain't goin' quiet."

"I mean out there on the road."

"Don't do nuttin' witout Chevy and Tau. Hope that puts yer mind at ease."

Abedni has got him all anxious and worked up. I tell him, "Better slow down. You're bold pushing. Your hair's getting whiter."

Pa just says, "I harks hard," and moves away.

What will happen when his book is finished? Will he have fulfilled his earthly purpose and want to move on? I think he should start on a new book right now, so I advise him to throw all his energies into an attack on motor mania and nail those Triffids but good.

"But take your time, Pa," I caution. "There's nothing that makes us more vulnerable to the Triffid poison than being pressed for time. Serenity, Pa. And don't forget, your book could be a springboard for the Party. The beginning of a new order."

My argument must be having some effect, as I hear Pappy muttering title proposals.

DR. ABEDNI SUMMONS
THE PRIMAL PERSONALITY

One Sunday in November we are about to depart for Dr. Abedni's when Gloria says she'd like to drive. We make the usual excuses, whereupon she produces a driver's licence with her name on it. It's the standard Ontario sugar-corn prize, blue in colour and very authentic-looking. And lately, they've added a photo of sorts.

"Yep, it's genuine all right," I have to admit, "but nothing to be proud of. And it doesn't change a thing. How long've you had it?"

"A week."

"Subterfuge!" says Pa.

Gloria and I sit in the back and sulk all the way to the Doctor's. I feel betrayed; haven't I told her numerous times she's not ready for a licence? She's a real pain when she wants to be.

I had one hell of a time persuading her not to go alone to Doctor Abedni's. She seems to regard the idea as an adventure. I must say, Abedni has an infernal nerve inviting her for hypnotic testing without even telling us!

I also asked her not to wear her short red dress. "You're going to distract him," I argued.

She poo-pooed these reservations, saying my mind was prone to focus where it had no business. "Besides," she told me, with a gleeful chortle, "I intend to test his mettle."

And so, as we enter the house on this day, and the black cat, followed by the white one, slinks up for a coy brush against Pa's polished boots, we can tell by the vibrations that

Abedni is not happy to see Gloria in company. Still, his eyes do light up like tropical fireflies at the sight of her.

"My dear, please come into my lair, ha-ha-ha. Never mind, the Professor is only kidding, heh-heh. You are welcome anytime, anytime you feel disposed. What can I get you? A cup of tea perhaps?"

The living room is strewn with books and tomes, and before sitting down, we must remove some of them from the sofa. "Evidently you have been busy, sir," I remark, but it appears that the great mind is not inclined to humour Pa and me. He busies himself with the interview paraphernalia.

Pappy, for his part, has all his faculties in play, and is sniffing like an airport hash hound hot in pursuit of any unauthorized references to Triffids, in the event the Professor should stoop so low.

Abedni gives Gloria a little test for hypnotic susceptibility, so expeditiously we scarcely note it. "Now, my dear," he says, "the purpose of this interview is to examine your own special relationship to your car – in your case, the car you will soon be driving – and also the fundamental attitudes you have toward the driving activity."

"Gee, Professor, that's cool." Gloria gives a bashful flick of her lashes.

"Heh-heh, you are going to be a marvellous subject, Miss Gloria. Now, I will ask you some questions, and you will respond briefly and frankly. Short, honest answers, please. Then, when that is done, I will put you under and I will ask the same questions again. Finally, we shall compare the two sets of answers. Anything unclear? No? Here we go."

Doctor Abedni activates his equipment and plunks a pillow into her lap. "Knees distract me, my goodness. All right, I want you to imagine you are out for a drive on a fine sunny day, not much traffic. Imagine how you feel. Describe those feelings for me."

"Well, Professor, I feel fine, I guess. I always like to be out for a drive on a sunny day."

"Now, Gloria, picture heavy traffic. You can see it, hear it, smell it, taste it. How do you feel now?"

"It's no fun driving in traffic, Professor."

"Is the design of your car important?"

"Sure. For looks and for safety."

"Who causes collisions?"

"People who can't drive—who aren't paying attention. They may be in a hurry. Speeders—"

"As you know, Gloria, driving is risky. Comment on that."

"I try not to think of it. If we thought about all the risks we run, we'd never get out of bed in the morning."

"How does your car affect your status as a person?"

"Are you kidding, Professor?"

"Great answer!" I cry, interrupting the proceedings. The Professor gives me a vexed look.

"One last question, my dear. How does your car affect your sexual image? I mean, the way others perceive you, sexually?"

"Really, Professor, that's pure cow dung."

Great answer again. Pappy and I are amazed.

"All right," says Abedni, "that is that. Now I shall proceed to put you under. Are you comfortable, my dear? Ah, please retain the pillow. Here is another to sit on, if you wish."

The Doctor then speaks to her in a very soothing and monotonous voice, while he dangles a peculiar phallic-looking key chain before her eyes. Gloria, who began with an air of wanting to make things difficult, soon surrenders; the muscles of her face slacken and her eyes grow vacant.

"Sooooo good. Sooooo relaxed. Are you ready to answer my questions, Gloria?"

"Yes."

"All right then. You are out driving on a really nice day. What are your feelings?"

"Freedom…power…invincibility…"

Poor Pappy gives a mock slap to his forehead. I feel the same way. We both know that the interview is about to take a serious turn for the worse. Professor Abedni is poised to uncover the naked truth about Gloria.

"What do you mean by 'freedom'?"

"I can do anything I want."

"What do you mean when you say you feel invincible?"

"I'm Number One. I'm God."

Boy, what an evil glint I detect in the eye of that Abedni! He gives us a wink, as if to say, that's how you draw out the Triffid.

"Now, Gloria, the traffic is heavy. Picture it. Can you see it, smell it, feel it?"

"I hate them. They're in my way. They're all idiots! I want to kill them."

My poor Gloria, Abedni's getting right inside her. Pappy's beginning to enjoy it.

"It's de real her. That's Gloria right enough. It's de way she drives."

"All right, my dear, let us talk about how your car should look. Are you happy with the cars you see on TV? Do you know what you want?"

"Sexy. It has to be sexy. Elegant. Sleek. Sexy."

"What or who causes collisions?"

"Sleek and sexy."

"That is fine, my dear, but now let us talk about collisions. Smashing up your car, getting killed. Who is to blame?"

"Idiots. All those idiots who can't drive. They're in my way and I want to kill them."

"When you buy a car, how do you think it will affect your status?"

"They will envy me. They will want my car. They will look at me. They will want me. I'll get respect. I'm young, I'm cool, I'm smart, I'm good looking, I'm ready for anything, I'm sexy, I'm—"

"Fine. Anything else?"

"Better not get in my way."

"Be more specific on how you want your car to enhance your image sexually."

"It's like lying in the sun. It makes me feel sooo good. I'm having sex with my machine. I'm Number One. I'm God. There's nobody but me."

"Good gracious!"

The cushion drops from Gloria's knees. I can see Abedni struggle with himself. "Look here, sir," I intervene, "we get the point. Enough is enough."

Gloria perceives my voice—she later will tell me—as

though I'm lost to her in a fog. "Is that you, Rufus? You're a wimp, you know. You're always hanging back and letting others get the jump on you. Your old man is senile."

"You see," Pa says, "what a down-by-de-watershore tally-wack and moocher she be."

"Gentlemen, gentlemen! I am just concluding, dear me!"

"See that you do," I say, my patience at an end. Abedni gives Gloria a pinch and a shake and it's all over.

"Well, heh-heh, there you are, gentlemen. That is my little contribution – the driving persona of one of your Triffids. Oh, pardon me, my dear, you were a charming subject. You have been of inestimable assistance."

"Golly. Hey, wait a minute, what do you mean, 'one of your Triffids'? Are you talking about me?"

"My dear, I am only a humble seeker of truth, who desires to shed some light on this Triffid creature. God only knows, there are those who would obscure the facts to gain notoriety – "

Gloria makes a face. "Get to the point. Never mind the innuendo."

"Of course, my dear. Let me see, how shall I put it? Ah, yes. Social science distinguishes in each of us two personalities, a primal and a secondary. The primal personality is also called hypnotic or robotic. It is the heart and soul of the beast, so to speak, heh-heh. We all have it. It has been with us in water and on land throughout the eons of evolution. When we experience a visceral response to a problem, you may be certain it is the primal personality asserting itself. It is the raw motivator of the brute, heh-heh. Instinct, impulse, that kind of thing..."

"So what?"

Boy, is Gloria ever on a short fuse with the Professor!

"Just this, my dear. I had hoped Mr. Pappy and Mr. Rufus would recognize their mysterious alien. I submit that the primal personality and the Triffid are one and the same."

"It just looks dat way," Pappy says.

"Does it matter what we call them?" I protest. "Why can't we just concentrate on dealing with them?"

"What's it got to do with me?" Gloria asks.

"Goodness gracious me, dear me, can I finish? Rein in those primal appetites. Hold onto your chains, heh-heh. Now, we know what the primal personality is. The secondary personality – also called the conscious personality – is very, very significant. It is the part of us that has to dominate in order to be a good driver. In other words, you have to be fully conscious. One hundred percent conscious. The secondary, or conscious, personality uses the more developed parts of the brain to perform complex tasks such as visual searching, preconceptualizing, and so on. As Mr. Pappy would say, these are the Vulcan skills the Triffid is unable to master."

Pa and I certainly agree that the good driver is always fully conscious. But Gloria is livid. You can see she's out of control by the way she keeps biting her lip. And she even has lipstick on her teeth, giving her a bloody, vicious, primal look.

"I suppose I'm in your primal category," she fumes. "Does that mean I'm not a good person? Does that make me an animal or what? Oh, never mind. Play back what I said, Professor."

Abedni plays back the recording. Gloria's eyes are darting from one to the other of us like some killer ray. "That's what I said!" she exclaims in disbelief. "Are you saying this is the real me? Explain yourselves, you – you pack of kooks!"

"I's got an answer for ye," says Pa, who has more courage than Curry-Funk. "Ye be unfartunately a Triffid, and there's nuttin' we can do for ye."

Gloria turns those sad blue eyes on me. They ache for a kind word. But now is the time for truth. "I love you, Gloria, but you weren't fooling anyone. Triffids can only fool each other, never a good driver.

"Why do you think Pa and I, after that one terror ride you took us on, would never let you drive Chevy? Heck, I'm sick of worrying about you, I'm tired of wondering how long it'll be before you have to pay your dues. Maybe you're gonna be all ripped up, then put together again like a broken rag doll. Maybe you're gonna be roasted alive in your own sauce. Or worse, maybe you're gonna kill somebody else, some little innocent, drag him all the way to Hamilton.

"Sorry, Gloria, we like you a lot. When you're on your feet, you're a normal, sweet chick with nice pins. But behind the wheel, you've got as much subtlety as the Frankenstein monster. Behind the wheel you're as ugly and brainless as anyone else in the crowd."

"An enemy of de people," Pa can't help adding.

Gloria folds her arms. Her face reddens. "Are you finished now? Why should I listen to any of you? They gave me a licence, didn't they? The Ministry of Transportation. The Minister signed it. The government thinks I can drive. I'm no worse than anyone else. You can't say everybody is wrong. Three crackpots, that's what you are. Huh!"

I try to calm Gloria. I tell her that reality is a very hard thing for most people to get a grip on. "It's not something you can run after, or acquire in a hurry," I tell her. "You can't get it in a fast car, can't get it by listening to loud rock, can't get it by surfing the Net. You see, Gloria, *it has to come to you.* And if you can't sit still long enough, it won't. It comes like a lazy butterfly, when it wants to, and you have to be ready."

Gloria looks dubious. I tell her to bear with me. "You can lie on your back in a meadow while bees buzz and clouds skitter. You can do a thousand things folk used to do before the world got small, fast, and busy. But racing after it will get you nowhere."

Gloria gives a nervous little laugh, like one who comes suddenly face to face with some absurd and disgusting truth about herself. "The rule of men is over," she tries desperately. "Haven't you gotten the world into enough trouble? Work on your own sex — men are the real experts when it comes to making do with the brain stem."

Doctor Abedni, frightened into the shadows by the peal of thunder, ventures to attempt reconciliation: "Calm yourself, my dear. May I get you a nice hot cup of tea? My dear, no one in the whole wide world will admit to being a Triffid. No one ever has. And in fact it is not required. Good heavens, no. But will you not let us help you? Just think of calm, clear waters, and pebbles in a fountain. Go ahead, do it right now. That is the way. Nothing stirring, nothing moving, just the water rippling over the pebbles. Your thoughts are tranquil, you are at peace with the world —"

"Don't touch me, you pervert!"

Doctor Abedni, who was poised to give Gloria a comfort-
ing pat on the arm, winces and withdraws, like a child at the
zoo who backs off after seeing the animal's teeth.

Oh no, Gloria's checking her watch and eyeing the hall
closet. Next thing, she'll be grabbing her coat and making a
run for it. She'll be just another memory. Another dumb
broad who didn't like my sandals.

So I try to soothe her. "Please, Gloria, we're your friends.
It's not the end of the world, you know. After all, most peo-
ple are Triffids. But you're one of the lucky ones; you have us.
And we can help you find your way into the Kingdom of
Reason. Please, let me help you."

These last words I coo into her ear – women are very susceptible to a man's cooing. She allows me to give her a little
peck on the cheek.

"Remains to be seen wedder we can help her," Pappy says
unhelpfully. "I tinks we should irradiate her wit red light to
kill off de Triffid."

Gloria makes a face. "Just try it!"

Abedni cackles sarcastically. "That will not be necessary.
However, you will have to undergo a transformation, my
dear. I think you should start with your schedule – throw it
away. Slow down. Get rid of your cell phone. The world does
not care about you, and you should not care about it. The
universe is in no hurry. Why should you be?"

We scramble to offer Gloria encouragement, even Pappy.
We're so solicitous, she forgets her watch, her coat, and her
pride, and begins to behave like a rational creature. At least
for the moment, her conscious personality gains the upper
hand.

"All right," she says, "deep down I've known it for a very
long time. I couldn't shake this feeling I was an idiot. But
whenever an inkling of truth presented itself, I'd drive faster,
make an ass of myself on the freeway. Sometimes I'd take
another course at night school, anything to be busy, to fill up
time, to avoid gaps, spaces, quiet moments. I was driven. I
had to obey every voice in my skull. The more I did for me,
the more it wasn't enough. Is that what it is, being a Triffid?"

We're all standing round nodding our heads. "You got it," I say.

She looks terrible. I feel an overwhelming desire to take her in my arms and tell her it's all right, to brush back the blond hair from that tear-washed face. I'm ready to say and do a thousand foolish things.

But she stuns me by saying, "Well, I guess we're through, Sweetypie."

"Gloria!" I take her hand and I plunk us both down on the sofa. She's sniffing and pouting, and she says, "I know you don't want to be going with a Triffid."

"Right on," Pa says. But I throw him such a fierce look, he ambles off to the kitchen, and so does Abedni.

"Do—do you really think there's hope for me, Rufus?" she snivels.

"Why sure there is, Sugarplum. It's your mind, that's all. The rest of you is just as lovable as ever. Some people don't even care about the mind. That's what a dumb blonde is. But don't worry, your mind is closed, that's all. We're going to open it for you."

"Then, you're not calling me a mindless vegetable?"

"Course I'm not."

"Yes, we is," comes Pappy's voice from the kitchen.

"Still, I'm a Triffid."

"Yeah, Gloria. It's just the way you drive, and a few other things—I think we can fix them."

And so, during the days that follow, I try very hard to ease Gloria into a full realization of her essential Triffidness, as I am certain some tiny spark of humanity still resides in her. If this were not so, we would not like Gloria the way we do. Even Pa's railing is often only the assertion of long-honed defensive instincts.

It's also clear that Gloria has the will to fight back—a sign full of hope, not only for her but for all humankind. If Gloria defeats the Triffid in her, we may then know the way the masses might be brought back from their mesmerized state of lowness.

I can't help thinking of that super-great movie, *Invasion of the Body Snatchers*, an all-time classic. It's the tale of a human tragedy shockingly similar to our own. But folk who had had the BS seed planted inside them were lost forever to Body-snatcherdom the moment they fell asleep, because in sleep they were transformed into mindless copies of their former selves.

I keep seeing it over and over in my head. The main guy and his girl are trying to get away. The girl falls asleep while he reconnoitres, and so she loses her brain to the aliens. *Surrender, my love*, is her siren song when he returns, and discovers her transformation through a kiss, which is without passion. *It's such a wonderful state to be in. Who cares if we don't have our brains? We'll still be together.*

Nothing doing. Without her brain the girl is worthless. So he runs for dear life, knowing he may be the last person with his brain intact in all the world.

And I know what he's thinking: No brain, no freedom. Without a brain we're no different from the rest of creation. Without a brain, who will carry the torch for planet Earth? Who will put things right in the galaxy? Who will boldly go forth to demand answers? Who?

He runs and he runs, till he comes to a highway. Those people driving by—they must be normal, because they're coming from outside, uncontaminated parts of the country.

He bounds onto the road, desperately shouting, waving his arms. *Stop!* he cries. *Before it's too late, stop! You're next! They're going to get you!*

But there's one basic fact that hasn't occurred to him: most of those who are not Body Snatchers—nine out of ten of them—are Triffids. And to them he's just another idiot on the road. They give him Word and Sign, and it's only by sheer chance they fail to run him over.

Well, I thank my lucky stars it's not like that with Gloria. Gloria still has a spark of divine reason that yearns to be free.

"Prove it," says Pa. "Wedder or not you do will have serious consequences for all de world. Teach her discipline and control, so that her drivin's always uniform, not subject to impulse or whim, de late appointment, or de god of gogogo.

111

Last Days of Driving

Be sartain she don't read de wheels section of de paper, for verily I say unto you, it be full of false gurus, who worship at de slippery altar of this god, and those of udder manipulator deities, bowin' down naked and entirely witout shame before them.

"This teach her above all. It be easier for a Triffid to pass through de eye of a hurricane than to drive as though havin' all de time in de world. Truly, ye may as well say to de tiny nectar-sippin' hummin' birds as they feeds and hums on de wing, 'Get ye up on high and soar like eagles.' Now, all these busy little birds tinks they's eagles anyway, and they tells themselves, 'Hey, we can be this low, and still seem to soar.'

"But afore they knows it, they's gone. They never seed de view from above. And they's missed all chance o' seein' it, ever."

13

HOPE FOR GLORIA

I keep my fingers crossed for Gloria. Though Word and Sign have not been evident in her driving, she's still been as blind and mean a scurrier as anyone else in the crowd.

"Is this what women propose to do to achieve the long-sought equality with men?" I slyly ask. "Do you really want to come down to their level? Word and Sign are not the pass-words to equality, you know. You women only degrade your-selves. Men, like Nature, are there for you to surmount."

Gloria has had a different understanding. "We intend to beat them at their own game," she tells me. "If men can be air-force pilots and front-line combat troops, then so by God can we. If they can mug, cheat, steal, and drive like idiots, then dammit so can we."

Her thinking is fallacious. It's the way kids reason. They see the Triffids doing it and they want to do it too. It's absurd, but it's the way she thinks. It's what comes of watch-ing the women's channel on TV. Men swear, women have to swear too. Men are idiots, women should be idiots.

I keep telling her, the majority can't drive. The majority are not a good guide in almost anything.

"Golly, how do they manage to keep it a secret?" she naively wonders.

"Excellent question, Gloria. It's because they all believe they're Number One. The schools and the commercials have drummed it into them. I'm worth it. I deserve it. I do it for me. They've killed humility. People think they're good, no matter how bad they are. It's just one big incredible lie. But the Triffids, they buy it, because their brains are off. The Triffids'll buy anything.

"Look at it this way, Gloria. Everybody can't be that worthy. It's not possible. Many deserve very little. Some deserve a kick in the butt, others deserve to be crucified. In olden times they knew that."

She's not going to be easy. I can see the struggle in the furrows of her brow.

"Why do they let this happen, then?" she asks, like a little child discovering the world.

"Listen Gloria, it's all part of the great sweep of history. This just happens to be the Age of the Common Man and Woman. Industrial societies had to come down to some very broad common denominators in order to accommodate the masses. It suited the Triffids to a T."

"Golly, Rufus, I never learned that in school."

"No, and you wouldn't. The Triffids wouldn't allow it."

I give Gloria the dialectic in small doses, never obtrusively. I plant the seeds of doubt. I wait till she's ready. I almost always wait till she asks the question before I give the answer. Lots of bun, tiny slivers of meat.

And so we practise a thousand traffic lights, ten thousand times.

"You don't have to go through on those amber lights, Gloria." Countless times I have to tell her that. "In fact, you shouldn't, unless you let Ally Oop in a gravel truck stick to your bumper. And when the light turns green, you don't have to floor it just to please the guy behind."

"I don't? I mean, I know, but – they have their expectations, don't they? I hate to disappoint them. Besides, they won't like me if I don't get moving."

"Girl, you must let go of that. Now, I know it's hard. But you give them their due by driving sanely. Beyond that, you don't owe them a thing."

"I – don't – owe – them – anything."

"Perfect. That's my girl."

Later, Gloria's driving my car on a small two-laner highway I've specially chosen. We're approaching a group of cyclists, and beyond the bikes is a bend in the road. Gloria on the brake gently. String of cars behind us. I ask her, "Those guys behind, what do they expect from you?"

"Horn for the bikers. Swerve around them. Go for available space. Squeeze by. Take a chance."

"Right. And you're going to do what?"

"Nothing. Stay behind. Be patient. Wait till I can see down the road. Wait till I have space and time. Hurry is only a state of mind. Hurry is the ultimate hubris."

"Good for you, Buttercup, now you're in control."

Behind us the others all bunch up. They angle left and right as they look for a hole to put their snouts in. What the hell's she waiting for, they all wonder. Some are already composing a letter to the paper: How slow and indecisive drivers endanger us all.

There is no relief. The road continues curvy. Choice is clear: persevere or take a chance. Great test for Gloria. I ask her to give a running commentary, so I can follow her thoughts.

"Well, all right. I–I'm waiting till it's safe. Till I can see up the road. The bikes are not really in my way; that's my old program and it's been cancelled. Being in a rush will not get me anywhere faster. The hinder's in my mind, not on the road…"

Boy, do they rant and rave behind! Just look at all those fingers in the rear-view mirror! Look at them scream! "Take a chance, idiot!" – that's what they're saying. Some are biting the steering wheel, others are mistreating their families by mouthing the foulest of expletives, pulling on their Hyde personae to frighten the babies.

"Golly, the bikes are not in my way. They are not keeping me from my destination. The bikes are not making my life difficult; only I can do that. If somebody passes, I will not lose my place in line. I'm not really in any line. The line is only a frame of mind for those who can't wait…"

"Super, Gloria baby. Excellent. Fantastic."

We all know, even Gloria, that sooner or later some Triffid behind will break out. That's where the danger lies, and we're ready. That's why we stay well back of the bikes. But while I'm thinking of reminding her of this, the road straightens.

Now we are able to pass safely – or would be able, were it not for the rush of Triffids behind. All together they lurch into the other lane and race by us, nose to tail, saluting with their fingers.

Gloria has anticipated – Triffids are predictable. After all, we know a lot more about them than they do about us.

"Golly! So I am last to pass the bikes. Does it matter? No. I've just found that out. It doesn't really matter at all, except I'm glad I don't have that pack behind me any more. I guess that's a bonus."

As we pass the riders, who all the while had been casting nervous glances back, they wonder why it has taken us so long.

Gloria is with the Professor and me, practising her 777th left turn. It's a T-intersection and Gloria is making a left into the stem of the T. An oncoming pedestrian is two steps away from the curb and preparing to cross as we drive out into the intersection and assume our waiting position with car and wheels straight.

"Tell me what you're doing," I say, even though Gloria's doing fine.

"Okay. I'm signalling for my turn. Keeping straight, so the pedestrian knows I intend to wait. Also, this car coming up fast behind me – if he hits me, I won't plough into the pedestrian."

"Super-duper, Gloria."

"Marvellous, my dear," says the Professor. He's perched in the back, like a great wise owl, sure of being a grand influence by his mere presence.

Pedestrian hesitates. She has never seen anything like this before. She thinks it always has to be a game of chicken. But Gloria gives her the wave-on. Not the get-going-dammit kind. Just a friendly, old-fashioned, you-first one.

Pedestrian smiles and walks. But lady in car behind us hits the horn; what the devil is going on here, she wonders. Pedestrian, startled, gives us a what-the-hell look. I ask Gloria what the horn means.

"It's a signal," she says. "It's not what horns are made for, but it's definitely a signal. She's telling me, smarten up! She's telling me, I know you're not behaving like the rest of us. She's saying, I know you're not a Triffid."

"Hey Gloria, right on, babe. You got it. You're beginning to take their measure. Now you see where it's at. This is what dumb is. It's the essence of dumb. This clown behind with the South American army ants in her panties, she thinks we are the problem."

"Gloria is becoming a wonderful driver," says Professor Abedni.

Once back at Gascap Bend, Abedni gives us his interpretation, rather academic but entirely valid and noteworthy, of our little run-in with Mrs. Anty-Panty.

"That rude lady was threatening your bubble, my dear."

"My what?"

"Your bubble. Your personal space. All creatures have it, you know. When anything enters that space, an alarm goes off inside us. We feel threatened. Especially if the intruder is a stranger. Yes, indeed. Dogs have it. Fish have it. We have it.

"Dear me, if the lady only knew how rude she was being! But perhaps you cannot expect people to know. The Triffids have been whittling away at personal space for such a long time. They detest it. They want everyone nose to bum, so to speak. It is a nose-to-bum world out there, and if you are not sniffing up somebody's arse, they do not like you.

"What we are talking about is a force field, you understand. It defines the proper spacing between individuals. The proper social distance. It is one of Nature's little tricks to permit – notice I do not say 'ensure' – the survival of the race. Simple observation of Nature will provide ample illustrations of the existence of this field of force."

"Gosh, Professor, I think when I was very young I knew that instinctively."

"I am sure you did, my dear. We all come into the world with our brains intact, but then we lose our native smarts through the bad examples of our parents and others, who do their best to lead us into the labyrinth of good intentions, thus putting us on the road to hell."

"Gee!" Gloria considers for a moment. "Professor, isn't it that bubble that tells us it's rude to breathe down somebody's neck? No wonder you guys were always so serious. They were threatening your personal space. Yes, they were intruding into your force field. They were bursting your bubble."

"Precisely," the Professor coos.

Now we know the wheels are turning. There is hope yet for Gloria. "When you're driving," I explain, "you need a force field much bigger than the one that serves on foot. The brain has to modify Nature for survival, so all our moves are in harmony with Nature's physics. That's why the Triffids are always in trouble – they haven't been able to make the adjustment."

"Golly, what stupid clods!"

"Yes indeed, my dear. The bubble is not something to be taken lightly. Without the force field, you are in the behavioural sink. The sink, my friends, is a term coined by an old colleague of mine, one Calhoun, an amazing ethnologist. He did some experiments with rats, depriving them of the space they needed. They became dysfunctional – mind you, I do not think rats should be treated this way!"

"Of course not," I agree.

"Never," says Gloria. "So what happened to them?"

"Well, my dear, deprived of their bubbles, the rats became, as I say, dysfunctional. They ceased to care for their young. Sound familiar? The males went in packs and gnawed each others' tails, just like the Triffids on the Don Valley Parkway. That is what you do when you are in the sink."

"The sink. Golly, what a horrible image! I guess your friend – what was his name? – Calhoun. I guess he just wanted to say we're all going down the drain. Is that where our future lies, Professor – in the sewer?"

Boy what a jump-start we gave her brain! Now it's all keyed up and working overtime. And like to go on running for a good while all on its own. And the longer it runs, the more the Triffid in her will suffer.

It has to die. That is our determined objective. To kill it.

BRASS KNUCKLES

We take some time off. Gloria needs it. We all do. It's her idea. "Pickle the polemics," she insists. "I want all of us to dodge driving for an entire day. Can all car conversations. Ban anything brainy." So we take the streetcar into town to spend a few hours doing nothing.

Toronto flashes by, a staid old maid who recently learned to dance and paint herself in bright colours. The trees all have bare arms and are crying for snow. Gloria chatters to keep our flights of fancy from getting off the ground. What she doesn't understand is, you can't take a holiday from a revolution, not when it's your own.

"Spadina-Spadeena-Spadinski!" calls the driver. It's our stop.

Gelato and cappuccinos, then a stroll in Chinatown. I don't know whether the sights have anything to do with it, but Abedni turns very serious without any warning – what can you expect of an academic? We've just passed a few shops with smoked ducks hanging in the windows, and Gloria has just been telling us about the Peking-duck ritual at Champion House Restaurant, when the Professor starts to fume.

"Dear me, I hate bazaars!" he croaks.

We're all taken aback. We ask him what it is he can't stand. We hop aboard a tram. As we find seats at the back, he says, "I see the world of tomorrow. One big marketplace. Picture it, the whole world is one big bazaar. It is all city. They sell water in bottles – you will not find it anywhere else. Birds hang by their feet or flutter in cages – there are no other birds. Everything is tame, everything is regulated. Nature is confined to tree farms and gardens. All large animals reside at the zoo. Some of them in sperm receptacles at frozen zoos, in the hope some future time will find space for them, though perhaps not in this world at all. It is very depressing."

Several well-dressed middle-aged ladies who are seated across the aisle from us begin to cast anxious glances, wondering no doubt if Abedni is prone to violence, and why a nice girl like Gloria would venture out in the company of three perfect weirdos.

"Professor, did you know that in the time of Robin Hood the forest primeval stretched all the way from Brittany to Moscow and beyond?" I ask him this to get him off his topic. But it's too much for Gloria, who sees it as just further proof we can't get our brains to gear down.

"Stop it!" she cries in a shrill voice. "You promised not to think!"

That's all right for her to say. Easy when you're not in the habit. The ladies opposite turn to look at us, though carefully, perhaps thinking some indecency is in train.

Radshak and I apologize. We all get off at Queen's Park, where we feed the pigeons, without any thoughts but bird-feeding ones. Then we take the subway, still minding not to say anything that doesn't have the dull ring of banality. Pa has been quietest of all; I get the impression he's communing with Tau and saving his energies for something unexpected. There's a certain glow at the nape of his neck.

When we get off, we have to ride the escalator with a bunch of unruly kids. Their computers are off but their mouths are wide open. "How can so many jerks be together at one time?" Gloria asks. Radshak is petrified. The noises they make—racist slurs—are straight from the brain stem.

We get to the top with a great sense of relief, gasping for fresh air, yearning for wide-open spaces, groaning because we've all suffered damage to the force field. There was hardly a person on that escalator whose private space had not been violated. But the poor Professor has suffered far more; he has been insulted and humiliated.

It's not over. Ahead of me, a female brat of about 14 starts screaming into the face of this lady. Lady's trying to avoid her but can't. "Why did you touch me?" the kid is yelling. "Why did you touch me?" Hell, I'm glad I didn't touch her; think I'd want my fingers amputated. I don't believe anybody really did touch her, either. I think it's a signal, because now they swarm around the lady in a pack, taunting and pushing her.

Pa and I are pretty darn good shovers. One look at each other and we spring into action, like Batman and Robin. We grab the Triffid cubs by their collars and fling them to the floor. We take them by surprise. But they recover and swarm us, kicking and punching. We fight desperately. We can't let ourselves get beaten up merely because our opponents are small, dumb, and protected by the Constitution. Lucky Pa brought his brass knuckles. He breaks loose and spins like a top, brass arm out. Faces crack; I hear them. Blood spatters, and it's not ours.

Can't beat them all, though. Soon we're on the floor, under a heap of the vile vermin. We have no space at all. No bubble. Absolutely nothing between them and us. Hell, this is it, then, I think. I'm going to suffocate in some young Triffid's crotch.

Luck is with us. They come off us one by one, as though the gods have come to our rescue, till Pa and I are looking up at a bunch of cops and security guys. "Are you all right?" they ask us. "Where are you hurt?"

A cop takes a close look at Pa, whose hands and shirt are bloody. "Poor old gentleman, where did they hurt you, sir? This man needs an ambulance!"

Gloria too is bending over us. She's bawling. She thinks the blood is ours. Radshak's face emerges from the throng. "Dear me, what a noble sacrifice! You have restored my faith in Anglo-Saxon virtue."

We get to our feet, dust ourselves off. "Got a few bruises," we tell the officers. "Cancel the ambulance." We give the cops the relevant information, then get the heck off home.

Imagine, kids doing that! Imitating Nature. It's absurd. But of course they're not real kids. A Triffid kid is no more a kid than a rabid dog is a dog. Once smitten, you're gone. We have no regrets about the broken jaws.

Freedom! It's a heady drink. Not everyone can take it. Some go around begging to be put down. Charles Bronson in *Death Wish*, that's who I feel like. What a feeling – to look evil in the eye and strike it down! Wonderful! Many go their whole lives in the midst of evil, without ever doing anything against it. As if a battle never joined can ever be won! Yet surely that is why we are here, to join battle. Honour Woden. Conquer the forces of darkness.

On this day Pa and I have joined the ranks of the dragon-slayers. Like St. George, we stand ready. What a shame, that True North should have come to this! The land of snow and hard realities. The home of law and order and the Mounties. This pillar of Empire. This proud kingdom. This independent jewel. What a shame!

"Forgot to wait for de press," Pa says regretfully.

"Write a letter now, Pa. Say you're the old guy who got beat up in the swarming. Can't miss."

"I'm after tinkin' de same. Jigged if I doesn't."

And what a fine letter Pappy writes, telling everybody off for bringing up kids without brains! A super commentary. But I warn him not to use the term "Triffid." "It's a red flag for all the Triffid bulls who work for the paper," I say. "Once they know we're out to get them, they'll put your letter in the waste basket."

And of course, as Pappy does not heed my advice, that is precisely what happens.

The day after this adventure, the paper reports that three teens had their noses broken in a subway swarming:

One of the injured teens claims that Mr. Albert Prince was wearing brass knuckles. "How else do you think I got my f— head busted?" he said. This account has been completely discredited by police and other witnesses at the scene.

In the same paper, we're happy to read about a bunch of kids at Lord Lansdowne Public School, who all appear to have their heads screwed on tight:

The Lansdowne kids have made civic history by being the first group ever to persuade a committee of the city of Toronto to lower the speed limit on one of its roads.

"People underestimate what we kids can do," said student Monica Kim. "The fact is, we're tired of not being listened to. We're tired of being targets whenever we need to cross the street."

The students also won a recommendation to build a $25,000 crash guard between the road and the sidewalk. "It's the real protection," said Monica. "Speed limits don't really mean anything." Many community groups have tried to get speed limits reduced, but to no avail.

"Speed limits are there to keep traffic running smoothly and quickly," said Transportation Commissioner Dagwood Fuddle. "Tampering with them could really screw things up."

Pappy says it's an awful shame we can't have the kids at Lansdowne trade places with the jerks on these committees. The kids would know what to do, he believes. He thinks all committee members, commissioners, and government ministers should get six months off to look for their brains, failing which, they might be invited to undergo synaptic reconstruction at the public expense. Or better yet, just step down and let the kids tell us how to regulate driving.

I am convinced the victory of the Lansdowne kids is a sign of things to come.

BRINGING HOME THE SHAME

In an old and tired voice, Julie tells me how her sister died. Maria was only 10 at the time. It was her birthday, and she couldn't wait to get home from school, where there would be presents and a cake with icing and candles. As the school bus turned into Gascap Bend, Mummy was waiting on the lawn. Julie and Maria said bye to the nice lady who drove the bus. Seconds later Maria was lying dead on the road.

"She ran because Mom was waiting on the lawn," Julie tells me. "The driver of the car didn't stop. I still dream about it. I still see Maria lying there with the disbelief in her eyes. She wasn't dead yet. She was just looking up at me as if to say, 'How could this happen?' My mother went crazy. She–she attacked the bus driver. Ripped open her face with her nails. The kids were all crying, their faces pressed against the windows. It hurts me to think about it..."

I thank Julie for telling me this. I remind her there are countless families with missing members, and they all endure the same memories and the same kind of pain. "Whoever killed your sister, Julie, also wounded you, and your father and mother."

"I hate bus drivers," she tells me.

I ask about the car involved. "Didn't they get the guy?"

"Yeah, they got him. They charged him with leaving the scene. There were no other charges. No one knows if he was speeding. No one knows if he was impaired. But what really got him off the hook was the fact that the bus driver forgot to put the flashers on when Maria and I were getting off. The judge ruled that, since drivers were not being warned, they could not reasonably be expected to exercise sufficient caution. I don't think that judge knew what he was talking about."

"No, Julie, I don't think he did. Judges are as much in the dark as most everyone else, sometimes more so. For a judge who rules in the shadow of ignorance, compounds whatever evil comes before his bench. And yet they do rule where they have no expertise."

"Gee, what's wrong with this country?"

"Well may you ask. No judge ever said honestly, 'I know nothing about this; therefore I'm not qualified to judge.' Nor has any one of them been heard to say, 'I drive like this myself.' Instead, they think they can compensate for their inadequacies by taking to heart the ancient dictum: Judge not, that ye be not judged. And if that does not persuade them, there is always: There, but for the grace of God, go I. In other words, they're not putting people in prison for doing what they do themselves."

"Oh no! It's all so cynical!"

I congratulate Julie on her insight and am very pleased with the excellent progress she has shown. For the next time, I ask her to consider the relative responsibility of those involved in the death of her sister. (I think also it will ease the pain. As she brought the subject up, I believe she needs to talk about it.) As well, I ask her to consider whether or not it is important that the warning flashers on the bus were on and working at the time of the incident. "When all is said and done, Julie, what is the real importance of those warning lights? For homework think about it. But be careful, a good answer is scarce as hens' teeth."

I leave her, certain she will dream of vengeance. The world is not as it ought to be. That is why Pappy and I will have our army of malcontents.

Between this lesson and the next I think of other judges who distinguished themselves by the asinine quality of their decisions.

I had a student once who worked at a variety store. The

building had a glass door that opened outward. One day my student opened the door into the path of a manoeuvring Cadillac. The glass shattered, cutting him badly. His face was totally disfigured. He sued the driver.

Did it do any good? Not a chance. Judge ruled in favour of "the other guy." No one could reasonably be expected to know that the door would open, the judge said.

I guess not.

Nine out of ten judges will make that ruling.

Another student of mine was one of three people killed by a lady who fell asleep at the wheel. The lady was acquitted of dangerous driving causing death. The defence argued that the dangerous driving was caused not by the defendant but by something beyond her control – namely, sleep. Moreover, the defendant could not be expected to have known that she would fall asleep.

Of course not.

The words of a medical doctor, an expert in sleep disorders, who testified in the trial, are quite telling. He said: *Driving is an automatic activity, mechanical rather than cerebral in nature. Drivers can hardly be expected to anticipate what is rare and unusual. That includes sleep.*

This is what comes of relying on Triffid lawyers and doctors. For them the brain is *never* involved.

At least I have no reason to worry about any future milk-store heists while sleepwalking. If I get caught, I'm certain the magistrate will understand. All I have to do is point out that my brain was not on.

My next lesson with Julie is a real eye-opener. She tells me her boyfriend, Ennio, is going around with a sawed-off shotgun in a bag. She asks me if people can be Triffids even when they're not driving. I say of course, you just don't notice it as much; because when they have to deal with you face to face, they're adept at concealing their Triffid natures. To be stupid and rude, as they are in their cars, would be too risky. Somebody might hold them accountable.

"They wouldn't have any friends either," Julie says.

"No, not one."

"My poor Ennio, he's a Triffid!"

"When you rub them the wrong way, Julie, it all comes out. They lose perspective. Thousands of years of culture, five million years of human evolution, count for nothing. Triffids are never in control. But in a tight spot, they lose it completely, taking their recourse to Word and Sign, knife, gun, baseball bat, or hockey stick."

"Poor Ennio!"

We do some heavy sighing together. Then she searches the great-blue-deep through my windshield, as though focusing on eternity will be rewarded with some special insight. "He thinks he's defending my honour," she says. "Just because somebody wrote something stupid about me. Oh, it's so pointless. What can I do to make him stop?"

Of course I say the obvious. "Haven't you told your dad? You want to keep him out of trouble, don't you?"

Later same day, I'm resting with my wheels behind the Donut Delight, eating pomelo and listening to the news, when I hear:

A Toronto high school student told police it was a rude message written in his girlfriend's workbook that sparked an ugly confrontation this afternoon.

Apparently, the young man's girlfriend is being stalked by the leader of a rival gang, a hot-rod enthusiast and troublemaker of long standing, who has recently been expelled from Hillcrest High. He is believed to be the organizer of the weekend drag races at Blind Summit, a dangerous stretch of road north of the city, where five teens died last summer while racing.

Thirty students, armed with shotguns, bats, machetes, knives, and hammers were facing each other down when police arrived. According to Sergeant Gordon McDuff of the Toronto Street Violence Unit, police made several arrests and seized two sawed-off, 12-gauge, pump-action shotguns, and numerous other weapons.

Later, Julie tells me her boyfriend, Ennio, as well as Joey Slimeball Snookums, are being charged under the *Young Offenders Act*. They must remain at home, or in the presence of one parent, when not in school, and they must report to the police once a week. Their fathers have to put up $5,000 surety bonds, which will be forfeited if any of the conditions of the sentence are broken.

I read in the paper that Julie is one of 250 children and young adults taking part in some serious research called, "The Voice of Youth":

> ... *What the researchers found really disheartening in their study of young people was the lack of self-confidence in many of them.*
>
> *One eight-year old, when asked what she didn't like, replied, "Myself."*
>
> *Parents are finding the report very disturbing. "No one talks any more," several of the youngsters said. "They don't know how to parent." Some kids suggested compulsory parenting courses.*

Julie is not, like some of her friends, demanding a kids' seat on school boards, a youth prime minister sitting in Parliament, or youth courts like the Courts of Peer Review in some U.S. states. But she did tell the researchers that adults are too rushed and self-absorbed to be tuned in to young people. *Their minds have been hijacked,* Julie told *The Star.* She also had some great things to say about punishment:

> *You have to bring the shame home. It must be obvious there are no rewards for wrongdoing. Let them suffer the disapprobrium of their peers and the wrath of the people.*

"Great!" I tell her when next we meet. "Now you're ready to fight them hammer and nail. Did you say everybody should learn to drive, I mean, not just pretend? To make the roads safe again and put the fun back in driving?"

Julie looks away. I know she had trouble with that one.

"I tried, Rufus, honest I did. But it seemed as if they didn't see any problem there, or any connection with their study."

"I see."

I can't stop the disappointment from welling up inside me.

I feel betrayed. I know my eyes are moist. And yet, it's not her fault. How can I expect one kid to openly declare herself against almost the whole population? Make a pariah of herself?

"I really did try, Rufus. I said to them, 'Can't you see how everything is connected? How all the evil has a single source?' They were university kids; I thought they'd understand."

"And what did they say to that?"

"They said I was quite the philosopher."

"Hmmm. Lucky you didn't say anything about Triffids."

"Yeah, lucky."

16

THE ABEDNIMOBILE

Soon be Christmas. The rush is on now in the malls. People trudge around shopping and arguing. Paper says we don't have fun at this time of year. Also, average person spends seven years of life waiting in lines, and one year waiting at traffic lights.

That's because they know nothing of pacing. Pappy and I try to get the green lights. But the jerks race up no matter what the colour. Result: they wait longer and they wear their brakes down faster.

Paper also says sniping has increased along every freeway, with an average of 6.5 incidents being reported across Ontario daily. This is attributed to the combined effect of yule rage and road rage, a particularly potent mix. Apparently, people nurture more hate for one another during the Christmas season than at any other time of year. Since the late 1990s, 10,227 separate types of rage have been identified. The police estimate that at least ten shooters are at large on the freeways. This is in addition to the 401 Bomber, who, for the last four years, has blown up overpasses and vehicles, resulting in a toll of 311 dead and 1247 injured. The bazooka attacks on rush-hour traffic last summer, which killed 70 and injured 211, are thought to have been the work of the Bomber.

One scuddy morning with the odd flake falling, Pappy and I are on our third cup of coffee when the phone rings. We let it go about eight times just to eliminate wrong numbers. If they can't wait that long, then we don't know them.

It's Doctor Abedni and he's very excited. Says he wants us

to see some work of his. If we come at once, he will introduce us to yogic flying.

Pappy says fine, we'll come, provided there's no flying.

"You ridiculous Ministry man!" Abedni teases. His lilt is very honeyed. "Next to the ultimate transmigration, it is the most wonderful thing you can do for your soul. I am very sorry for you. Very sorry. Quite sincerely, I am at the threshold. Yes, I am going to achieve absolute levitation … No, there is no doubt. I am going to fly, ha-ha-ha."

Pa butters him up, telling him he's a man about to cross many thresholds. "I's used to a more quiet pace," Pappy says. "I likes to sog along. This flyin's too frenetic. All right for yuppies maybe. I ain't lookin' for excuses. Me joints'd crack. De cartilage in me knees'd snap. No, I don't tink it will help me arthritis. We has no desire to fly and that's final."

"Ha, ha, ha. You are a strange person, Albert. But do not worry. I fully comprehend the reticence of an old MTO man. You are too used to guiding others to be guided yourself. Well, all right, I agree. No yoga. Please come immediately. I am very excited. I need you and Mr. Rufus. I need your advice. You old dog, of course. Of course you will get credit if there is a paper. Heh-heh, naturally."

"Why do you call me an old dog?" Pa asks.

"No disparagement, Albert. I love old dogs. And by the way, I do not put my fellow creatures on the dinner table. When I have a burger, it is always a veggie burger."

"Eat what ye like, sir, and allow me to do likewise. Meself, I's a meat-and-praties man. Time was when I ate lots of fish, but nowadays de Icelanders takes de best and sells it to Japan. What they has in Toronto ain't fit to be mentioned."

"Well, Albert, the great Leonardo da Vinci would not condone your eating practices. He was a man far ahead of his time. He said animals would eventually have the same rights as we do. He was a vegetarian, you know. But I understand how hard it is to give up bad habits. Sometimes I think what we need is a sustenance replicator, such as they have on the starship *Enterprise*. That would provide you with a facsimile of prime rib, spring lamb, or roast chicken. And you would

131

Last Days of Driving

not need to murder to get it. Dear me, I am inclined to think that we humans will never succeed in resolving our moral dilemmas by reason and force of will. Rather, technology will make it possible for us to absolutely forego the bother of making difficult choices."

We arrive at Doctor Abedni's, as planned, well past the hour of curry. The Professor comes to the door giggling and chattering like a schoolgirl. The two feline slinkers, the black one and the white one, parade themselves between our legs.

The Doctor shows us a full-page ad from *The Star*. We missed it at breakfast, as Pa and I tune out all commercial messages, whatever size, shape, or colour they may be. It reads:

Kids!!!
Your Parents Can't Drive!!!
Do not let them maim or kill you
Find out now how you can make them get their brains back
Refuse to ride with them
Phone: 1-800-REFUSE and stay alive!!!

"Hey," says Pa, "This'll learn us to peruse de paper wit more scrutility. Look at that, Rufus, a direct appeal to de little ones. Amazin'!" Then he goes into a trance. But it's only a trance of an eyeblink, and only I notice it. A wry smile comes to his lips. "What de devil be ye up to, Radshak?"

The Doctor's full of himself. This is obviously his own advertisement. "Gentlemen, we are now become fishers of youth. We must cast our net wide. We must catch them before the parting of the way. Before they gain insight into the nature of the beast – human nature, that is. Because then there is a fork in the road. Either they accept what Nature gave them and run with it, in which case they use their inheritance as an excuse for a low, mean, and miserable life; or they take the other route and see Nature as a hinder. They resolve to surmount what is given. This is the high road that few take.

"Do not worry, Albert, I shall not attempt to yank the carpet of righteous Anglo-Saxon wrath and just revolt out from under your feet."

"Radshak, bear in mind me ancestors come from Ireland."

Boy, the Professor really put his foot in his mouth there! It's the second time he called us Anglo-Saxons. I'm half and half, taking Ma's side into account. But Pa—I think he's pretty well a hundred-percent Celt. Not that we really mind. We never were ashamed of being British. Nor did we ever feel like colonials. Hell, you don't build an empire and then turn around and say, "I'm just a poor, used colonial." Triffid talk, that's what it is. The beaten of this world will always find someone to blame for their troubles. Speaking for the Prince family, we were never ashamed of the Empire, because we're the ones who bloody well built it!

"A thousand pardons," says the Professor, oozing apologies. "Unforgivably clumsy of me. I shall take myself to task for being so insensitive—"

"Forget it," I say impatiently. "Doctor, do you really think this ad of yours will do any good?"

The Doctor shrugs and gives an odd little chuckle. "I am not worried, Mr. Rufus. Your so-called Triffids will not have their ears tuned to our strident clarion. But that is fine. The youth will hear it and be haunted. They know what is true. Some will be stirred to rebel."

I picture Abedni as a kind of latter-day Pied Piper, advancing up Bloor in his flowing robes, while he sounds a golden clarion and a long file of enthralled kids marches behind.

"Well," I say, "it's clear that trying to educate the parents is a waste of time."

"Precisely, Mr. Rufus. A great waste of time. I think all serious reformers have come to the same conclusion—parents are not to be trusted. Have you ever noticed how little kids take to the computer like baby ducks to water? They are ready to communicate. The generation gap is ready to crumble. But it cannot happen yet because adults are not ready, and will not be while their minds are in hock."

Abedni then praises us for long years of slogging, saying it took great courage to buck the tide the way we did, but that our sacrifice has laid the groundwork for what is to come. "Dear me, you have both done a wonderful job. But what we need to do now is get all the kids organized so they become a force."

"Like de Scouts?" Pa asks.

Abedni give an evil little chuckle, way back in his throat. "Heh-heh-heh. Not quite as benign as that. Here is a story I cut out of the paper last summer. Let me read it to you: *Parents are becoming more and more blind to what goes on in the home. The police are confiscating huge numbers of weapons and other stolen goods from the homes of kids who hide the loot under their parents' noses. Some of these imps have padlocks on their bedroom doors, and parents either don't care or are afraid to intervene. Besides robberies, the weapons are obtained through drug deals and swarmings.*

"Well, gentlemen, there you are. The little peckers are armed to the teeth. There is an arsenal out there, hidden among the teddies and the roller blades. I tell you, the older kids are taking charge. They are not putting up with this decadence any longer. My point is, can you imagine what we might accomplish if we got them all out with their guns together? Can you see it in your mind's eye? Gentlemen?"

Pa is not impressed. "Mayhem," he says. "De end of civilization as we knows it. Far worse than any youth riot of de past."

"Tut-tut, Albert, do not exaggerate. Their energies could be channelled, I am certain of it."

The Professor terminates the discussion, saying we have more important matters at hand. He points to some large drawings propped against his Harley.

"Are they UFO's?" I ask.

"UFO's? Why no, Mr. Rufus. Better than that. These are drawings of my car, the Abednimobile." Pa and I have a closer look. This certainly is one weird contraption. "This, gentlemen, is the world's first fool-proof car. Any fool can drive it and still survive."

What a genius the Professor is! He never ceases to amaze us with his truly, almost divine, ingenuity. Just think, a car for fools!

"Is this circuitry?" I ask, pointing to some lines in a cut-away drawing.

"Bioelectronics," Abedni proudly replies. "The computers I put in this car are going to be powered by real brain cells. Yes, that is right, human brain cells. Ironic, is it not, that machines will make better use of them than the individuals they came from? Thinking cars, my friends, that is the future. Not smart drivers, smart cars."

"Gosh, Professor, I guess that's one way to deal with dumb drivers." But I notice Pa appears ill at ease. I wouldn't be surprised if he's already in touch with Tau on this one.

Abedni continues to point and trace and babble, as if we ordinary mortals had any remote chance at all of comprehending the circuitry and chips and stuff beneath the skin of this incredible car.

"Gentlemen, the Abednimobile will require energy only in minuscule amounts. And the devices in this car will learn much faster than any human brain. Dear me, Doctor Frankenstein would be quite envious, heh-heh-heh."

"How do dis ragged-arse ting work?" Pa asks.

"How, Mr. MTO-man? Well, take the brakes. ABS was a first step in solving braking problems. A driver did not have to know how to brake anymore, just when to brake. But in my car, you do not need to know either."

"No? Not at all?"

"Nope. Let us say you are approaching a bend in the road. In my car no judgement is necessary. You do not need to think, you do not need to slow down. It is all taken care of. Dear me, you may be enjoying a coffee and talking on your cell phone; it does not matter."

"That so? No judgement." Pappy's eyes are racing over the plan, as though recording it all for the inspection of his Far Friends. Then his eyebrows rise, he looks askance at Abedni. "Damnation, sir, this vehicule don't *need* no driver!"

The Doctor gives a little maniacal laugh. "What better revenge, eh? It is the next best thing to taking their toys away from them — mind you, I do not rule that out. They will love this car. It is packed with gewgaws. Talk about fully loaded! What a head-turner, they will say. What a flashy, sexy set of wheels! I can do anything in that car. No more risk threshold. I will be perfectly safe no matter what I do. I can drive with perfect abandon. I will not need to wear out my brain. I will be Number One!"

"Professor, you're a marvel." I can't help but admire this sly man. "It appears you have removed the average driver entirely from the equation."

"Exactly, Mr. Rufus. That is precisely what I have done. Your son, sir, has a marvellous grasp of what I have accomplished here. Their days of maiming and killing are over. Your Triffids will still be around, Mr. Pappy, but this car will neutralize them."

"Gee, all you do is push the gas pedal and steer," I say, thoroughly astounded. "And I'll bet you could have eliminated that too, Professor, but you wanted to give them the illusion of having some input?"

"Certainly. They can steer like crazy and push the gas pedal to the floor. That is all they have to do. They can have an old-fashioned brake pedal as well, since they are used to it. I think they will appreciate having two pedals to work."

"Sounds like you have a winner here, sir. Fabulous car. Forward-looking, sexy, loaded, fast, and safe. What more could they ask for?"

I'm a bit concerned about the way Doctor Abedni cackles, drools, and rubs the palms of his hands together. Could it be he's not immune to the lure of the golden calf after all? Or is this merely a yearning for power?

"Yes indeed, gentlemen. My car is also in conformity with the first law of modern collectivities, which is that the people are always right. And the people want what they want. And with this car, I have given them what they want, heh-heh-heh."

"Bananas!" Pa says.

"Professor, I still don't see how the friggin' thing will work," I confess. "You say it will just fly into bends and corners with the gas pedal to the floor? How is the average cluck going to manage that?"

Abedni gives me a pitying look. "The car, Mr. Rufus. It has dynamics. It measures and adjusts everything at any given moment. Continuously. Attitude, yaw, everything. Activating this, deactivating that. From moment to moment."

"All by computers?"

"Certainly."

The Professor points to the various functions and the

pathways of communication, all of which tell me absolutely nothing. But from his verbal description, I do get a pretty good sense of what the car can do.

"It is all right here, gentlemen. Here, you see? The on-board diagnostics. They monitor and control engine operation and transmission. They monitor and memorize engine misfires, catalyst efficiency, engine knock, fuel evaporation parameters...

"Here, my friends, is the ultrasonic sound device to ward off animals. Here, a near-object detection system to cover blind spots. Here, an early-warning device for bugs. A baby-goose detector – birds are different, you know. A black-ice detector. Here laser and radar scanning devices – the computer-controlled vision camera – well, you get the idea. Everything is there. The car is foolproof."

Still, as I look at the Professor's amazing creation, I must confess to doubting.

"It ain't drivin'!" Pappy declares. "Won't be no place for grand ol' Chevy."

Abedni takes a long, hard look at us. For a moment it seems he might throw up his hands in disgust at this unexpected opposition.

But he says, "Now, Albert, do not fret. Do I look like a quasher of classics? An annihilator of antiques? A heaver of hot-rods? Of course not. We can work this out. We can have hobby tracks for people like you. Recreate the good old times with curvy roads, limited traffic, green fields full of colley-cows, but – ah – all in a finite space. You do not like that, I see?

"Now listen, Albert, my friend, you must understand that if we are going to control the Triffids, we need vehicle uniformity and absolute control of all variables. Spacing will need to be electronically regulated; we cannot leave anything that important in the hands of Triffids, now can we?"

"Na," says Pa. "Chevy wouldn't like it."

"Albert, you are a stickle. Just what do you want us to do? Kill off the Triffids so we good guys can reclaim the roads? All I am saying is, let them drive crazy, and let us be safe. They can drive crazier than they ever dreamed possible.

They can have all those thrills of mindless abandon which the vacant mind is so fond of. But they will not torment you and me. We will not have to be looking over our shoulder at any given moment. We will not be carved up by some cretin, crushed by a clown.

"Dear me, still not convinced! Well, you know my scheme is not written in stone. I can see it might be a sacrifice for people like you. Suppose we were to consider a dual-road system – one set of roads for the Triffids, one for us. Sure, that is the solution. Why should you and I be hooked up to an advanced-tech babysitter?"

"Sounds reasonable," I say. "What about it, Pa? A dual system. One for us and one for the nerds. We all get what we deserve. We all get what we want." As an afterthought I ask, "What the heck does your contraption run on, Professor?"

"Available CO_2." This he says with a straight face. "Right, the stuff we all exhale. Got the idea while reading about the Mars mission."

I have a feeling Pappy would laugh at this if he weren't afraid of getting the hiccups. He gives a wry grin and says we have to be getting on home. Abedni offers us tea. We thank him, no. "Enough slops for one day," Pa mutters on the way out.

Driving home, Pappy is connecting with Tau. This I know by the deep breaths and the glow over his eyebrows. "Me lungs be full o' de rare air of revolution," he tells me.

We're heading east on Bloor. Folk on either side scurry like pinballs and pop out with their parcels from between parked cars. There's a feeling of snow in the air. It's a time for True North to celebrate. The Triffids, though, gnash their teeth and plan to visit Florida.

I tell Pappy to go ahead and say what he has to say. I know he has some plain talking to do.

"Is I green round de brows again? Is that how ye knowed? You be right, my son. When you was a little gaffer, ridin' beside me, I taught you to hate de Triffids, hate in this case being entirely justified. Udder pappies was teachin' their little ones to imitate them."

"That's true, Pa."

"I taught you to use yer eyes. I taught you to never be content, long's de world be run to please de dregs. And so yer spirit yearns to be free in a world of reason and justice."

"Sure, Pa."

"De years are passin' quicker now. We has bided our time. We has learned de lessons of Tau. And we has sown. But we has not reaped in accord wit our sowin'."

"Right to the point of being fed up, Pa."

"We're losin' de war against de Triffids, son."

"I know that too, Pa. We lost it long ago. I think when we all got radios and cars. And they made the roads straight, and paved them so we could go to movies, learn about the world, and drink in strange places. And we all left our farms and our fishing and moved into town. And we didn't take bread for the road any more, because we weren't afraid of the fairies any longer. There was no more mystery. They killed it, Pappy. They killed the mystery."

Pa looks real sad and tired. "They killed a lot of tings. I fears they ain't done yet. I sometimes wonder why I come up here to Toronto. Strange place to be for an anti-confederate man. Right in de enemy heartland."

"All the Newfoundlanders in the world wouldn't make any difference, Pa. This is a Triffid planet we're on now. We can fight until we drop. The mind-snatchers have won. No use to run out into the road trying to warn people. No use to cry, 'Stop, your next.' Too late. The war is lost."

"Yeah, seems dat way. I hates to admit it. Soon there won't be any of us left. Yer students regress, most of 'em, de minute they gets a licence. They forgets about force fields, everyting. They lets de Triffid inside, then there's no udder rule than monkey-see-monkey-do. De police are no good. Politicians, judges, lawyers, teachers – all Triffids! That's why we's paid for our pains in ridicule. I supposes any day now they'll stop pretendin', and so come right out and declare themselves. World's first Triffid republic."

"Looks that way, Pa."

"They'll make us mow and spray our lawns wit nauseatin'

Last Days of Driving

regularity. We'll have to snog every bug and spider we sees and carry a can of annihilator wherever we goes. No more puttin' de bugs and spiders we catch down in de basement in wintertime. We'll be expected to step on 'em or swat 'em wit a rolled-up newspaper. You and I and de Professor will have our heads stuffed wit de pulpy marrow of a Triffid seed pod. Word and Sign'll be everywhere. They'll have a new flag. One wit de Finger on it. De Finger Republic – now there's a grand name!"

We ride in silence for a while. As if in consolation, snow comes down in earnest. Then Pappy sings himself a song. I can barely hear it. It's an old ditty, but it sounds oddly relevant to right now:

So now Confederation
A shameful death has died;
'Tis buried up at Riverhead
Beneath de flowin' tide.
O may it never rise again
To bodder us, I pray …

First flakes of winter are magical, I learned as a little boy. They glisten like diamonds. They're telling us: this is the kingdom of snow and the season of celebration.

"And now it's my turn to talk plain," I say to Pappy. "I'm not teaching any longer. I'm quitting Galaxy Drivers."

I thought Pappy might slide under the steering wheel, but instead he greets my declaration with a cheer. And when we get home he fetches the rum and calls for a mug-up, saying, "Byes, we'll all hands make good cheer togedder." We toss off a couple of draughts and Pappy does a jig. Then he gets his bag of Harbour Grace knobs and invites me to pick one. And I know he takes my quitting as a grand occasion, because only once before did we take candy from that bag – the day Pappy was forced to quit at MTO.

I pick one with a good dark stripe and pop it into my mouth. The white is peppermint, the dark is molasses. In the old days, Grandpa Prince would make the trip to Harbour

Grace a couple of times a year expressly to buy the knobs. And when Pa left Newfoundland, he brought a great bagful with him. Now there are only four left.

"De last four Harbour Grace knobs in de universe," he declares, smacking and rolling the candy with his tongue. He wraps them up and puts them away.

But I think the candy did something to him.

"Rufus," he says, "There's one ting we ain't tried and that be war. Get yer guns out now. This ragged-arse town's gonna blow up like a meadowful of overripe harses' farts!"

CONCEPTUAL DEAD ENDS

At Galaxy Drivers they can't believe I would desert the cause. They think my employer jests as she makes her announcement. But then they see the teardrops tumble from her eyes, and all of them are numb and start to tremble. Then they weep or bawl, like a troop of kids hearing that all the candy stores are closing down for good.

I take some toilet paper from my pocket and pass it around. My employer is already on the floor. She's in deep pain. And yet, she has a stake in Triffiddom, just as Sergeant McDuff has a vested interest in crime.

It shows how much she loves me.

For several minutes they sob and wail, but then my employer picks herself up and orders us all to run around the block. I think it's an exercise in grief control she picked up in Japan.

Debbie keeps pace with me, and between sobs she asks, "What is this tripe we keep hearing about? What the devil is a Triffid?"

We're both huffing and puffing. Folk point at us and laugh. There go those idiots from Galaxy again, they say.

Between breaths I tell her. "You already know that, Debbie. You just got – a different name for 'em. You know, it was my Pappy's great contribution to humanity – to point out that we had to call the evil by one name. Otherwise – how would sane folk ever know what they were talking about?"

She gives me a certain look as we turn the first corner. She's trying hard to wrap her brain around the whole thing. "Are you talking about rotten drivers?" she asks.

"Yes – You're a jewel, Debbie – and a crackerjack. I knew you knew, even if – you weren't sure what to call them."

"All of us know," she says. "But at Galaxy there's the bottom line. Bottom line is business. Gotta be careful."

"Yeah, Deb, you're telling me. Gotta know a lot about hamburgers."

During these weeks, Gloria makes remarkable progress. Some people are like that. They reach a plateau and do not make progress for a while. But as they sleep, the magic catches up with them. This is the meaning of the word "overnight" when we say that somebody underwent a radical transformation overnight.

On the day of Gloria's flowering, I give her a bouquet of red and white roses. This is the day Gloria joins the Party and becomes a card-carrying member.

Doctor Abedni's current project is to demonstrate that most drivers have a severe identity problem. He tells us this as he and the two cats usher us in.

"My dear friends, they do not recognize their own driving personae. It is quite amazing. What they do is construct a fantasy identity, and they swear by all that is holy it is their own true self."

"Really?" I say. "A fantasy identity?"

"Yes, that is so. A mere imaginary figment. A virtual reality of the mind. But it is a fake."

Gloria says, "Golly, Professor!"

"Right, my dear. It is worth a barrel of 'gollys.' Now, I would like you all to help me make questionnaires for our little survey. We are going to ask our sample some very basic questions. The answers we get will help us determine what are their values, attitudes, and skills, all in relation to good drivership. We will also ask our sample to evaluate themselves with reference to a standard. Is that understood? Marvellous."

In spite of our compliance, the Doctor steadfastly refuses to concur in, or in any way connect his name to, Pappy's hypothesis. Pa makes the mistake of pressing him. Irritated,

Abedni condemns the Triffid concept and does not mince words.

"It is unnatural, unnecessary, and asinine," he says.

Pa reddens around the nose, like a lobster in the pot. His combat boot actually leaves the ground. But not by much. Pa is exercising prodigious will power. The muscles around his mouth tighten. Through his teeth he hisses, "High-learnt brin bag, wonder o' de East!"

Pa is so upset he accidentally steps on the black cat's paw. It skreeks and shoots under the furniture.

"Okay," Pa says, "All right. What do you want to call dis chummy, then?"

"Stop prevaricating, Professor," Gloria rails, coming to Pa's help.

Abedni gives his best Peter Sellers smile, but the regard he casts us over his horn-rims is pitying. "Dear colleagues, what we are concerned with here is no alien. It is merely a particular configuration of the mesmerized state in which the mass of humankind has always gone about living. It is a state of semi-awareness, in which one focuses on the transient and the petty, the low and the mean, near rather than far—"

"A trance?" Gloria suggests.

"Yes, my dear, a kind of trance."

"But golly, Professor, who put them in that state? They weren't born into it, were they? I think there has to be a Triffid there somewhere."

"Good girl," I say. "Professor, no one can dispute your knowledge of science. Pappy, I know you have your powers, except in the dead of the moon. I have to respect both of you. But is it really necessary to have this argument? Do we want a rift in the Party?"

"Have you seen any aliens, apart from the likes of me?" Abedni taunts.

"Curry-funk!" Pa retorts.

"Can't we be civil?" says Gloria. "Think of the good of the Party."

I respectfully request the Professor to elaborate on his

thesis. "Supposing, sir, you are correct and the majority of drivers are just some kind of benumbed low-life, how does that idea account for the astonishing similarity of negative behaviours over a whole population? Is it likely there would be such a development without a plan or a guiding force of some kind?"

"That's tellin' 'im, Rufus bye."

A shadow of exasperation passes over the brow of Abedni. "You westerners are always looking for devils. Why? Do we have to find a devil here? All I am saying is, people cannot drive in a mechanical and automatic way any more, with their minds in neutral and their thoughts hither and yon. What is needed for today's driving is unbroken mental engagement. Full utilization of faculties. It is more like flying a plane than old-time driving. You need a quality operator, someone who is focused and alert. That is what I am saying."

All this while, Pappy is making signs and silent threats behind the Professor's back, which puts Gloria in a very giggly mood, and causes Abedni to cut short his harangue. We decide to go home before things get entirely out of hand. I can't help wondering how we four can ever hope to bring a political party out of the wilderness and into the light of power.

Once we are home, I therefore suggest to Pappy that the outer-space connection will be impossible to prove. I also point out that science looks first for the more obvious and nearer explanation before going further afield.

"Look at all those times we've been to the Bradford Triangle without seeing a thing," I remind him. "We've seen neither Tau nor Triffid. All we do up there is get stiff necks and buy cucumbers. Suppose we did see some aliens, how would we know who they were and where they were from? They're probably not gonna tell us, you know."

What an awful look he gives me! Then he gets this mystical glow and his eyes are set to infinity. "Oh, son of mine," he says, "creature of minuscule faith, heed me now. De Tauans is great biders of time. Wit them it be a cardinal virtue never to be on time, but always behind it. And so they tests our mettle, for whosoever cannot wait, cannot be called de friend of Tau."

"The friend of Tau! Come on, Pa, where's your proof? I've never seen any Tau."

"You'd seed 'im if you knowed how. I understands de fallacy of yer thought, my son. Yer sayin' I can't be right by meself alone. How can I wander in de desert alone? How can I lie in de marsh under de stars wit me eyes tuned and never doubt? You wonder how I knows what I knows. But verily, those who be born to move mountains will stand alone."

Sergeant McDuff comes racing down Gascap Bend in his cruiser and pulls up alongside us as Julie and I are about to commence a lesson. He seems apprehensive. Lately, Pappy and I have been browbeating him.

But he says, "Have fun!"

"See how normal he appears?" I say to Julie. "Looks almost real, doesn't he?"

"Daddy, you have to take lessons. It's the last time I'm telling you." This she tells him with surprising authority. "Otherwise, I'm not riding with you any more."

"Right!" I put in. "Can't you see we're on the verge of a revolution?"

McDuff looks embarrassed. "Hey, I'm a cop, remember. I'm the good guy. What in thunderation do I need lessons for?"

I give him a steely-eyed look and we drive off. I can see the day coming when my methods will not be so nice.

Now I must hurry to prepare Julie McDuff in the few weeks I have remaining as a driving instructor at Galaxy Drivers. Julie has made remarkable progress. But that very success in her pilgrimage has brought her up against the titan of challengers, against whom all who wander alone in the empty desert must do battle. Self-doubt is the name of this foe.

"How can I be right and everyone else wrong?" That is her crushing question that comes crashing like a seaside breaker over my preoccupations. Yes, Julie is just an average mortal. And the friends she has are average, mocking friends.

I have Julie pull over so we can talk this out.

"They make fun of me," she wails.

"It's only a social tool to keep the pack in line," I tell her. "It's something Nature taught them. But you and I are pledged to independence. We choose to obey the laws of the mind. Ah Julie, I know how the others bounce and cluck like nervous fowl with a fox in the coop. I know they hiss and honk and flap their useless wings. They think the only reason we drive, you and I, is to annoy them, the ordinary drivers of this world. It's as far as their thinking goes. It's what they have against us – we're not ordinary. We don't fit in. They have no knowledge at all of our high, holy purpose."

Her look is not encouraging. I can see she doesn't know what to believe. But I tell her it's late, too late to waste time doubting. I tell her there aren't many left like us. But a new day is dawning. You can hear the tranquil purl of water if you know how to listen – the gentle beckoning of Aquarius. And you can hear the clarion call of Reason. I tell her that all over the world people like us are beginning to come together to save humankind from the Triffid. To banish pack and herd. And to bring to this Earth the Age of the Individual.

I consider telling Julie about the Party, but I veer off and ask instead if she knows how lucky she is to have me, since I alone teach the Triffid.

I'm amazed at her shocked reaction to my words. "The other instructors don't teach it?" she exclaims.

"No, Julie, they don't."

She looks like a caged animal. I don't know what the problem is. I tell her not everyone is blessed with my insight. I tell her she's very lucky.

"Now I'm really upset!" she says, her teeth clenched. Heck, I never saw her like this before. It's the kind of face Gloria likes to make.

I tell her most instructors are Triffids. Obviously, they're not going to let the secret out. They're not going to undermine the Triffid conspiracy. But most of the instructors at Galaxy, I tell her, are pretty well clued in on the Triffids; they just don't call them "Triffids," that's all. "A dung ball by any other name would stink just the same," I say.

Poor Julie, she's really having trouble with this.

"I–I'm confused. Are you absolutely certain about these dung balls–that is–I mean Triffids?"

"Dead certain."

"And–and you say they're not people at all, but only copies of people?"

"Just copies."

"They don't have a soul or a mind?"

"Just pap. Pulpy stuff like the inside of a squash."

"But that's so scary! You say they're lurking everywhere, just waiting to kill us? Are you sure? You know, I can't sleep at night because of this. Oh, I wish I could hear something about it on TV. I can't find anything on the Web either."

"No, Julie, Triffids are in total control of the media. They're not ready yet for you to know about them."

"My God! And my parents haven't got a clue."

"Apparently so."

"My God!"

"Now, Julie, buck up. We can slay the dragon. The day is coming. *Le jour de gloire.* On that day all the Triffids will be called to account before the tribunals of Reason. It's our destiny to crush evil. That's what you and I are here for. We have given ourselves that destiny because we're unhappy. Someday all the evil in the world will be overcome. And on the day the last evil deed is done, on that day we shall grab the Grand Master of Revels by his beard, and in the name of all creation we shall make him tell us why. Why did you do it? What rational explanation can you possibly offer?"

"Uh, I'm so confused. So tired. Day of glory, please come soon. Will I ever get to be a good driver, I wonder?"

"Of course you will. Stand fast, Julie. You're not alone. It seems as if you are because they outnumber us ten to one. But you and I belong to a partisan army of heroes. Today we may be scattered, hounded and ridiculed, but tomorrow the world will call us the iron arm of destiny.

"Always remember, Julie, the Triffids are no match for you. While they are almost blind, you have the restless, seeking eyes of a bird of prey. And while in Triffid brains the neurons are often unconnected, and the cells unlinked, your brain is a fully wired one, ready for anything.

"In years to come, your record will be a perfect blank. Theirs will be filled with citations, court appearances, seedy ticket-lawyers, collisions, body shops, huge premiums, suspensions, interviews, reviews, dead life-forms. Yes, such is their litany of misery."

That is my unusually meaty hamburger for Julie. I drop her off. But then I think, hell, aren't I leading Julie and the others into the same conceptual dead end where Pappy seems to be? It's clear that Julie is not taking the Triffid as an allegory, something real but earthbound. No. What Julie imagines is an invasion of vapour-like aliens, insidious extra-terrestrials. She thinks the earth is under attack from the Big Deep Beyond.

Maybe the baggy-panted Professor is right to ridicule us after all.

I resolve to persuade Pappy to take a more common-sense line. But what about Julie? I don't think I want to tamper with her young mind. I'll let her sort it out for herself.

She will in time. The bright ones always do.

THE BOAT CREW

After getting a very excited phone call from Dr. Abedni, we pick up Gloria and drive to the Professor's to learn the results of his study on driving personae. The two cats come out into the hall to greet us, like fashion models swinging in fur.

We're not at all surprised to learn that 88 percent of respondents reported having collisions over the last few years, while 12 percent had no collisions.

Nor are we surprised that 97 percent of survey respondents consider themselves decent, honest, true, well intentioned, patient, understanding, polite, law-abiding, careful, skilled, sober, relaxed, and focused while operating a motor vehicle. Indeed, while doing almost anything.

Also, they never exceed the speed limit by more than ten to twenty kilometres, and then only to drive safely, to pass, or to discourage someone else from passing. They always adjust speed to suit conditions, mainly in pea-soup fog, winter white-outs, or cat-and-dog rain. They usually leave enough space, almost never follow too close, almost always obey signs and signals, and they are generally more courteous toward other drivers than other drivers are toward them.

"Gee!" says Gloria. "How can that be? What happened to all the idiots? What happened to the ones you hear about every day in the news? Not to mention all the idiots you see with your own eyes when you're out driving? They're not being truthful, are they, Professor?"

The Professor chuckles at such charming naiveté. "Dear me, is it not wonderful? But, my dear, they have no idea they are so far from the truth. They think they are good, ha-ha-ha! They think they are models of virtue."

"My gosh, you mean they can't even tell the difference between good driving and bad?"

"Not a chance, Miss Gloria. Forget driving, they cannot tell good from bad, period. They cannot see the misery of their own evil. They are just as much in the dark as you were before you chanced to meet with present company."

"So that's why they treat us good drivers the same as they treat each other, isn't it, Professor? Because they can't tell who's a good driver and who isn't."

The Doctor's brown eyes are deep pools of intelligent cunning. "Certainly, my dear. They have the virtue – or so it might seem – of treating everyone alike. As far as they are concerned, we are all just part of the herd. Our good driving gets in their way. They don't know we do it for survival. They think we do it to annoy them."

"Gee wilikers, that's awful! I feel sorry for them. They're just the way I was, proud and confident, yet totally in the dark. Just waiting their turn to do something horrible – something that will torment them forever. They're all going to screw up. They're just waiting their turn! There must be something we can do to change things – I mean, besides just sniping and plotting and wishing."

"Great speech," I say, patting Gloria on the back. "Too bad your newspaper ad calling on kids to rebel didn't get any response, Professor."

"Your sincerity, my dear Miss Gloria, is very touching. I love those who see the little sparrow fall. And you are correct, Mr. Rufus, my ad was a flop. But not to worry, I think I know why it was a flop. Nobody really trusts an ad, you see. You have to run it a million times before they decide to buy anything. Brainwashing can be an expensive proposition. You need big bucks to do that. No, we do not want ads. We want publicity. It is far more effective, you know, because they think you are not selling anything. Best of all, it is totally free."

"Publicity? How does we get it?" Pa asks.

"Easy, Mr. MTO-man. Sorry, I should not call you that,

Albert. My friend, it will be easy for a man like me. All I have to do is burp or fart and they come running to see what I have discovered. Now, the best way to start is with a press release, then follow with a press conference – Distinguished professor proves alien ether detrimental to the adult brain – something like that. That is a health issue, and health issues are big. This one has a slant that will blow their silly socks off. The threat is from another world. Oh boy, that sounds scary!"

"That's a grand idier," says Pa. "Alien ether, just as I been sayin'."

"Dear me, soon you will all see with eyes of wonder the splendour of the deeds we do. And so, to tighten our firm resolve, I propose that we four plotters join hands around this great motorbike, the supreme symbol of free flight, to solemnly commit ourselves to be the avengers of all little sparrows everywhere."

And so this we do. And the Doctor speaks to us in words of fire, calling upon us to radiate hope into the far reaches of remaining minds, especially the minds of youth, through whom we aspire to teach the people to drive and to live, if there is still in the minds of adults any spark that might be used to rekindle their native intelligence, however uncertain that may seem.

I am rather disappointed in the good Professor when he phones me clandestinely. At first it appears he only wants to chat.

"Did you know, Mr. Rufus," he tells me, "in the 1600s it was proposed that tiny aliens were the cause of disease? It is quite correct, of course. Pure guesswork, that is what it had to be…Imagine the classical Greeks trying to penetrate the microcosm, not with optical aids but with pure reason. They had an unwarranted faith in brain power – well, apart from the soothsayer, what other tools did they have? Their minds would not accept that a particle might be endlessly divided. They probably reasoned that no rational being would create something like that. Hence the gods would not. It would be a useless boggle. You would have people trying to get to the end particle, wasting resources in a search they could never know would be futile ... We are bound to figure it all out, you know. It is just not supposed to be too easy ... "

"Professor, what is the purpose of your call?" I ask, having a shocking notion that his harangue could theoretically go on till one of us dropped.

Long pause. I imagine the Doctor is taken aback by such a brazen consideration.

"Why, I thought you knew, Mr. Rufus. I desire of course to know how he does it. How does your dad communicate with the Tauans? Is that where he gets his powers from?"

What a shocker! I never expected the Professor would ever take an interest in the matter. But the worst is, he doesn't believe me when I tell him I know very little about it.

"Why don't you ask Pappy?" I suggest.

"There is something odd about your garage, Mr. Rufus. I happened to drive by a couple of times and I noticed a strange, eerie glow emanating from around the door. Is there — ah — Is there something in there?"

"Certainly. Chevy's in there. Sometimes Pappy forgets the lights."

"Oh dear me, I really do not think it was car lights making that greenish glow ... "

Abedni won't quit. Even when I terminate rather abruptly and hang up, as politely as I can, he phones back. He's like a kid at the supermarket who whines and bawls to get the candy bar.

What the heck, I tell him what I know to be done with it, which isn't much anyway, in exchange for a promise to keep it under wraps.

"Did you hear anything when you drove by?" I ask.

"No."

"Well, there are strange sounds too. Sometimes at night when Pappy can't sleep he goes down to tinker with Chevy. He has something going with the car, you know. But that's not all. He's intimated that he communes with Tau inside Chevy. Anyway, just last week I heard an odd hum that seemed to come from the garage. At the same time there were loud snores coming from Pappy's bedroom. And so, thinking there might be a prowler, I grabbed my Glock from the dresser and went down to have a look — "

"Yes? Yes? Were they there, Mr. Rufus?"

"Was who there?"

"Little bald guys with long arms and large saucer eyes?"

"Let me tell it, Professor. What I saw was a strange, misty light, and yes it was greenish. I suppose you might say unearthly — "

"Yes? Yes? Go on. What about it?"

"There were creatures there, right enough. I say creatures because they were ephemeral. They were transparent. I could see the back of the garage through them. They looked like old-time Newfoundlanders — a boat crew, by the way they all seemed to belong together. They had their rubbers on and carried tackle and clubs. They looked like they were getting ready to hunt."

"Hunt? Hunt what?"

"Seals, I suppose. But on the other hand, some of them were carrying hammers."

"Hmm. A boat crew carrying clubs and hammers."

"It was their primary unit of organization, you know. It rivalled the family as an anchor for a man's thoughts and passions."

"What did?"

"The boat crew."

"Oh, I see. Yes, yes. A boat crew. Newfoundlanders. Hmm."

"They were a grand bunch of lads in sealskins, Professor. Just like the ones Pappy tells me about — honest and ready. They all had a certain look of — something you don't see much these days — a look of — the word that comes to mind is 'mastery.' They all had it. You could see it in their eyes. Their eyes were rather oversized, come to think of it."

"Oh-oh!"

"And ... there was also a fascinating murmur that came from them. Very soothing. Like the purl of a brook in a country meadow, in some place where roads don't go."

"Oh dear me! Did they say anything?"

"Well, they didn't speak, if that's what you mean. And yet, somehow, I knew what they wanted to say."

"Yes?"

"The cull must proceed. That was the message. That's all. The cull must proceed."

"Holy Jupiter! But who the devil were they? Did you ask them?"

I have the feeling Abedni knows more about them than he's letting on. "Friends. That's the impression I got. Maybe that's all they wanted to tell me. Or maybe I took them by surprise. They were there only for a moment. They climbed into Chevy and vanished—"

"They drove off in Chevy!"

"No, they didn't. They just climbed in and vanished. In a slew of yer eye, as Pa would say."

"Amazing."

"Yes. Immediately afterward I thought I must have been somnambulating again. But I couldn't've been. It wasn't a dream. I remained awake till daylight, and several times I went down to the garage but found it quiet and empty, except for Chevy. When I told Pa, all he said was, 'Shame I missed 'em.' That's his way. He won't talk about it."

"Strange, Mr. Rufus. Very strange. Dear me! I would like to have a look around in your garage, if you do not mind?"

I tell him to talk to Pa. Abedni mutters something indistinct and hangs up. He's an odd turkey, all right, just as Gloria says.

REVOLUTION

Doctor Abedni was certainly right about the value of publicity. His press conference is sensational. All the media attend it. We get headlines in every paper. The Professor is on radio and TV. Everybody has discovered our cause.

Pa and Gloria and I sit in front of the TV and watch openmouthed. The CBC has it all:

Authorities are profoundly baffled by a bizarre phenomenon which seems to be occurring spontaneously all over Toronto. A student at Hillcrest High told this reporter: "Enough is enough. We're not accepting this pretend world any longer. We don't care what adults say, now we know they're Triffids. We won't ride with any of them till they get their brains back."

As at most schools in the city, only about half the student body showed up for classes today. Those who did attend spent the day harassing the principal and staff, most of whom took refuge in the school office. According to an unnamed source, the principal, Priscilla Pea, known to her students as Pee Pee, has been advised to call in the police. So far, Ms. Pea has refused to do this, saying she has the situation under control.

Late this afternoon our camera caught Ms. Pea climbing out a back window into the parking lot. As you can see, she can't drive off, since all her tires are flat.

Boy, I have to hand it to that Abedni! The news has never been so much fun. At last our Revolution is under way. The Triffids are about to get what they deserve. Young people are joining the Cerebral Drivers Alliance in droves. The Professor – that sly old crow – already had thousands of Party cards printed and ready for signing. The card carries an oath obligating the holder to abstain from riding with any unqualified drivers – for our present purposes taken to mean anyone not Party-approved.

The dads are resisting, says one young fellow on the tube. *They say they know how to drive and all that, but like, we're not buying that crap. We've seen their driving. We know the trouble they're in. We know they can't tell up from down. They collide, run over squirrels, and get tickets. We've heard the Word and seen the Sign. Our parents are lower than the basement drain. So we're saying, get real and get your brains back. Until then you can ride alone.*

There are some who complain they can't get to hockey practice or figure skating, or to whatever, either because of the oath they swore to the Party, or because their friends won't let them get in the car with mom and dad. Of course, there are some ugly incidents. But we enjoy every minute of watching, and we're well supplied with beer, cola, and popcorn.

Several days go by. Each is better than the last, as we watch, munch, and guzzle. All kinds of fantastic rumours are circulating. Business is languishing because kids can't get out to buy. Hardware stores are experiencing a run on hammers and nails, no one seems to know why. In Toronto, taxi drivers and pizza couriers are being dragged out of their vehicles and beaten. Gloria, Pa, and I are keeping count and applauding these promising developments. Other organizations are scrambling to make common cause with the CDA. Senior citizens' organizations are among the first, as well as many of the city's thousands of Newfoundlanders. The city is in complete turmoil.

But then a cloud envelops our joy. Our Revolution is getting away from us. Everything is Abedni this and Abedni that. Every paper we pick up has his name on it. The noted doctor, the famed neurologist, the brilliant brain professor – it's sickening. He never mentions us!

"Bet he's wishin' we'd all pack up and flee to Mexico," Pa remarks.

"I told you he's an odd duck," says Gloria.

"You can't both be nobody and lead a revolution," I point out. "Pa, it's high time for us to stand up and be counted. Time to shuck our Newfie modesty. Let's get us some publicity, so they know who the hell we are."

The schools are soon empty. Nothing anybody can do about it. For a while, the teachers wait around in empty classrooms, or wander lonely halls, the corridors of pretence, like the last dazed batch of dodo birds. They squawk and look forlorn and trust in a better tomorrow.

School boards hold emergency meetings. So do government departments and agencies. They call in specialists and debate, debate, debate. Everyone stymied. As one official puts it, *Whoever would have thought kids could do this? We'll have to pull up our socks pretty far if we ever hope to get their attention again.*

Pappy, Gloria, and I are reading up on publicity when they start to come to us anyway. Just a trickle at first. They come down Gascap Bend in twos and threes, knock on the door, and want to shake hands with us. We grin and laugh and clap them on the back. Sometimes, if they look famished, we let them share our rice, potatoes, or codfish balls. And if Pappy's in the mood, he entertains them with a song or two. Soon there is a steady stream of youth that abates only at nighttime.

At last we're mentioned in *The Star*. It's an interview with Doctor Abedni, who refers to Pappy as *founder of the Party*.

"Hum," says Pa, "maybe he ain't such a cracky little dung sink after all."

Maybe not. Or maybe the wily Professor is just trying to take the pressure off himself for a while. It's a vicious game we're in now and it behooves us to be watchful.

The kids are telling us to get out of the house. They're saying we should take things in hand, put an end to the chaos. No government, they cry. Do something. They're so helpless and needy. But with each day our power grows. We sit on it while the generator hums.

Pa is making ominous noises. I tell him there's something demonic in his thinking.

I fear his heart is set on revenge. "Tink now what we can do to all them little horned devils they let loose on de roads," he muses. "We treated them as heroes, as if they was old-time hockey stars from de forties or fifties. What did we get from them? Torment. Being good drivers, we had to turn de udder cheek. And they thought we'd cower forever in de end zone. Now dey'll have to pay de piper."

I wonder if Pa isn't trying to make himself into another Mao, the way he keeps pumping hands and patting shoulders, and calling the kids "my children" and "my soldiers." He tells them he's far too modest to play a leading role in the Revolution, though he always has some good advice on how to get things done.

"Mind now," he tells them, "ye needs a body to protect de Revolution and de gains of de people. A body that can strike like lightnin' on a cloudless day. Call it de Committee of Public Safety. 'Tis a grand old name that will reassure good folk and lull de udders."

"Yes, of course, Great Captain," they say, kissing his boots and even licking the dust off. I'm afraid Pappy encourages them in finding ever more colourful epithets to dignify his person. They thank him with tears in their eyes. Some faint, others scream.

"Let a tousand flowers bloom," Pa tells them. "'Specially dandelions. Let every lawn be covered wit 'em. Let de venomous flies be swept from highways and byways. Let their dronin' and buzzin' cease forthwith forever. That's me personal message to de youth of Toronto. Got that? Look lively now, mates."

Meanwhile, on TV we watch the politicians scramble to keep up with events. A few are making interesting adjustments. One is Sheila Pots. They ask her what it's all about. Is it a real revolution?

Oh, definitely it is. It could change the way we drive forever. Even the way we live. That's what they want. They want us to drive like real people. They're saying it's not enough any more to just have this corn-pops licence. And I think they're right.

Yes, of course the ideas have been around for a while — it was the political will that was lacking ... Of course driver training will be mandatory. The bottom line is to get drivers trained to a real standard. No more pretending.

Well, there will be a real road test, periodic reviews of driver performance, and upgrading when necessary. Collisions will result in automatic interviews. Drivers will be held accountable. Police, school bus, taxi, and public transportation drivers will no longer just follow the crowd, but will be models of excellence for the rest of the driving population.

And something entirely new, we're going to enforce the laws and regulations as per the Highway Traffic Act.

Boy, there's one chaw of a lady! Have to hand it to her; she knows about survival. The reporter asks Sheila if she doesn't think it's an awful lot to be asking of a drivership that, some say, has very little upstairs:

Oh, I agree. There's an awful lot missing. But when we're done, we'll be the best. A model for the world. And our people will be safe again. Look, I don't need to tell you what the toll has been up till now. Yes, it's true that an astonishing number of drivers will lose their privileges. We estimate that anywhere from a third to one half of all current drivers will be unable to adapt to the new standards. Well, so be it. You don't expect me to miss any sleep over that, surely? The reign of chaos is over, period!

No, the reign of terror has not begun. I don't think we will have a police state. I think people will get used to driving like people instead of like maniacs. The world will envy us.

Pappy loves her. She's practically toeing the Party line and she's a Liberal. "When de time comes," Pa says, "see that they treats her wit kid gloves. I'd hate to see her wasted."

The arguments and interviews go on and on in an orgy of desperate good sense and instant inspiration. Pa says most of the speakers are pretenders. I myself doubt whether we shall ever be able to separate the good from the bad, the innocent from the guilty, the redeemable from the depraved.

After Sheila, we get to see an interview with the president of Betcher Auto and Life Insurance Company. Billy Fleesom comes on grinning and glowing in support of the new order. After predicting a great revolutionary future for Betcher, Mr. Fleesom proudly announces that all the company's policy

160

THE
SINK

holders, new and current, upon completion of any CDA-approved driving course, will have their premiums cut by five percent, and by five percent yearly thereafter on the base amount, providing that their driving remains flawless. Eventually, the premium falls to zero.

Pappy, Gloria, and I applaud as President Fleesom confesses the sins of his company:

It's really a vote of trust on our part. We know there are people out there who never have acci—I mean collisions. We believe that most people, given the new standards, properly trained and expunged of alien influences, can approach or even attain the same level of excellence as these few.

And yes, it grieves me to say, it really is true. All these years we have been fleecing the good drivers, the ten percent who all along knew what they were doing. We made them pay practically the same rates as the others, the rotten-egg majority. To the ten percent we robbed, please accept our sincere apologies. We are sorry. A plan for reimbursement is under consideration...

Sure and high time too! Lucky for him he said that! It just might save his neck.

Suddenly, we're shocked at the faces we see. There's Professor Abedni playing cars with tots at the Ontario Institute for Studies in Education. It's a report on the Ministry of Education's pre-school driving program. According to the host, it's *a preparatory indoctrination into the good-driver mind-set, designed by Professor Emeritus Radshak Abedni, eminent neurologist and foremost thinker of the new order.*

"Foremost tinker!" exclaims Pa. "There's a wrinkle fer ya. High-learnt mattress thumper!"

The camera comes in near for a close-up of Abedni's face. He looks ridiculous among the tots. He's got a sheepish, self-conscious grin that makes him look not so smart at all.

Helping Doctor Abedni is Jake the Rake, the biker guy who almost got creamed on the 401 by a flying brake-cylinder pod. Scruffy jerk! I see Gloria's on the edge of her seat watching him. He has a group of tots to himself. They're all pushing little plastic motorbikes.

Dear me, kids love to play with cars and motorbikes, Abedni says, when the microphone is thrust in front of him. *It is a great opportunity to instil into their tiny minds a set of positive constructs to counteract negative impulses from their parents, the entertainment industry, and commercials, which until now have been their only formative contact with the driving ethos.*

Pa continues to scoff. "Foremost tinker. Foremost dickiebird!"

"Yeah Pa, and did you see that silly biker trying to insinuate himself into the good graces of the Professor?"

Gloria throws her popcorn at us. "Oh grow up! They deserve praise for what they're doing. They're not just sitting at home hoping things will turn out."

I jump out of my seat and put popcorn right down the back of her neck. "What the hell is that supposed to mean? You think we're having fun sitting here? Watching upstarts get the accolades? Take all the power and glory? How do you think that sits with us? You want us to jump on a train or a plane, I suppose. Take the first flight to Ottawa. Rush into the fray and forget to take our underwear, like Lenin when he discovered the revolution had started without him. Well, Miss Pretty, this old man and I have read all the handbooks. We know about timing, you see. If you take that train too soon, you're dead. Do you know what happens to unsuccessful rebels in this country?"

I pull an imaginary noose tight around my neck.

"Poo," she says, unimpressed.

"I do feel de press of time, girl," says Pa.

I'm just telling Gloria not to worry, and that we have big plans for her, when Abedni's face is on the TV screen again. We think it's Abedni but it's not. It's only a dummy—has the face of Abedni but the rest is built like a turkey. Oh no, they're burning him in effigy. Triffids at Queen's Park. Triffids out in the open at last. Self-admitted Triffids, on foot, no wheels. No one has ever seen it before!

Pa jumps clear out of his seat at the sight. "Ain't it wonderful?" he cries. "Yarry bastards! Don't ever again tell me there ain't no Triffids!"

It's true. Pa was right all along. There goes a pack of

Triffids. They're carrying signs with slogans such as "Triffids have rights" and "Hard hockey/tough beans." They rage into the cameras just as we've seen them do in our rear-views. They're screaming that the Constitution protects them, that driving is a matter of personal expression and instinct, that the foibles of the people are sacrosanct.

The reporter's mike is thrust into the face of one frothing Triffid. *Drivers don't kill people!* she screams. *Accidents do!* Another rushes up to shout, *You can't legislate the way a Triffid drives!* In the background you can hear them blaming the weather, wimps, low speed limits, and photo radar.

They set fire to the Abedni turkey and prance and jeer as the flames consume it. Pa seems to get quite a kick out of this part of the newscast.

The Abedni effigy disintegrates and fizzles and the Triffids jump up and down on it. Then the shadow people assemble behind a huge logo, which is a bare bottom with superimposed finger, under a crown of nuts. They march rag-tag to the Spirit of Unity monument and attempt to destroy it. Failing in that, they proceed to the Spitting Stones, where the names of the small in heart and mind are to be engraven. They bow down and kiss the monument. Then they tramp to the great oaken doors of the legislature, upon which they uselessly pound, expending their ill-humour in foul oaths and other menacing tactics.

Let them rant and rail. It may be the last they do.

Finally, the man everyone's been waiting to hear from, Jean le Beau, the prime minister. He's a careful, cautious guy, lean and nimble as Jake the Rake, and fresh from the Log Drivers' Waltz. Scrappy when he wants to be, yet more cunning than the Wizard of Oz.

Jean handles the overtly Triffid reporter with his usual superb and earthy aplomb:

Wad do you mean I taig de fun out of driving? Wad fun? De infrastructure is nod bil' for fun. Idz to save time — who for, I dunno. Would you call it fun to drive from Toronto to de airpor'? A sane person feel grateful only to arrive alive. De udders have no idea of de risks dey run.

No, wad do you mean I try to maig life safe? Wad do you mean you can't lie and cheat? Doz are your God-given rights. Nobody expec' you to be angels. You guys can taig your wheels to de raiz track — it's only fifty bugs. An' I promise you, we will buil' special idiot roads, right across de country. You guys can arrange wid your insurance companies exclusive privileges on doz roads to do wad you wan'. Doun' try to screw tings up!

NUMBER ONE, SORT OF

What a fantastic dream I have! Could it be the sci-fi novel I've just finished reading that brings it on? Is it the fault of *Tau Zero*? Is it because a starship makes it to the end of space and time and matter and energy? To the end of the universe? Yes, it makes it to the end of the universe.

It's an accident, of course. They can't stop the craft from accelerating. Thus velocity approaches the speed of light, stretching time for the crew. Endlessly.

They make it beyond the far reaches of the universe, the farthermost galaxies. And as they do, matter begins to turn in upon itself and crowd together. The universe is collapsing. The crew, because of their velocity, have survived billion-year cycles that were experienced as mere moments. It's the end of creation. And they witness it. A new universe is about to be born …

Or maybe not. Pa says the universe, our universe, will go on expanding forever.

I believe it's the parade that prepares me for this dream, as it really gets my neurons and synapses to snap, crackle, and pop. I'm right behind the Professor in the big march. He's a white apparition in that bedsheet, a spirit with long black hair and a swinging, golden clarion.

Today we do some serious strutting, Glock and I. Right up University Avenue. It used to be University Avenue. But Pa has now renamed it Grand Alley of the Relentless Furies of Retribution. Years ago we marked it as the main triumphal thoroughfare of our Revolution.

The Professor and I are first to arrive at Queen's Park, and so we get to watch the arrival of each contingent. Pappy is first in, leading the Upholders Clarion Corps, all of them in their snow-white military dress with the red steering-wheel logo. Behind them come the Heroes of the Revolution, a fine crowd of adolescent goons.

A raving, idolatrous mob follows us into the park. Only the pikes and bayonets of Special Detail keep them from crushing us in their crazed determination to touch. Many fall on the ground where we walk, eat the grass in our footprints, or lick up the sandy soil with their tongues. Such is the nature of their devotion.

A kiddie corps of drums and trumpets swings into the park, looking business-like and fanatical. They blow and beat like furies from hell, savagely, with faces grim. Behind them comes the League of Newfies in Exile, wearing red and white shirts and carrying sealing clubs. Next is the feared Gee-Gee or Grey Guard, the savage shock troops of the Seniors' Coalition. The League Against Addictive Advertising and Other Toxic Pap arrives, a thoroughly sour and vindictive bunch, whose stormy faces testify to the wounds of twentieth-century business ethics. They carry signs that say, "Crucify the Corporate Bastards!" Behind them come several thousand homeless and street people, all of them armed with hammers and nails and a thirst for blood.

The bad drivers, like ancient Rome's parading remnant of a conquered army, stagger into the park dragging their chains. Along the route, each one had the care of an old tire, one of the last he or she had ridden on. They had a choice of either rolling the tire along, or wearing it around the neck. Whoever lost a tire got a bath in squirrel dung. Now they throw themselves down and make pitiful cries for mercy, while the crowd greets their misery with jeers and a shower of sticks and stones. But I doubt the felons are any more culpable than many of their tormentors.

Right on their heels, and a great worry for them, a strange object advances in fits and starts. It's Doctor Abedni's car. Driving it is a guy with a lethal record. He's having a wonderful time. In any other car he'd be leaving a trail of misery. But in this one he can't, because the car won't let him. Still, the bad drivers fear for their lives. Not only are they chained and managing their tires, but they are also worried by the idiot in the strange-looking vehicle behind them.

More bands, and then a thousand vintage motorcycles. And out in front it's Jake the Rake. And – Gloria! Yes, it's Gloria. She's holding on to him with tight arms too. What a nerve! The bike's a mess – customized to death.

I know it's all going straight to my head, making me heady. All this adulation – what is one supposed to do with it? No wonder Caligula and Nero, and the pop and hockey stars of today, allow themselves to be persuaded of their divinity.

We hail the people from a dais. The Professor, white, mes-sianic, a fire-tongued visitation from on high, puts all of them under his spell. And when he has them there, he asks them what they think they are worth.

"Nothing!" they cry, all in one voice. "We're worth noth-ing!"

"Wonderful, my dear friends! Now, I would like you to tell me, please, what should be done with those who are worth nothing?"

Again the crowd responds in one voice: "Crucify them!"

And at that very moment in the sky a cloud appears, which takes the form of a cross, and all who see it marvel and say, "Here is a sign!" And all Toronto falls to its knees and pros-trates itself. Some pray, others wail or moan. But they all feel sorry for themselves for having become worthless nothings, deserving only to be nailed to crosses.

And the crowd all cry woe. "What are we to do next?" they ask, as they are not quite willing to ask to be crucified. "Tell us what to do, Great Guru Abedni."

The Professor has been waiting patiently for this moment. He is ready with his answer. "A Sacrifice is called for. A terri-ble atonement. I shall be first to do it. No, no, none of that, dear people. I do not mean death. No, I am not suggesting collective suicide. Nothing like it. Have no misapprehen-sions. Calm yourselves. Calm yourselves."

The Professor waits. The tension builds. "This then is my sacrifice, dear people. I promise you, and swear by all things holy, never again to drive. Yes, that is right, I will not drive again. Never again. I will never again get behind a steering wheel. All privileges of the road I hereby renounce and relinquish. That is my awful, my terrible sacrifice to the god of Reason."

The crowd is struck dumb with disbelief. They gasp and look around at their neighbours. Can it be he said what I thought he said? Then someone cries in a voice of agony, "No!" And the whole assembly cries, "No!" Someone yells, "You can't do it!" And another one, "You're crazy!"

The Professor gestures for calm. "All right, my friends. It is all right." When it's quiet enough to hear a pin drop, the Professor says, "It is logical, you see. I have no aptitude for driving. To speak very plainly, I cannot drive for beans, heh-heh-heh. I cannot even do a simple curb park – I never know where the wheels are. I bang the curb. I ride up over it. I could seriously injure someone at any time. Therefore, I have no moral right to a licence."

The crowd is still crying no, don't do it. A fire is going now. A roaring, heathen, fire-festival fire, a bone-fire fire, a sacred fire to leap over with a maiden, a fire to take ashes from and put under your bed to protect against lightning, a fire to burn a straw- or wickerman in, or even a guy, a witch, or a heretic.

Something comes out of the Professor's wallet. Something blue with a picture on it. It's the Professor's driving licence. It's real. It's a bona fide Government of Ontario corn-pops permit to jackass on four wheels. He holds it up for the crowd to see.

"Garbage!" the crowd roars in unison. "Garbage-garbage-garbage!"

Some in the crowd are hurling less civilized epithets. Others betray their true loyalties by giving the Triffid salute, the infamous Finger Sign, or by baring their bottoms and yelling, "Ass wipe!"

Triffids abound. We know that. But it will not hinder the agenda. On the contrary, as the Professor solemnly commits his worthless document to the sacred fire of Balder, evoking amazement and delight in this mixed crowd, we see an opportunity to strike at the Triffids. And so we challenge the multitude to throw their own dirty papers into the fire, which many instantly do.

The rest trickle forward toward the fire under our encouragement. We praise them lavishly, giving many of those who come forward a delicious, juicy hamburger, though a practically meatless one. That's what they want – the great taste of beef, but no meat. That's the way a Triffid wants everything. And so they throw the pretend papers into the flames. And at each toss, a little red devil with horns escapes into the air over Queen's Park, giving a wee wail like the squeak of an unoiled door hinge.

And all the while the mood is building. Hallowed is the glow this night from our Balder's fire. Many are giving the steering-wheel salute, raising their arms to form a circle. The multitude begins to sing one of the great songs of the Revolution, "We Will Teach the World to Drive."

During this eerie ritual, the Doctor grabs my arm, gives me the look of a wounded beast, and cries, "You see, Mr. Rufus. See how easy it is." Then he laughs demonically.

Is he in his right mind, I wonder? What kind of strange bird have we gotten in bed with? But oddly enough, after he touches me I feel in my bones that the gods have something to say to me. I jerk loose from his vulture claw. "Keep your space," I say. "Stay out of my bubble." He doesn't even appear to hear me. But the truth is, I can't wait to get home and have my dream.

Lo and behold, I no sooner hit the sack than I find myself crawling around in some far-flung kingdom of the Great Beyond. In fact, I'm eavesdropping. I'm hiding behind a great ball of cotton and I see these two guys strolling in the fluff. One has a golden clarion and looks like Pa, except his hair is also golden, and on the back of his corduroy jacket is crudely sewn the name "Gabe." He also has a huge pair of white wings coming out at his shoulders. The other one is like the turkey effigy of Abedni the Triffids burned at Queen's Park, and he's wearing a T-shirt that says "Number One." I have a feeling this guy is really big in the scheme of things.

From what I glean, they appear to be talking about big bangs and basic principles. Turkey Feathers has a fancy clock. It's on Divine Time and it's set to zero. Hasn't even started yet. By heaven, they appear to be planning the universe!

"Let it be a place where all living things must eat," says Number One, grinning hugely. "And let them desire to eat each other."

The other fellow – Gabriel, judging by the name and the horn – is obviously shocked. "Eat each udder!" I hear him retort. "My God, forgive me, but that would be a cruel waste o' critters. Gives me de ditties to tink of it."

"Heh-heh-heh, dear me, I do believe you are correct. But you know what we agreed on, Gabriel. Each universe has to be fundamentally different. The fact is, we have run out of options. But look on the bright side of things. This will not be one of those dull clusters where all the life forms cooper-ate and dine together on silica. This will not be just another paradise where every creature evolves toward everlasting life. Dear me, this one will be far more lively. Now it is time we had some fun, you and I. Nothing says we have to be dour and perfect all the time, you know. Picture it, Trumpeter. In this new scheme of things every creature will want a plant or an animal on the table. They will always be hungry because most of the plants are fibrous, poisonous, or prickly; and most of the animals can run like hell, and sometimes bite or sting as well. Can you picture that, Angelpuss? Every crea-ture has some other creature at its back. Sniffing, stalking, waiting for a chance. Oh, I tell you, if any good can come out of such a creation, you and I are true magicians."

Gabriel gives a couple of lazy toots on his horn at this divine plan, a sort of angelic throat-clearing. "My God, I hears de knell of a danger bell. It were a dung sink yer after creatin'."

That grin on the face of Number One – sure looks like Peter Sellers.

Number One fans his turkey feathers. "It is, rather," he says. "Dear me, good thing I am not answerable to anybody, what? Now, take the clock and let us get on with our big bang."

The two of them go off in a hurry, but return immediately.

Divine Time, it's only been a moment. But on Earth, billions of years have gone by. Gabriel is not happy. "I told thee this ting wouldn't work," he rails. "'Tis a Meso-zoic house of horrors. Those dinosaurs wit their big maws and cruel claws is disgustin'. They got no brains. Look how they picks on those poor little crackies hidin' in de under-growth. It looks to be anudder dead end, High-and-Mighty." "Yes, quite. I see your point, Hornblower. Without brains that place is going nowhere. I wonder ... "

Gabriel gives a little toot of his horn, obviously a note of optimism. "Yes?" he says hopefully.

"Some of those cute little mammals you mention, cower-ing in the shrubbery—given enough time they might evolve into half-intelligent bipeds. What do you think? I mean, providing we find a way to neutralize those terrible-tyrant-kings with their over-sized choppers?"

"My God, yes! Anyting but those loathsome reptilians!" Gabriel gives a few triumphal blasts of his horn that seem to say, "I told you so!" Then, after a moment's reflection, he says, "What about de Prime Directive, chief? Override again?"

"You got it. Hit the buggers with an asteroid. Just be sure to cover your tracks."

Gabriel winces. I imagine he's trying not to think of all the suffering he's about to unleash. "Ya know, Number One," he says, "those frightened little mammals really is quite cute. Too bad they hides in their cubbies and eats only blueberries. Once de big guys are outta de way, I tinks dey'll be more curious and covetous. A race of tinkin' malcontents just might spring from 'em."

"Goodness, I cannot wait to see. Well, let us hurry up the process, shall we? Get those mammals moving. Send them dreams to spur them on. Once they get up on their hinder legs, some of them will settle down where the fishing is good and the sweet corn grows. Then they will have time to sit and think, play tiddly, and make beer. Before you know it, they will be civilized, have priests, sacrifices, sports, animal shows, snacks, and loud music. Ha! That is when the real misery begins. I tell you, Gabe, it is always the same old process, no matter how we throw the dice."

"Yeah," Gabriel says listlessly, polishing his horn in his

huge wing feathers, as if angels ever left dirt or a fingerprint on anything. "That be right, Number One. Once they're up on de old hinders, in a slew of yer eye they's inventin' some kinda contraption wit foot pedals. It always gets away on 'em, 'cause they puts 'em up to great speed while their minds be still in neutral."

"Dear me, do not worry, Buglepuss. They will screw up, believe me. But they will have just enough grey matter to get off the ground, so to speak. And sooner or later they will make a machine that is smarter than they are. The androids take over and, of course, the real progress begins. Nine times out of ten that is what happens."

From my hiding spot behind the cotton ball, I plainly comprehend that the archangel is not convinced. "Are ya sartin, Number One? Suppose our bipedal hopefuls wind up like de reptilians, all hormone and a brain de size of a dumbledore's. They may be cute, but they got teeth and claws, and a bad temper. Suppose they kills each udder off afore it be time for de androids?"

A not-very-becoming sneer crosses the visage of Number One. "My, my, dear me! Do I always have to get bogged down in the details? Okay, okay, make sure a few of them get an extra dose of sense and sensibility. A little more grey matter than the others. One in ten, shall we say? Just as a little insurance against such a development."

Having said that, Number One floats off and disappears.

Gabriel sighs and looks wistfully out over the eternal stretches, which are soft as cotton and white as new-fallen snow: "We be a ragged-arsed bunch, we deities, but our work be ticklesome." He gives his horn a few low toots and starts to sing:

When I was out walkin'
me sea stock to buy,
got tricked in de liquor
an' bought bung-yer-eye.

Oddly, though I remain hidden behind a pile of cotton, I have the feeling this fisherman's ditty is being performed for my benefit. I try to shake it and plan to wander off and do some exploring. The sameness of the landscape presents an over-whelming impression of sterility, as if they've suffered some major environmental catastrophe. But these thoughts are interrupted by a horrible blast all in my right ear. It com-pletely destroys my hearing. It's that infernal archangel with his trumpet!

"Oh, you bastard!" I cry. "Only dorks go around blowing horns in folks' ears like that!" But then I look at him and, except for the wings, he looks just like Pa.

"Sorry," says Gabriel. He gives a little toot that drives away the pain. "That any better?"

"Yeah." If he didn't look like Pa, I swear I'd break his bloody trumpet.

"Ah-ah. None of those thoughts around here, chummy."

I guess they knew I was here all the time. Stupid of me to think I could fool Number One and his trumpeter. "Sorry," I say meekly.

"Ya don't need to spy on us, Rufus bye. We wants ya to come back tomorrow night as our guest. And ah, bring de old man's Chevy."

Chevy?

I'm about to reply to that when I find myself lying in my bed on Gascap Bend with a mild sting in my right ear.

I DON'T LIKE YOUR MODEL

But next night I arise like Dracula. Somnambulating, I climb into Chevy and accelerate. Don't even need to open the garage doors. I push the pedal to the floor. I get her up close to the limit – almost 300,000 kilometres per second. I arrive in jig time and drive right through the Pearly Gates. Front entrance this time. Gee, it's summer. Everything's green.

I find Number One and a bunch of archangels hanging out in a meadow by a little brook. I drive right up to them in Chevy. They all have wings and turkey feathers, and they're wearing huge self-satisfied grins, like the CEO's of earthly conglomerates when the market is bullish. They're sitting or lying at weird angles to the grass, not being bound by any physical laws.

After they've all had a good look at the car, except Number One, who appears distracted, I put to them a rather stupid question: "Are – ah – are you male or female, as I'm damned if I can tell?"

They snicker at that. "A little of both," one angel says. "Number One likes it that way."

"Oh, I see."

Now I notice they all have lines in the water. The water is the clearest I have ever seen. I have an overwhelming urge to drink it and to take my shoes off and put my feet in it.

"Not up here, you don't," a black angel cautions me.

"I can't help thinking," I say, somewhat annoyed.

"How's yer ear?" Gabriel asks.

"It's all right."

"Your universe is a frightful mess," Gabriel remarks. "I suppose ye blames it on us?"

Another angel, a skinny one who looks just like Jake the Rake, points the tip of his wing at me and says in a cautioning tone, "Hey, buddy, you're on your own down there, you know."

How am I supposed to respond to talk like that? "Caught any fish?" I ask, attempting to initiate a little light conversation.

Jake sneers. He flicks his dirty blond ponytail. His wings are frayed. "Fish? You want us to torment the fish? You're not on Earth now, buddy. Holy shit!"

"Sorry. I just couldn't help it. This looks exactly like the streams and rills we used to have at home. So sparkling and inviting—"

"That you feel drawn to kill whatever's in it," says an angel with zebra-stripe wings and a malicious mouth. The black angel is nodding in agreement.

I'm looking for a chance to address Number One himself/herself. But Number One is contemplating the stream and pays me no heed. I notice his T-shirt is faded, just like the ones Doctor Abedni wears.

"Little kids wit paint sets," says Gabriel. "Ye've mixed, stirred, and slopped till de water's all dishy."

I ask them why they've got lines in the water if they're not fishing.

"It's how we contemplate," says the one with zebra wings. "What of it?"

"Nothing."

"Hey buddy," says Jake, "Con-tem-pla-tion. It's one of the really cool things you can do in the All. See those little bubbles? Crazy, man! Course, down where you are they don't do it. Bad neighbourhood. Shit!"

All this while, Number One just sits there, apparently unconcerned with my presence. He looks like Abedni but he's not even smiling. He smells like haldi powder and garlic. "Hey there, Number One?" I try. "Number One, sir, I have questions."

He or she—Number One has bumpers—darts a glance in my direction, then goes back to his contemplation. I feel like a brazen, buzzing cluster fly. Or a whiny mosquito, droning into the reverie of a Beethoven or a Newton.

I want to understand, but I can't. Nor can I keep the indignation from showing. "How the hell did this guy get to be Number One?" I ask in a voice loud enough to ruffle all their feathers.

"Now mind who ya be twitin', bye!" cautions Gabriel sharply. Then he says, "Truth is, Number One been like this ever since yer Big Bang. It bodders 'im, you know. Yer whole universe is out of control. There's galaxies slidin' 'cross de path of travel of udder galaxies. Dreadful tings happen. Horrible tings. Evolution didn't work out. On your planet de reptilians went haywire, then de simians threw off Homo sapiens—oh, sorry…"

"It's all right," I say. "I'm not ashamed."

"Yeah, don't worry about it. Your part of de All is filled wit creeps."

"Your universe is the sink," says Zebra Stripes maliciously. "Most of the sentients are idiots."

"But why can't the Big Guy straighten things out?" I ask Gabriel. "After all, it's his party, isn't it?"

"'Fraid not. Prime Directive, you know. Non-interference is de rule. Past a certain point we almost never intrudes."

"Really?" I say, astounded. "Not even if a race of beings is taking their whole galaxy to hell?"

"Not even."

"You humans are the worst that ever came out of the primal soup," Zebra Stripes declares, obviously bent on tormenting me.

"Hey, buddy, can we take a closer look at your wheels?" Jake asks.

Except for Big Guy and Zebra they all crowd around Chevy, taking turns behind the wheel, poking at the upholstery, and sniffing at the engine.

"Hey, what a sweet thing this is!" Jake says, sliding in behind the wheel. "All it needs is some chrome. Take it to the Rod Shop. Holy shit!"

While they're checking out Chevy, I decide to amble right up to the Big One. After all, I didn't come this far just to shoot the breeze with a troop of celestial pigeons. So I clear my thought and I say, sort of off-the-cuff, "Ha! Never thought I'd get this close to ya, Number One." I almost give the Deity a thump on the shoulder but catch myself in time. Number One does not budge. No sign even of having heard me. So I try a more serious tack. "Sir or Madam, can you tell me why we're so fragile? Would you care to answer that one? Your laws often make mincemeat of us – Don't care to answer that one, eh? Well then, how about this one: Is there any point to it all? – You fudged it, didn't you?"

Maybe Top Cock is not into philosophy. I try again with a little friendly banter.

"Number One, Your Loftiness, have you seen any of those old *Star Trek* episodes? I'm thinking of the one in which Captain Kirk meets Apollo. Apollo, son of Zeus? Remember that one? We find out that the Greek gods were really extra-terrestrials? Yeah, that's what they were. There came a time, though, when the Greeks were no longer prepared to bow and scrape to them. So Apollo and the others got fed up and went back to where they came from. Do you feel you can identify with this story? Care to comment on the lack of fervour among your devotees? No, eh?"

I quit in disgust and turn to the others: "Is this guy aware of me? Does he know what's going on? He's not senile, is he? Or maybe he's just stuck-up? No offence."

"Hey buddy, his eyes are bad," Jake says. "Doesn't hear so good either."

"He won't answer strangers," Zebra Stripes says sourly.

"Are you sure he's alive?" I think the question is justified.

"I say, that is bloody cheeky!" says a dapper little angel with a trim moustache and an English upper-crust accent.

"Blasphemy!" cries Zebra Wings, outraged.

"I'm not trying to be rude," I say, responding as best I can, "but the good old days are gone. You can't expect us Earth folk to kowtow the way we used to."

Gabriel gives an angry little blast on his horn and says, "No, 'cause yer too big for yer boots. Yer grandpappy went barefoot to town every Sunday. There were a rock he'd sit on at de edge of town, and there he'd put his boots on. I some-times misses 'im when I sees that rock. I sometimes tinks what a pity ye be mortal."

"You really remember Simon Prince?"

"Yep, I seed 'im sog along to church all right. And once or twice a year I watched 'im sail to Harbour Grace to get those knobs. Wish I had a knob right now. Like all good tings, they doesn't make 'em anymore."

"Well, son of a gun!"

I'm just thinking maybe I should knock Number One into the water to wake him up, when the thought is intercepted by Gabriel: "Don't let 'im bodder ya. All de Number Ones is like that."

I'm taken aback by this statement. I give him a puzzled look. "How's that?" I say. "All of whom?"

"Why, all de Number Ones, of course. Oh, I see. Yes, I'm afraid so. There be more Number Ones upalong than you can count. Lotta folks wanna put that Number One shirt on."

Well, that's it, then. I should have known they'd do their best to confound and obfuscate when confronted by a mere mortal. Isn't it what they've always done since the clock first started to tick? Never give a straight answer to anything. Never be direct when you can take a detour. Promise what-ever is necessary, but never bother to deliver.

Gabriel gives a la-dee-da, ho-hum sort of toot on his horn. "They's not all as quiet as this one," he says, "though they's all wonderful self-absorbed. Would ya like to meet some o' de udders?" Gabriel puts the horn to his lips, no doubt to call up other Number Ones to torment me.

"Forget it!" I say sharply.

"Hey man, you little Earth mammals are so cute," says Jake.

I scream. I can't help it. Just like a bayman fallen into the liver butt. "If you're not really fishing, then what the hell are you doing?" I sound so angry they all take a step away from me. Then they laugh like loons before dawn.

"He's only tryin' to be dispassionate," Gabriel says, indicat-ing Number One. He takes me by the arm and walks me off aways from the others.

"Yeah. He's doing a super job. But now I know he doesn't

see the little sparrow fall. They told us that in Sunday school, you know. St. Paul's, Halifax. We had to sing these songs about how he's looking out for us. I thought it was suspect when I got a little older. But some believe it all their lives."

"Tell me now, bye, how are ye gettin' on in yer universe? It be a place of deep awe and wondrous mystery, idinit?"

"Yes sir. We stand at the threshold and wonder. Sometimes we ask ourselves, why can't we have it all now? Our lives are short, you know."

"How's tings in Canadicker Land? Yer pa's an anti-confederate, idinim? See de Yanks 've stolen yer game. You folks is busy as dumbledores, buzz-buzz here, buzz-buzz there. Tell me, has ya got enough space in yer sector of de All?"

"Well, you know. Have we ever got enough of anything?"

I can tell by the way the archangel is examining his horn that he is about to reveal something significant.

"Rufus bye, ya wouldn't believe how I had to fight to get ye what ye've got. High-and-Mighty wanted to cram everyting into practically nuttin'. 'Put them all snout to arse,' 'e says. I got that changed."

"Well, just imagine! Somehow, I'm not surprised."

"That ain't all. I had to push for a built-in finite velocity – you know, an absolute speed. A limit. Try and guess what ol' turkey fedders said to that. He said, 'Dear me, let them break their fool necks if they wants to.' Yep, that's what 'e said all right. Tinks 'e knows it all. But I set 'im right. 'If there ain't no speed limit,' I says, 'we'll soon be overrun wit those glorified apes from Earth and all kinds of udder upstarts, all lookin' for favours.' Yep, woulda been far too easy to get here."

This archangel looks so much like Pa that I can't help feeling that's who he is. I ask him if we're related in any way. He laughs at this and immediately gets a fit of hiccups.

"Well," I say, "I'm glad somebody up here shows a little common sense. I applaud your efforts to get more space and a limit. I'm big on those things myself. But I have to tell you, sir, I don't like your model."

"Oh, is that so?" Gabriel looks really concerned and that encourages me to tell him precisely how I see it.

"Just take a good look at it," I say. "Stars are dying. Suns die

179

*Last Days
of Driving*

on a daily basis. They get super hot and destroy the very creatures they brought forth. Throughout the All, countless life forms are desiccated, starved, bombarded, and scorched into oblivion. Some are great civilizations. Then you have your ordinary bastards, like us on Earth. Whole galaxies collide and you deities don't give a damn. The slaughter is of astronomical magnitude. To me it's a great crime. The greatest crime of all time. And the gods are responsible. Shame on you! Have you no pity?"

"Now, now, don't be gettin' tissy wit me, Rufus. I does what I can. Remember, I's only de hornblower. Maybe I can blow a blast to wake de harbour, but me influence be limited for all that."

"Well it stinks. You've got your little lambs together with bright-burning tigers, sparrows falling into the cat's maw –"

"Dreadful, idinit? Believe me, bye, ya has me sympathy. Sometimes I has to wonder. But de only one to know what it all means, or wedder it means anyting at all, that be 'Imself.'"

No doubt finding my questions so uncomfortably to the point, Gabriel leads me back to the others and Chevy.

I give them all a defiant look and say, "Down on Earth we're getting ready to assume full responsibility." I think they might find this defiant remark a bit enigmatic. But apparently they know my meaning, as I can tell by the raised eyebrows and the looks they give one another.

"It's about time," Zebra Stripes sourly remarks.

Gabriel gives a couple of glad toots of his horn. "Hope ya learnt someting," he says.

"Hey man," says Jake, "reality's where it's at. And you folks ain't found it yet." He gives me a wink, as if to say, here's a tip to help you understand things.

The others have backed away from Chevy. It's clear my time is up. They want me to get in and blast off.

"A few innocent last questions before I leave?" I ask. I get the nod from Gabriel. "Well, this may sound simple to you but, is space curved because matter is curved, or is it curved independently – sorry, I never got past Grade 11 physics? Is there space without matter or matter without space? What's left when you take space away? Are the gods in, or outside of, the All? What is nothing? Can you tell me that? Just once I'd like to hold a candle to Doctor Abedni. I have a right to know, don't I? Do I need quantum physics, or can I just have an answer in plain old English?"

But even before I finish my questions, I know by their faces they aren't going to answer. They laugh and pretend not to know. And maybe they don't know. It would not surprise me at all.

I can't help adding a defiant remark: "We humans will know it all one day. Before we're through, we'll be the masters."

Transports of mirth at these words of mine.

"Hey, buddy, how close can you get this thing to Tau Zero?" Jake asks, when I've climbed into Chevy and am ready to go.

"*Tau Zero*? Isn't that a sci-fi novel? – Oh, you mean how close can I get to the limit. Pretty darn close. Just over a billion kilometres an hour."

Buzz of astonishment. Whispers of amazement. The Zebra is sceptical.

"My pa's a wizard," I explain, as I push my foot down on the starter pedal. The engine fires immediately. I can tell the angels are impressed.

"Be careful," Gabriel warns. "Look out for de fairies." I'm very surprised when he gives me a piece of fairy bread to put in my pocket.

"Hey, buddy, hope you know what happens if you reach 300,000 klicks per sec – Poof!"

"He won't make it home before the end of time," says Zebra Stripes, just as I push the gas pedal to the floor.

Wait a minute, what does this sourpuss angel mean by that? Isn't the universe just going to expand forever? Isn't that what Abedni said? Too late! I'm already close to the limit.

I wake up in the morning with a deep sense of betrayal. I feel as if I've paid a visit to the Marx Brothers in *Duck Soup*. I hope I will never go there again. I'd rather journey to a doomed star than meet up again with that bunch. Only one among them with an ounce of sense was Gabriel. Too bad he can't take over up there. Out there, wherever. Things would certainly change for the better.

I will never again use the word "hubris." If ever we humans had a sacred mission, it could only be to defy the gods.

I tell Doctor Abedni about my heavenly visit. I don't bother to say that, apart from the feathers, Number One looked just like him. I ask him what he thinks is the future of humankind in the cosmos.

"Dear me, as far as I can tell we have no future. Our destiny is to die off and be superseded. To some, it may appear that we have subverted the process and escaped our fate through technology and science. But in fact, I would hazard a guess that technology is part of the evolutionary plan. Technology is about to cause a quantum leap in the whole process. It will start with ourselves but will end with something rather different. Metamorphosis, yes. We shall all become beautiful butterflies and escape our confines. Our descendants will not be just like us. Dear me, far from it. You and I will soon be obsolete. Just like our ancestors way back when. Does it really matter?"

THE SLIMEBALL MAKES HIS MOVE

After inhaling the adventurous breath of the forest, having feasted our eyes, dreamt, and remembered, we snatch the ornaments from our yule tree, pluck from it all its feathers, and drag it naked to the curb. There we cast it down with shreds of tinsel clinging and let it wait dishonoured, like the pumpkins after Halloween, to be taken away with the other spent and used-up stuff.

Not really. That's not our way. That's the way Triffids do it.

At our place we have a lopping-off ceremony. We reverently cut the branches off and tie them in a bundle. They'll be used for the Balder fire at Midsummer. The stem of the tree is always used in the garden. After all, even in the Stone Age they knew what a sacrifice was, and they treated it with rite and reverence from beginning to end.

On our first and last lesson after the holiday, Julie turns those dark, beguiling eyes on me. Why are they so mournful? What problems could she possibly have, now that the Party is claiming victory everywhere? Still, I fear our Revolution is about to plummet into the darkest depths of human experience.

"Drive safe," she says. It's the new Party greeting and it's in vogue everywhere. Actually, it's supposed to be "Drive safely," but what the heck.

Julie's having nightmares about her sister's death, she tells me with moist eyes. Perhaps I erred in encouraging her to talk about it. She feels she should have been holding her sister's hand more tightly. Then it wouldn't have happened.

"When a robin chick falls out of the nest, it's gone forever,"
I tell her. "If it's missed, it's just for an eyeblink. The other
robins don't torment themselves. They can't afford to."

I'm not certain how helpful that is. One thing I do know,
she can't drive now. I recline my seat and get comfortable.
"You were doing your homework, I suppose, when you got
that dream? Did you come to any conclusions about the
relevance of the bus flashers?"

Julie has a great answer. She says they had no relevance.
"The guy in the car was not thinking. I guess he didn't care.
He was letting technology substitute for brains, like the
jerks who zip over railway tracks without looking. All he had
to do was slow down. Instead he took a chance. He had the
stereo on. His mind was miles away. And my sister paid for
it."

Julie's more than upset. She yearns for vengeance, I can see
that. Retribution—is there really any justice without it?
Haven't we been kidding ourselves long enough? Haven't we
been shunting off responsibility onto some cotton-candy
tribunal way out in Forever Land, light years beyond our
jurisdiction, a realm of turkeys? Julie only wants the mad-
ness to stop. She desires it with a passion. I believe she is
ready.

"He didn't care," she tells me. "He wasn't sorry. He had no
regrets. To him it was just something that happened. As if it
was just a matter of having bad luck. It could have happened
to anyone, he said. He didn't mean to kill Maria; why should
he feel guilty? So his life was disrupted for a while. Very
inconvenient!"

"Julie, Julie. You will not be free till you strike out against
this evil. The beast who killed Maria is still out there, alive
and unrepentant, ignorant and dangerous as ever. Vengeance
is what you crave. Use your sting, girl. Sting the bastards!"

The bright eyes come in from infinity to focus on me. A
cunning smile begins to flicker at the corners of her mouth.
"Sting them. Yes, that is what I would like to do. It's what we
used to do before we had police and courts and the Constitution. And now with the CDA we have the chance at last. The

chance to make them pay for what they're doing to us. Yes, I will sting them."

"Now you're talking!"

As if on cue, the winter clouds roll back. And the sun's rays, launched at more than a billion kilometres an hour, breach my windshield instantly, illuminating us in glory. And so she begs me earnestly to recommend her to the Party, which I swear I will. And it seems to me my engine is humming Alte Kameraden.

"Wait," she says as I drop her off. "Daddy wants to speak to you."

Gordon McDuff, police officer, looks as forlorn and worried as a kid lost in a department store. His Triffid world is in the throes of death. He asks me what he has to do to get the Triffid out of his brain. I feel like laughing and crying at the same time.

"Beware of deathbed conversions," Pa has warned me. Pa should know. He's spent years reading up on revolutions. How to make them. How to keep them.

I ask McDuff if he isn't just trying to save his skin. He plays dumb, says it's Julie he's worried about. Latter-day altruist. "We can't get her in the car," he says. "She's taken that – ah – that oath. Brainwave of your Professor Abedni."

"You bet. I suppose you're proud of her?"

McDuff shifts and mutters something I can't make out.

"You want my advice, Sergeant? Take the course. You get your brains back – and Julie." I can hear the wheels whirr and grind in that cop skull of his.

"Well, I – ah – maybe, for Julie's sake. It can't hurt, can it? Sure, if that's what you think I should do."

Kids are beginning to straggle up from the other end of Gascap Bend. A few have already planted themselves on our lawn, or on Jinkerdiddle's, and are watching us like the birds in Hitchcock's movie. I'm sure that's the way McDuff feels, though the kids come mostly to get an eyeful of Pa and me, sometimes to get a bat, a whip, a gun, or a hammer autographed.

I grin at them, striking a pose. I take my Glock from the

holster and fire one into the air. It never fails to give them a thrill.

"Cute kids," McDuff remarks, trying to sound unconcerned. But his moustache is bent like the tail of a shy and nervous dog. Poor McDuff, he can't admit he's been wrong all those years. He's a bad cop, because somewhere along the way he got his brain all screwed up. Got it all sucked dry, toasted, and dehydrated, just like a Dutch rusk.

"Relax, McDuff. Go sign up with Galaxy Drivers. They'll fix you up. Won't hurt a bit. Guaranteed."

"Is – ah – is it automatic?" I can see a faint ray of hope in his eyes. "If I take the course do I – ah – do I get my brain back?"

Wow! Never thought he'd bring himself to say it.

"There's no cause for optimism, McDuff. You see, you not only got that brain of yours steeped in foggy preconceptions, but then you had to let it dry up as well. And now you're just a straw man, with a brain no better than a rusk. A rusk is mostly air, you know. Probably the great Oz himself couldn't help you now."

A shadow of utter panic crosses the face of McDuff. "Oh God! Oh no!" His moustache quivers, as if it wants to detach itself in disgust from the rest of him and drop off.

"Afraid so, McDuff. You have only a slight hope. There is nothing automatic about brain power. That's what the wizard of Gascap Bend says. Pappy's the best wizard around. And you don't need a twister to get to him."

"God, Rufus, I can't believe how he got things stirred up the way he did."

I take McDuff inside, out of sight of the scruffy types shuffling baggy-panted up the Bend, so he won't be nervous. And I tell him the main thing is not to weaken, but to fight the Triffid in him hammer and nail, and to get into Galaxy on the double. Also, I give him some pointers on the exercise of his faculties, and tell him to try some serious thinking, to see if it might move some of the pathway straw in his cerebellum.

"Otherwise, McDuff, your only chance is synaptic reconstruction."

"What? Rewire my brain? Is that what it is?"

"Calm yourself, McDuff. We'll cross that bridge if and when we come to it."

I leave him. I feel so sorry for Julie, having a parent like that. She still loves him, though. She told me she does not intend to keep her promise not to ride with mom and dad. She believes he's fighting to get his brain back, and she thinks he's going to win. She says he needs her support, and that's why she's going to ride with him.

Who knows, she may be right.

I've taken Lenard Klutz for his road test. Splendid result. I had every confidence in him. I was not worried about him. What's on my mind is the climate of fear and intimidation. As a reaction to the successes of the CDA, road rage is every-where. It's completely uninhibited. The Triffids are coming out into the open, now that the CDA is threatening their very existence. Main roads and bridges are especially bad, with rammings, fist fights, duels with guns, knives, baseball bats, and anything at hand the order of the day.

Klutz seems to thrive in this climate. After postponing his road test five times in a row, I give in to his pestering and decide to take him.

Mostly, Triffids are killing Triffids. What a boon that they can't tell good from bad! If they could recognize their enemy, we'd be dead by now. But they can't. Just to be safe, on the way home I ask Klutz to suspend the good habits I taught him, so as not to rouse the ire of the Triffids. I've also taken the sign off the roof.

Besides the independent snipers and bomb throwers, sev-eral new clubs and secret societies are terrorizing streets and highways.

The worst of these is the Bandits. Their ringleader is none other than Joey Slimeball Snookums, the same imp who shadows Julie in his pink Mustang while she's on her way home from school. In letters to the paper, he has called us alternately, *the new commie threat in disguise* and *fascist scum*. The avowed objective of the Bandits is to fight the CDA, and generally to thwart the forces of law and order by creating mayhem on the roads.

According to several career officers, our society failed to respond adequately during the watershed years from 1980 to 2005. That quarter century was crucial to the formation of the current driving ethos, which fosters rage, risk-taking, and violence. Nothing short of a revolution could turn things around now, they believe. That is why these officers support the CDA.

I'm at the intersection of Danforth and Pape, heading west with Lenard Klutz driving. We've had to make an unexpected detour. Klutz has just told me he's not living at home any more. He's sharing a place with a young lady.

I have to keep reminding him: "Don't bother congratulating yourself, Lenard. The corn-pops licence they just gave you is a necessary evil that will soon be swept aside. I want you to remember that. This licence is worth nothing. The Triffids designed it for themselves, so they could drive without standards and without review. That's why any idiot could get one. The real testing you did with me, not with MTO."

"I know that, Master," Klutz replies.

He's leaving twice as much space as I taught him to, really irritating the Triffids to no point. It's sheer bravado. The Triffids drive round us while we're stopped at lights, giving us the Finger. I'm afraid we're going to get rammed from behind. "Madonna!" he says to himself. "Hulk!"

"Who are you trying to impress?" I ask.

"I'm setting the example, sir. I intend to be the best of the best. I intend to leave more space than God himself."

I smirk at this witticism. I hope that's what it is. Klutz has always been way too serious. I still fear he's too self-important to be a good driver. But right now, other than an occasional exaggeration, it's hard to fault him.

Klutz cuts his space cushion down a bit because of my concerns. "Still think I'm nothing but a little turd, sir?" he asks, driving masterfully along the Danforth. I can tell by the grin on his face he's certain of the answer. He turns off onto what used to be the Don Valley Parkway and is now called the Valley of Death Parkway because of all the crucifixions that take place there. Overnight, the Parkway has become one of the most scenic city drives in the country. There has, however, been a slew of collisions for obvious reasons.

"What do you think?" I respond, turning the question back to him for answering.

"I think I'm ready to join the CDA," he replies, throwing me for a loop.

"Whoa! Hold on there, Lenard. You have a bunch of driving skills that put you in the top ten. But the CDA is more than that. The CDA is a way of life. It requires many years of practice, commitment, a certain view of things –!"

As I say this, a suspicious-looking black Caddy with tinted glass pulls alongside next to Klutz. I can tell Klutz is aware of it too. On my side, an old pink Mustang pulls abreast of us. I think I recognize the driver. Sure I do, it's Snookums. I thought I knew that old rustbucket. I give him a wave, forgetting he's the leader of the Bandits.

Snookums grins back at me. An unseen hand rolls down the rear window of the Mustang. I don't notice this until somebody shoves the barrel of a rifle at me. I duck just as I hear several discharges and Klutz slams down on the brake. Tires squeal, I lurch forward, belt activates, wrenching my gut. My head stops just short of dash. My mind braces for rear impact – It doesn't happen!

Our stop is so sudden, the attacking cars wind up hitting each other with their fire. Klutz pulls onto shoulder without skidding. I grab Glock. Throw myself into ditch. I see Caddy cross median, smash into oncoming traffic. Mustang's way up the road. I take aim at the Slimeball but I don't fire.

I feel like Dirty Harry. Klutz and I scan the freeway. "Jesus!" he says.

We examine the car, taking care to keep an eye on the Triffids so they don't get a chance to mow us down. We know they can kill us here with impunity. We don't intend to let it happen. There are holes in all four doors and the rear windows on both sides are out. "You're a marked man, sir,"

Klutz says with admiration. "The Bandits are out to get you. Still think I'm not ready to join the Party?"

I ignore the question. "Good thing there was nobody behind," I say. "Otherwise—!"

"Not necessarily, sir. I would have stayed off the brake and pulled onto the shoulder first."

I give him a look. A Clint Eastwood Dirty-Harry look.

I don't really believe Klutz has what it takes to pull that off, even though we've practised it. But he wouldn't say that if he hadn't been checking his mirrors. I'm impressed. I've taught him to check the rear-view every three to five seconds, depending on conditions. I don't tell him I didn't manage to make the mirror check myself. Not that it would have made any difference. If a student is going to slam down on the brake like that, not much I can do to prevent it.

"Let's get the hell out of here," I say, taking a look around in case there are other Bandits in the vicinity.

THE TERROR

In the days that follow I increase my vigilance. I'm in a hurry now to finish up with my students. No sense putting them at risk. As an added measure of security, I get bulletproof glass for all the windows, and Pappy and I put new reinforced doors on the car. At the start of the day, or when the car has been left unattended, I also do a bomb check.

We don't take Chevy out much any more, because she's not protected. If we're visiting someone, we make sure there is a garage to leave her in, or we go for a ride and come straight back home. Otherwise, we take my car.

In the last few weeks, events have moved at an incredible pace, and the Party has a foothold everywhere, government bodies included. The genie is really out of the bottle now. The CDA has an animus all its own. The Revolution is a starship accelerating at warp speed into the unknown.

On the bridge of this starship they play a game of musical chairs to see who will occupy the captain's place. So far, Pa and I, and even the Professor, are more or less aloof from the whole affair.

Louts and goons are everywhere, always in good supply. No more due process. Laws come into effect through debates in the street. They usually include a brawl and end with a show of hands and a declaration. The courts have been replaced by *doomstools*, the chief concern of which is to deal with the Triffids. The justices are called *doomsayers*, and must be no older than 17 or no younger than 79.

The kids come to us and we humour them. No question, though, of keeping them under control. None whatsoever.

We have influence as the founders of the Party. It is we who discovered and exposed the nature of evil. But the kids do quite as they please.

Pappy foresaw this but he's not worried: "'Tis narmal. De Triffids be de fog men of every great happenin'. They busy themselves like crazed flappers in a meadow full of hunters. And they does what they can to screw tings up. But de day will come when all their wrath be expended. That will be our cue. We steps in and imposes upon them de Dictatorship of de Competent. 'Tis a grand ting to say."

I tell him it's an ugly phase we're passing through. And I say we have to choose our words carefully, because what we say becomes the divine word and law of the oracle, sealing the fate of thousands.

I'm amazed at Pappy, who loves to harangue the pilgrims from the verandah. I wonder if he imagines himself to be Mussolini or Caesar. He should be more circumspect. He's been telling everyone bad drivers ought to be crucified. It's only a metaphor. But the Young Zealots (newly formed to re-place the Scouts) have taken it literally. Thousands of Triffids have, in fact, been nailed to wooden crosses.

Pound of flesh, some say. The people need it. And as has been said, the people are a great beast. No use either, to tell the Young Zealots this is not what Pa meant. They claim to understand our meaning better than we do ourselves.

In the valley of the Don, the crosses go up so fast it makes our eyes water. Not that we weep for the Triffids, oh no. They have it coming. And, in fact, we're getting used to the idea. There is something magnificent in the sight of these crosses. They echo the glory of ancient Rome. What a thrilling, chill-ing sight it is! Thousands of crosses, row on row. A tormen-tor hanging from each of them. It's a spectacle rarely seen since the defeat of Spartacus. The blood of these criminals does homage to ancient rites of sacrifice and purification. I have thought long and hard on this, and I find it a fitting, as well as a humane, punishment after all. To hang in the fresh air, with the high drama of the clouds overhead, till life ebbs away. What a grand death it must be, to tower over your per-secutors and look down on the world you are leaving! How preferable it is to the sterile officiousness of the electric chair, the gas chamber or the needle! Or even the lonely hospital death between four bare walls, while morgue and security guys lurk and wait to be first in line for your gold wedding ring. To die such a death is to die without any bond either to one's own or to Nature. I'm inclined to believe we have not done so badly.

These first Roman crosses are quickly superseded by the Celtic type, since the circular part aptly symbolizes the steering wheel of a vehicle, and has come to be painted red like the CDA logo. Our colours are snow and blood. Reason and Nature. A popular symbol is blood on ice, representing combat.

This morning Toronto City Council voted to rename itself "Toronto Committee of Public Safety." The first act of the new body is to officially recognize the Upholders as "Protectors of the Party, the Revolution, and the People." The Upholders wear a white uniform with a red steering-wheel cross on the left shoulder. Very, very impressive!

The Upholders have conferred on Pappy the unique rank of "Great Captain." This in response to some ironic musings of his about not even being allowed a measly badge of recognition. Now he wears a white uniform with gold epaulettes and gold braid, and struts around the neighbourhood with friend Gerdie, who truly is not as meek as she used to be, but cultivates a hard look and wears army boots like Pa's.

Pa sure is enjoying himself. Only yesterday he was just another dull and faded old fart, bypassed by time, an exile in a foreign land. Now they worship the ground he treads. And no wonder. He turned the world on its head. He showed us that Fortune does indeed favour the bold and the brave. Now he struts like the top cock in the barnyard, like a dickie-bird among dee-dees.

Nevertheless, he's making an ass of himself.

"Stop this Mussolini posturing!" I insist. "Folding your arms and sneering over the heads of those that hail you — can't you see, Pa, it's ridiculous!"

"Now quit yer fessin', Rufus. Yer forgettin' someting. *I's de bye dat built de boat, I's de bye dat sails 'er. I's de captain. I's soon* to be master of all Upalong. Not bad for an old salt from Joe Batt's Arm. Don't ya tink dey's earned a few sneers, silly futters?"

Gerdie is getting names on a petition. Lots of names – she is, after all, a friend of the Great Captain. She intends to persuade our Block Committee that the dandelion ought to replace the trillium as Ontario's special flower. She wants to get at the Jinkerdiddles and all the others who can't stop rooting it out.

Gerdie has other demands. She wants the Committee of Public Safety to pass a law making it mandatory not to answer every second door knock or phone ring. Callers will not connect if the receiving party does not wait for at least six rings. Cell phones are being redesigned so they only work in closets. She wants the state to discourage phone use. Her aim is to turn down the tempo of living, which the Triffids kept slyly raising over the years to suit their own ends. She also wants all commercials to cease, and expects that those who tormented us with them in the past will be brought to trial and punished. She has recommended as well that the rock music be turned off at medical clinics, swimming pools, and bookstores. She is quoted in the paper as saying: *Have they gone completely nuts? What are they trying to do anyway? Drive us all bonkers?* The Triffids wanted us to dumb down, she says, while we were waiting our turn to have the juice sucked out of our brains.

I'm sorry to confess that Pa is not above a certain vindictiveness apropos of our good neighbours, the Jinkerdiddles. (Posterity will appreciate this honesty.) He does his best Mussolini poses in the street in front of their house, and encourages the crowd to admire him as he tramps back and forth on their lawn.

Small payment for years of torment from their side. We tried reasoning with them. We told them our space was sacred. We asked them to respect the force field. We warned them about our bubble. They did not understand. "We're no worse than anyone else." That was the best that Jinkerdiddle came up with.

So we built a fence. That was the last day we spoke to them.

Mrs. Jinker came out to watch. She had a little Jinker by the hand, teaching her to dislike us. She was also teaching the little one Fence Rage 101.

"You'll still hear us!" she threatened. "You'll still smell us! We'll pick your dandelions and mow your lawn!"

She was quite right. We heard and smelt them more ever since.

"What bad neighbours you are!" she said.

"Not as bad as we'd like to be," I replied.

"We've been here two years and you haven't said a word to us," she went on.

"Didn't know ye was lonely," Pappy told her. "Shoulda guessed it, I suppose, when Mister come over to cut de goose grass. Truth is, folk don't poke me fire less they knowed me seven years. Ye got five to go."

I ask Pappy if he's not inclined to bait the Jinkerdiddles.

"Nah, don't tink so."

"Well, do you need to spend so much time in front of their house?"

"I haven't kicked in their front door yet, has ya noticed?"

"At least stop gadding about in those seven-leaguers. You and Gerdie look like a couple of gnus newly fitted with horse shoes."

"That's yesterday's man ya be talkin' about. Today there's no shame to anyting I does, 'cause everybody knows me. Ain't that de way it works? They won't want to hear about me if I's narmal. Look around, bye, everybody's wearin' boots just like mine."

Gloria has a great new career. She has become the sultry voice of the Party on radio and TV. Today she begins her program by reading some aphorisms of Pappy from a little white book he authored, entitled, *These Self-evident Truths*. Gloria reads a few of her favourite lines:

1) *Triffids are never prepared, always impaired.*
2) *Triffid vehicles are time machines with the dial stuck on Mesozoic.*
3) *Triffids are always followers, even when they're way out in front.*

4) *In an emergency, Triffids will always react at a speed equal to the square of the velocity of their brain functions.*

5) *Triffids can wind their cars up to 100 in five seconds, and simultaneously accelerate their brains in reverse at the same speed.*

6) *Passing is the expression of the Triffid belief in unhinderability.*

7) *In the Triffid brain, rudeness runs in gear with the current level of frustration.*

8) *Triffids believe they are of the elect. That is why they think God Almighty had a hand in it when they collide.*

Way to go, Gloria! Great stuff! That's socking it to them! Pappy is so thrilled with that reading. He predicts a great future for her. Gloria's theme for the day is entitled *Number One.* She launches into it immediately:

Now ask yourselves honestly, folks: How many times have I regressed since the CDA took power? Go ahead and ask yourself. Nobody's going to turn you in.

Does the truth shock you, my dears? Yes? I thought it might,dear hearts. You know, it's not easy having the satanic wiles of Triffidus to contend with. You have my sympathy. Really you do. I want to reach out and touch you, embrace you, help you to conquer the evil inside you.

Those racy, primal images that have lodged in your skull pap—all those evil lifestyle videos you carry around inside you—they are just so, so seductive. So sexy. You know what they are, my dears. You know what they really are. That's right, our life of long, long ago. Those poor little critters we descend from. Yes, the ones who hid in the dandelions right under the belly of T-Rex. Doesn't it make your teeth rattle? We were small critters then, but we had appetites bigger than all the monsters of God's errant plan. We couldn't wait for our turn.

Can you feel that past of ours tugging at your little brain stem? Does it make you want to let your hair down and do something totally wild? Then you know what I mean, don't you? We're not trying to take it away from you. We wouldn't do that, now would we? You know I wouldn't deceive you. Not your dear friend, Gloria. You know I love you all. Honestly I do. But you knew that, didn't you? Sure you did.

A little harmless fun, that's all you want, isn't it? The lax life of the idiot. You know we'd never try to take it from you. Just don't try it in your car, that's all. Why, even the Wolfman locked himself up at night and threw away the key. That's why we loved him, in spite of what he did. And we will love you too if you can take a lesson from the Wolfman.

Be strong out there, my sweethearts. Fight impairment in its ten thousand different guises. If your brain is not up to it, leave your car where it is. Better still, call your Block Committee. They'll come over and pick it up. No more worries. Remember, take the tram or the bus and you get a free lunch.

And now, my dears, a little exercise for those who are feeling weak. Can you say these words after me? Sure you can. Are you ready? Here we go then: I know I can't drive. I don't know how to drive. I never did know how to drive. I have never known anything about driving. In fact, I was ignorant of just about everything. I was brainwashed. I was a slave of the toxic culture of buy and sell — a servant of Triffidus. I had no mind of my own.

That's wonderful, my sweet listeners out there. Now, take a deep breath. Again repeat after me: I am not Number One. I am a miserable blasphemer for the high-and-mighty thoughts I had. The world is not my oyster. The world owes me nothing. It is I who am the debtor.

There, now didn't that make you feel better?

Magnifico, Gloria!

Gloria drives the men nuts. It's necessary. Fight fire with fire. We must employ every tool at our disposal. We have ages of evil mind-bending to undo.

Even as Gloria speaks, folk line up to turn in their old plates — those with the number "1", or anything else that might be a sign of dangerous or delusory mental aberrations.

Gloria announces that this week the Silver Wheel award goes to the Toronto police for being, in her words, *the first force to admit publicly that nine out of ten of its officers can't drive for beans.*

Sergeant B.B. Granguff, accepting the award, promises that all officers will receive immediate instruction in defensive driving, and will not patrol in a cruiser until the Party certifies them. Sergeant Granguff admits the training is long overdue:

In the past, driving was a personal concern. All we did was instruct our officers in the physics, and occasionally in the ethics, of chasing down criminals. It's hard to believe, but we took it for granted that, when not so engaged, our officers would know what to do. The appalling loss of good women and men that has lately befallen us is an awful price to pay for negligence. From now on there will be no more racing to the donut shop. The Force apologizes to the Party and the People for its longstanding dereliction of duty. We can and we will do better.

Pappy and I are taking a break from the news. We find the crucifixion close-ups no more entertaining than when they zoom in on pavement pools of blood at murder and collision scenes. I guess those guys with the cameras have got their orders: If there's blood there, be sure you get it.

We're watching *The Blob,* starring the incomparable Steve McQueen. It's the intriguing story of a piece of galactic jelly. The jelly blob starts small but quickly grows by osmotically ingesting every creature in its way. It flows around its prey like an amoeba, completely enveloping it, and digesting it externally through the containing membrane.

A young couple are necking in a car, approximately same vintage as Pappy's. Lonely spot in the country. They're only having fun. But we know evil lurks in the dark woods nearby. We know the Blob will get them. We have our sadist expectations. We think, oh no, the Blob is going to get them! But part of us wants to see it happen. We want to see them pay the price for turning their backs to the dark, for feeling secure, for having so much fun. We miss our Balder fire and the stranger at the stake. Innocence pounced upon and brutally destroyed. It's a theme that endures and is dear to the human heart. Rape, murder and mayhem—it's what we love and live by.

Heavy thumps at the front door knock us off the edge of our seats. The Block Committee marches in. Bunch of kids, full of themselves. All dressed in white with the red logos brazenly flashing. Cleated combat boots biting into the hall floor.

Who the hell invited them?

What a nerve, they turn off the set! They terminate *The*

Blob! They cast probing, contemptuous glances. Abedni sent them – that's my first thought. The Professor is going to eliminate us. The mistakes we made begin to race through my mind.

But a glance at Pappy tells me I'm wrong. Impossible that we could have so mistaken the character of the Professor. Watching *The Blob* has predisposed us to fear. But Pappy quickly brings his wits to play. "Explain yerselves, young pucklins," he says, looking the ring-leader squarely in the eye. "What's yer name, young gaffer?"

"De-de-Dragon Slayer," the leader stutters. He can't take Pappy's withering gaze. Besides, he's just realized who he's talking to. So we imagine they've been going the rounds, terrorizing households at random. This time they picked the wrong one.

"Well, young gatcher, that's a fine name. Get down on yer knees now."

What a chuckle! What a nice way to say it! As though genuflection in Pappy's presence were a minor point of protocol!

They all fall to the floor. And Pappy's right. The nerve of them to turn off *The Blob*!

Dragon Slayer is making strange plosive sounds in the rug. Pappy seems to know what he's saying though. "Proposal? Is that it? What proposal?"

"Wa-wa-wa-"

"One Hundred. Proposal 100. Is that it? Thought so."

"Why," I say, "that's the bill that would broaden the Up-holders' mandate to allow them to deal with stupidity in general, and not just what's dumb on the road."

At these words, Dragon Slayer looks up at me gratefully and says, "Also-also- to get the ta-ta-ta-"

"Take yer time, Mr. Slayer. Dat's de stuff."

"Get the ta-ta-Triffids for their thuh-thuh-thuh-"

"Get 'em for their thoughts, is that it? I knowed ye'd be askin'. De Professor sent ye, didinim? Is he also larnin' ye how to fly?"

Pa goes to the window and looks out. The kids are sweating like pigs on a spit. Pa knows they can't stand waiting, because they're Triffids. They're like the mysterious voice at the drive-thru when you need to study the menu. If you don't know what you want, they call the cops. Silence has no value to them. To them it's a threat. Just as their snouts are drawn to empty space as though by a magnet, so are they driven to fill silence with noise.

Pa takes me aside and says, "They can nail at least half of humanity on actions alone. But thoughts! Wouldn't be nobody left. We all has bad thoughts. As for stupidity, why 'tis endemic to de race. Triffids tryin' to screw tings up, that's what they be."

"Yeah, Pa. Say you'll get back to them. They'll understand that. We'll have to figure some way to neutralize them. Just give me the nod and I'll see them nailed up tomorrow."

Pa gives Dragon Slayer a kick in the butt. "Get de hell out, all o' ye! Write me a letter! Don't dare come trampin' in here again!"

They can't be gone fast enough. But they leave behind a red and white envelope with the seal of the Toronto Committee of Public Safety. It's a warrant for the arrest of Gordon McDuff.

GOGOGO

At Osgoode Hall a young Upholder recognizes me with a fawning leer and ushers me to a pew in the front row.

A rather sensible-looking woman in middle age, prim and business-like, is being tried under the new *Nuisance Act*. From where I enter the proceedings, I gather she is one of those poor creatures imbued with the spirit of Gogogo, the tribal god of MCS, or Mindless Compulsive Scurrying. She calls herself a fast-tracker who knows how to get the most out of life. She wept when she was not permitted to have her electronic notebook and her cell phone in court, claiming she had a little girl's teddy-bear attachment to them.

"Blind, habitual rudeness," I hear the Crown Prosecutor say as I enter.

The doomer, a kindly octogenarian, obviously back from retirement, appears to take a fatherly interest in the defendant, and questions her in tones disarmingly soothing: "My dear lady, I understand it was not easy to get round the aggrieved, as the street in question is an ordinary residential thoroughfare with not much room to pass? What made you honk and race by the way you did?"

Her voice is clear and self-assured. "I was going home to lunch, sir. I usually hurry home – well, don't we all? Does there have to be a reason? We never had to give reasons before. This man was in my way, Your Honour. He was holding me up, and blatantly. He refused to go any faster than the limit."

The prosecution chuckle over these unguarded utterances, while the aged doomsayer looks despondent: "Madam, the

Court does not doubt that you were rude and in defiance of the law. I can only wonder what you do when on foot. Do you follow on the heels of strangers? Do you worry them, and when you can't get by, do you then make rude noises?"

"But, Your Honour, I only honked."

"The Court interprets your honk as, 'Get out of my way!'"

"Oh no, Your Honour. It was more like, 'Yoo-hoo! Here I come!'"

The doomer laughs. So also do the lady's three little grand-children, and her husband and two sons. Fine family, you can see that. Earlier, they had all told the Court how they loved her, and what a wonderful person she was, and other expres-sions of endearment and appreciation.

What a terror comes over this family now, as the doom-sayer's black mask comes down over those seemingly com-passionate eyes, closing them off and ruling out pity and help forever! This truly is justice that a Danton or a Robe-spierre would be proud to recognize.

I am preparing to follow the crowd over to the parkway for the nailing, when the obsequious Upholder approaches me: "We have someone special in custody, sir." This he tells me drooling.

Out of curiosity I follow him down into the dank of the basement. He directs me to an obscure grotto with cells on either side – the basement has recently been redone to serve as the ideal holding area for Triffid scum. I'm told the model used was a medieval torture chamber in the bowels of a German castle.

Peering into the interior of a particular cell through the grill of a great oaken door, I spy in the gloom a figure. A youngish man, it seems, in spite of the growth of beard, the dirt and the bruises, and other ravages of this hole. He's curled up in a corner and looking very abject and forlorn.

"I don't know him," I tell the guide. But even as I say it, I recall surrendering my black book to the Committee of Pub-lic Safety. In it are plate numbers, vehicle descriptions, and driver characteristics. Now they call it *The Codex* and are planning a mass execution for all those who made it into my diary of the road, my 'Doomsday Roster.'

"Page 56," he tells me, grinning lasciviously. He probably has the whole thing memorized.

"Was it Danforth and Warden? The guy who feigned a sideswipe and took out a lamp post just because I did two legal stops while he was behind me?"

"Not that one, sir. He's dead. Finished him off myself with that great new rack."

"I have it. It's Ally Oop, isn't it? The bastard who tried to make Julie turn in front of a Thunderbird?"

"That's him. That's the bugger all right. Want to give him a few prods with a hot iron? He's had a good rest since the last session, and I fed him some swine slops last night, so he oughta be nice and fresh."

So that's what our trucker looks like. A decent average guy. Not the kind you'd think would be driving around trying to frighten young ladies.

"Hey!" I call through the bars. "Hey you! Take heart, man. The cross is not near as bad as folk think. Once the nails are through, the endorphins take over. You'll look down on the world and smile, if I know anything. Consider yourself lucky."

He turns his face toward me. His gaze is vacant. Too bad, I think. His mother will be sorry. But he went through life, no doubt, as he went through traffic, elbowing and blowing his horn, like the true lout and nerve jangler he is. Who can say what his legacy may be?

"No last words of remorse?" I ask him. "A final word to edify the young?"

He barely gets his hand up to give the Triffid Sign.

"When is he due to be nailed?" I ask the Upholder.

"Tomorrow, sir."

"Tomorrow, eh? With gas and brake pedal hanging from his neck, the symbols of Stop and Go, the only two principles he had to guide him."

"Why, yes sir."

"Well, my good man, I have another idea." I take him by the arm and tell him my thoughts. Then I get on over to the nailing of the woman.

I arrive as they are affixing her to a fine tall cross, which happens with great agony and gut-wrenching screams from the lady – I can't believe any of it is really necessary. Then she is raised on the east side of the Parkway, about half a kilometre south of the Bloor Street Viaduct. She'll hang there till the crows pick her clean. I know in days to come I will not pass by this place without the wretched images of her family, especially the babies weeping.

From the Bloor Viaduct a line of crosses stretches away to the north and to the south. So it was in ancient times along the Appian and Flaminian Ways.

The bridge has become a popular place to view this grand though sombre scene from history. Folk come with binoculars and a picnic lunch, bringing their children and making a day of it. "Look," they say to their offspring, "all those bad people are paying their debt. They appear to get off lightly, as they'll soon be out of misery. But they never thought they would need to pay anything."

The children giggle and range over the crucified, in case they can find one who is "fresh," or at least alive. And often it is not difficult, since many of the felons linger for days. And when the children find one, they zoom in on the face to see what agony looks like – and if they're lucky, to catch the moment of death.

Nevertheless, on humanitarian grounds it is forbidden to taunt or otherwise torment the condemned from close up.

25

JUST SOMETHING THAT HAPPENED

As I pass through the regional forest, a strange mist partly dissolves the farther trees. But at a scrubby place with small deciduous trees and bushes, I spy the shadow of a premonition. Some part of Pa that's in me makes me shiver. So I head on home to Gascap Bend to eat pomelo.

I find Pa already eating his.

"What?" I say, when he gives me a pained look.

He shows me the daily paper and it's all in there. Twisted metal, the faces of the dead. Head-on collision at Blind Summit, the place where some kids go to race their cars. If you have enough speed, all four wheels will leave the ground coming over the crest. The kids call it "catching air."

But the only face that gives me pain is Julie's. Julie's dead, along with five others, including her father. Each face seems to say: "Look at me. I'm an idiot. I'm destined to die this way." But not Julie's. Her face tells me it doesn't belong with the others.

No, no, it can't be true. Not the Julie I knew, of such great promise.

I scan the details. McDuff was fleeing his date with justice. Julie was beside him, supporting him to the last. She would not abandon him. That's how loyal she was.

I skip the rest, my eyes picking out nonetheless words like *explosion, fireball, burned alive*. I throw the paper aside, sickened. I can't do anything for the rest of the day. I can only think of the horror Julie must have lived through during those last long seconds of her life. At night I lie awake thinking about what happened. Julie didn't deserve it. The others maybe, but not Julie. She would have been a great driver. I curse the gods, any power in heaven or hell that had a hand in it, or that let it happen, or that put such an illogical and unjust world in place to begin with.

At dawn I go downtown and arrange to have Ally Oop and others like him brought together in a school gym. The trucks are there when I arrive, two tractor cabs with fine horns. The horns are set to go non-stop and the felons are paraded around the gym. They walk defiantly and shake their fists at us, and make the Finger Sign, as we watch from an upstairs window. But on day two we refine the process, so the blast is infrequent but can come at any time – while they're eating, sleeping, or on the can. On the third day they're all deaf. On the fourth day signs of mental dishevelment appear – surprise, surprise! Some roll on the floor. Others go fetal with hands pressed to their ears.

At last they're getting their just deserts. They tormented us for years and years for no good reason. They blasted us because we wouldn't drive like them. They worried us for being good drivers. Who knows how many ears and nerves and hearts they ruined? They had no idea of what the horn was really for. They thought God Almighty had given it to Moses on the Mount for them to use against us.

Lenard Klutz, of all people! I encounter him there and he greets me fondly, daring to give me a little clap on the shoulder. I dart him a sulphurous look. He draws back. He tells me he's been doing well in the CDA. I wonder how he made it in but don't bother asking. He's risen from section leader to whip and carries an ugly black lash as the symbol of his authority.

"You won't get rid of them that way," he says cockily. "Too slow. What you want to do, Great Master, is build a gigantic horn specially for the purpose and set it up at SkyDome. You could terminate thousands at a time."

"Stick to your whipping," I tell him. Then the two of us have a go at the horns. I'm surprised to discover what fun it is to see them jump and cower and cry. I believe it's just what they felt in some way when they were tormenting us.

At this point their nervous systems are self-destructing. Some are having spasms, others are trying to climb the wall or hitting their heads on the floor. Many of them are fighting and trying to bite each other in the tail. A few just sit and weep or chatter incoherently to themselves.

Why, there's Ally Oop! My God, he's far gone! Hair's on end. Eyes are popping. He staggers about with one hand on a fancied steering wheel. With the other he gives the Triffid salute. He's trying to spit on everyone but he's too dry.

Torture! It's a time-honoured game for hurting souls. A remedy from the Stone Age. By Balder, it works!

I go from there bolstered in the certain knowledge the Triffid reign is over. Too bad Julie had to be crushed by the Triffids just as we are poised to crush all of them.

At least, I console myself, the Triffids will not mock and dishonour her memory in the old way. They will not dare raise their whiny voices, making time-worn calls for more bells, louder whistles, brighter lights, straighter roads, tougher penalties – whatever – as long as nothing changes. As long as they can keep the pap in their skulls. As long as the world is made for Triffids.

What about commercials – beer ads, car ads? What about images? What about videos, TV, movies? What about the way we live? The way we are? The people we've become? What about all that? These are the questions asked in the Party paper, *The Star of Reason*. Isn't there a lot we need to change? Haven't we been busy churning out the ether that Triffids love to breathe? Haven't the Triffids corroded our culture? Commercialized it to death, making it toxic to all but the brain-dead? Haven't they put us on a slimy path to the sink, where we smother in emptiness and drown in the ooze of alienation?

And yet the poor Triffids never cease to believe that happiness is just around the corner. That is why we call them counterfeits and shadows.

The Committee of Public Safety has acted swiftly and admirably, dragging off the parents of the crash victims in the middle of the night, Mrs. McDuff with them. Also roused and taken away are various media impresarios, ad persons and image-makers, corporate leeches, auto journalists, beer barons, and other low-life from the culture of exploitation.

They are all persuaded to sign a general confession acknowledging their collective responsibility, after which they are put on display at the Forum, formerly known as City Hall. Thus they can no longer hide from the people. A large cage protects them. Nothing may be hurled into the pen except rotten eggs and mouldy tomatoes.

In the days following the collision, the impact site is very busy with visits by relatives and friends of the dead, reporters, people who live along the road, police, and insurance investigators. They try to visualize or reconstruct the train of events leading up to the impact, according to the nature of their interest. And so do I.

I hear the friends of Snookums and the others talking in hushed voices. I think, no wonder you get it wrong. You have to counter the whole culture on your own. The culture of exploitation. I want to roar: Rejoice! Now you have the Party. Being stupid won't doom you. But instead I just listen.

A brassy snippet, with a modified Iroquois cut and a ring through everything that will take one, is telling off a reporter from *The Star of Reason*. I observed her earlier heaving her heart out in the bosom of a male friend.

"Fuckin' right they were goin' fast," she barks into the reporter's face. "So what? The fuckin' world runs on fast. Where you fuckin' been lately?"

The Star of Reason guy is not buying: "It's called 'the lemming factor,' girlie. Ever heard of lemmings? Ever heard of Monkey see, monkey do? Had your brain tested lately?"

You can see and hear she hasn't.

"Ya gotta go sometime, bud," her boyfriend pipes up. The girl laughs, showing her bad teeth stained with tobacco.

"There's a new spirit at work," the newspaper guy tells them. "This kind of wasting of lives does not need to happen. Young people are determined to put an end to it."

No surprise, the girl gives the Triffid salute, the infamous Finger Sign. It does what it always does. It magnifies her ugliness exponentially. It has, of course, no other effect on real people.

Then the vulgar tit tries another tack: "You know what the Party can do. Like, shove it. Ya know what I mean? Why don't you people mind your own business? This thing here, it's just something that happened. There doesn't have to be a reason. Like, people make mistakes, that's all. Sometimes things just happen, ya know what I mean?"

Sure, we know what you mean. We also know what you are.

The reporter's write-up, as it appears in *The Star of Reason*, tells us that this girl and her boyfriend have been brought to the New Age Sanatorium suffering from toxic culture shock, *to have their brains flushed of Triffid poisons, as we see that their minds are like broken toilets. The shit, instead of falling into the bowl, winds up in the box.*

TRIUMPH OF PROFESSOR ABEDNI

I am purposely late as I approach the steps. The honour guard comes to attention. One of the troopers is Klutz – I expect he assigned himself to the duty as a "friend" of mine. I've been told one of his first acts as an Upholder was to bring his own father to trial and to personally oversee the nailing.

The priest, wearing his robe of consoler, is right into it as I enter. Heads swivel as an attendant brings me a chair that creaks when I sit on it. There are some old uniforms – McDuff's comrades from the force. Mrs. McDuff, released from torture to attend, is at the very front with her head hung.

I hear the priest but I'm not listening. Somebody coughs. Somebody always does. Is there any purpose in this rite, I wonder? What can anybody possibly say? My stomach, it's going to growl. I take the fairy bun from my pocket and bite off a piece. Doesn't get down in time. The snarl comes just as a cop rises to give the eulogy for McDuff.

I admit I'm not feeling very reverent and tiptoe out. I hurry past the guard while I button my coat. Snow is falling and it squeaks underfoot. I can't help thinking, the crucified are going to freeze to death on a day like this.

"Tell me about those Tauans," I insist at last, one day when Pappy comes in from a séance in Chevy. "They're the guys in the garage, aren't they? Come on, Pa. Some day you won't be

here. Not even Newfies last forever. So tell me while you can."
Pa scratches his head like a dog, as though my question is
a bothersome tick or a flea. He says he's not sure what they
want. It's not something you find out right away.
Then he tells me again about his first meeting with them:
"There was lots of stars that night, Rufus me bye. I was
almost alone on de road, so me brain were on cruise. All at
once I hears this quiet babble – not like ordinary talk, mind;
more like de music of a brook or a little waterfall. I almost
jumps out o' me seat when I notices a lad in a sealskin sittin'
beside me. Though he were in shadow and wearin' a sou'
wester, his face shone like de glim on an ice field. There was
two just like 'im sittin' in de back. They all had eyes a bit too
big to be like ourn. Udderwise, I woulda thought they's
spirits of old comrades lost at sea. Or, dear God, maybe fore-
fadders of mine. Or just de fairies catchin' up wit me."
"Did they speak?"
"Well, yes, they did. We didn't talk, though. I just knowed
what was in their minds and they knowed what was in mine.
They wanted to go for a ride in Chevy. I asked them where
they was from. Down East, says one. Tau, says anudder. So
what's I to make of that? So me next thought is, what are ye
doin' so far from home? They says narmally they follows de
fishermen. But now as there ain't no fish, and hardly no
fishermen left, I's de bye to follow, cause I's born wit a caul.
They come to see me fish Triffids, and make de world a good
place to be again."
"Amazing!"
"They sartainly put de word 'Triffid' in me mind. I thought
at once of those classic movies, and I knowed what de sealers
meant. True North was goin' down de drain. People was lettin' themselves be turned into miserable zombies. Those
fairies or aliens was expectin' me to do someting about it.
Well, they come to de right man. I were ready for de message.
And before I got to Gascap Bend that night I had a twenty-
year plan. That were back in 1990. In twenty years, I said to
meself, there won't be no Triffids. And now very soon there
won't be neither."

"Gosh Pa, that puts you in the first rank with the great revolutionaries of our time. The world is in your debt."

Pa makes a few faces in the service of modesty, but I know he's enjoying his triumph immensely.

"So then, Pa, you're not sure where these — ah — apparitions in sealskins originate?"

"Oh, but I am sure. I knows what Tau is. A place where Newfoundlanders go when they passes on."

Pa, Gloria, and I go to see Jinkerdiddle in the hospital. He's suffering from hamburger disease, and when he sees us, he thinks we've come to finish him off. It takes a couple of nurses with strong arms to restrain him.

He blames us for poisoning him.

"It was one of your fanatics, Albert Prince, that served me that hamburger. It was full of meat and poisoned with good sense. But we Triffids are made of stardust. You can't destroy us."

"Silly man," says Gloria. "We are all made of stardust. We came because you're our neighbour."

"Brought ya some pissabed wine. Thought it might cheer ya up."

"It's all right," I assure Jinkerdiddle. "Made from the dandelions in our backyard. Nobody peed on 'em."

Jinkerdiddle makes a face and tries to get his fingers into position.

"No use to give us the Sign, sir," I tell him. "We warned you about those juicy hamburgers. You Triffids can take the beef only in small doses. That's why we let you mow our lawn. Didn't want you to feel threatened, you know."

I also explain to him that you can't force people to understand. You can't force them to be rational. You can't force them to be reasonable. It's up to him to get his head on straight. If he can't manage it, there will be consequences — very serious consequences.

"You're through mowin' udder folks' lawns," Pa tells him. "You're done pluckin' udder peoples' posies."

His only answer is to froth at the mouth.

Professor Abedni has one last surprise in store for us – a great one. What an amazing fellow! In all the upheaval of the Terror, he actually manages to bring his brain-scan experiments to a successful completion. This is what we read in *The Star of Reason*:

What a grand old guy this Radshak Abedni is! A fount of wisdom he is, and yet so unassuming. He ventures shyly forth to greet us from the shadow of his cyclotron, two cute little cats in tow, one black and one white. His manner is hesitant – timid even. He looks like an ancient hermit surprised in his cave. But when we broach his triumph, the pride wells up in those soulful eyes and he almost weeps.

"I've done it!" he tells me excitedly, again and again, trembling with feeling. The two cats go round our feet in circles, and in their plaintive mews seem to say it too: "He's done it!" What this amazing man of the future has done is prove beyond any doubt that the average driver gets from A to B with almost no use of the brain, and sometimes with no brain at all. How did he do this? With the help of a fine little instrument, a miniature positron tomography scanner, known as PET. Developed by the Doctor himself, it is the first PET in the world of such small size. It has the capability of showing the brain doing whatever it does, whether it's thinking, solving problems, or being sexually aroused. The Doctor assured me he spent long hours testing the device on himself.

The mild-mannered genius was interviewed at the Clarke Institute of Psychiatry, actually in the concrete bunker housing the cyclotron. It is the cyclotron which produces the radioactive material needed in scanning.

Professor Abedni has been holed up in the bunker for several weeks. We asked him if it were hard work or shyness that kept him locked up like that. A pained look came over his gentle visage. "My work," he said, "it's everything. Long live the Revolution!"

The first drivers were given brain scans last month. After being fitted with the mini-scanners, they were injected with a glucose substance (brain fuel) to which radioactive material had been added as a tag, thus enabling the scanner to follow the sugar. Areas of the brain that are active take up extra sugar. On a larger unit, active areas

213

Last Days
of Driving

would light up on a computerized image of the brain. But on the tiny mobile units, the information is merely coded for subsequent computer interpretation.

Three thousand drivers were involved in the research – half men, half women. They all followed the same route in their vehicles. The runs were spread over several days and were all scheduled between 1400 and 1600 hours.

With all the data transferred to the Institute's computer, Dr. Abedni was able to display a coloured three-dimensional history of each driver's brain during the run.

"Dear me, it is the first direct way to observe a living brain in action," said the gleeful professor. "Now, you may think I am contradicting myself, but most of the brains we observe here on this screen appear rather to be dead than living. Ninety percent of these drivers exhibit a predominantly blue and black spectrum, indicating an absence of brain activity. And please note, though the brains of men and women are not in every respect identical, this in no way influences the basic gender equality in the results of the experiment."

Dr. Abedni suspects the scans of some drivers that registered briefly in the brighter part of the spectrum may have done so as a result of sexual stimuli encountered along the way. "PET is very good at that, you know," he told us. I asked him if the proof were irrefutable: "Oh, my goodness, absolutely. Their brains are off. Period."

The Professor admitted he is also investigating certain molecules that act as an on/off switch for the genes controlling brain chemistry. "Yes, indeed, we may soon have the key to the greatest mystery of our race," he confided.

"What mystery is that, sir?" I asked. The two cats stopped pacing and sat side by side to look on, as if they too awaited the answer. The Professor smiled and gave me a playful poke in the ribs. "The mystery, my friend, is why we have brains but don't use them."

I have to admit, his experiment does prove the point. I suggested he had to take great satisfaction in a discovery with such enormous implications for a world on wheels.

He chortled and muttered something indistinct – the hum of the cyclotron played havoc with the acoustics. It sounded like "sweet revenge."

I then asked the Doctor, as the great guru of the Revolution, to comment on the amazing empowerment of youth and elders. But the only *words I could make out were, "Thank God, I'm free at last!" Whether he was referring to his own personal liberation in our glorious Revolution, or to something exclusively spiritual, or merely to the end of a scientific task, and a job well done – who can say?*

FACING THE VAST UNKNOWN

"C'mon, Pa, it's just Tom, Dick, or Harry in a rut. Or Sara, Jane, or Jill. That's what a Triffid is. A poor, used, little earth creature. You don't need to go beyond this planet. So let's have no more talk about interstellar influences."

It's so hard for Pappy to back down and abandon the stars. But Gloria is with me.

"Rufus is right," she says. "Triffids don't need to be aliens. Why can't they be plain, old-fashioned, dumb twits, like I was? But now I'm free. My eyes are wide open and I don't miss a thing. I'm not afraid of space and time, and when I hurry it's always slowly. We're all Vulcans now, Dad, thanks to you."

Boy, what a swayer of hearts she turned out to be! My sandals didn't matter after all. Gloria got her brain back and what a brain it is! And now everybody loves her.

"Well," says Pa, after some thought, "I ain't one to stickle. I harks to what folks say. There's no shame to comin' about if de wind starts to haul. But I knows what I knows. There's no goin' back, girl."

"Dad, no one can steal your glory. Everybody knows you are the one who put our planet on red alert. They know you hauled us back from the brink at the eleventh hour. You uncovered the Triffid. You showed the world just how numerous Triffids are. You laid bare the extent of their evil. You made them visible by giving them a name. And now they cannot escape. Now they must reclaim their brains as I did, or else be nailed. Everyone knows who did this. The whole

world thanks you. You have done the human race an inestimable service."

What a grin on Pa's face! He's waited twenty years to hear
someone say that.

"I'll be jigged, girl! That's a lot I done, idinit?"

"Gloria's right, Pa. No more talk about osmotic infusion or
brains being like tea bags. Okay?"

"Well, guess I couldn't prove it. Okay, I'll drop that. But
you ain't denyin' Tau—de guys in de garage, remember?"

"I saw them with my own eyes, Pa. But if they want the
world to know about them, they don't need you or me."

"Yeah, that's de truth."

"Tell you what, Pa. We'll call *The Star of Reason* and ask them
to send someone over. They're bound to ask us if we're really
under attack from the bowels of the universe. That will be
your chance to say, yes, the human race has been in retreat;
yes, an alien force is trying to destroy the human spirit; yes,
that alien force is the Triffid. But no, the Triffid is not an
invader from the Big Deep. The Triffid is a metaphor. An
ingenious figure of speech."

"A metaphor is it?" Pa scratches like a mutt roused for a
walk. "Chevy won't like it."

"It will get the Doctor off our backs," I try. "I'd hate to see
some of the things Abedni might tell the reporters."

"All right, Dad?" Gloria coos.

"I'll tink about it," Pappy promises.

We visit the great Doctor in his bunker. We discuss ways to
rein in the zealots, end the anarchy, curtail the terror. My
first thought is that the Professor considers the situation
hopeless. The hum of the cyclotron has mesmerized him. He
looks like Number One, fishing for nothing. We have no idea
this will be the last time we ever see him.

"My God, it is shocking what they are doing to each other
out there! It is unbelievable!"

That is the Doctor's first remark after our long pounding
with a rock, together with shouted reassurances as to our

identity, get him at long last to open the great door to the cyclotron.

Of course he's well, he tells us. Yet he ducks his own shadow. This is the man they call "the great guiding light of the Revolution," this flickering candle, who hides and cringes from the dark eternity outside. The two cats pace restlessly and mew neurotically, like the devil familiars of some olden wizard of evil.

"Dear me, what they will not do to each other! It is so dreadful! It is cataclysmic! They say the U.S. is going to invade. My God, I am afraid the Yanks are in for it again, poor devils!" The Professor gives a crazed little laugh, whether of gloating or hysteria we cannot tell. Perhaps it is both, perhaps neither. "Gloria, how are you, my dear? Would you like a bowl of rice? Not much to offer, now that the commercial infrastructure has collapsed like a house of cards. But we schemers will take the rice any day. It is a small price to pay to get our minds in order, what? You are such a magnificent propagandist. I mean it sincerely. You have seduced millions into following the Party line. You have done what the Soviets failed to do in seventy years – dealt this toxic culture a lethal blow. You shall be forever hailed in the annals of just revolt as the greatest upstart and rabble-rouser of them all. But I must caution you. We have remained aloof from the fracas for good reason. Lightning strikes first at those in high places. There is going to be plenty of lightning for a while. I would not want you to finish like Danton or Robespierre. I would not like to see you nailed to a cross in the Valley of the Shadow of Death. Please endeavour to be less visible for a while, my dear."

"Poo-poo," she says.

"Do not worry, Radshak. Pa and I will keep watch for her. We have our contingency plans."

"Yes, of course. So do I."

We ask the Professor for his opinion on the Triffid question, outlining for him the recent consensus we arrived at. We shall no longer represent the Triffid threat as an extraterrestrial one.

"Quite right. Excellent. Dear me, better not to take too hard a line either. I truly believe many of them can return to full humanity. But they need a great shock. They are getting it now, heh-heh. If we can make them slow down, they will be able to start their computers. They need some serenity. It is a key concept. Right now they are all smitten with MCS — Mindless Compulsive Scurrying. And so they are like crazed squirrels. Their larders are full, but they are still frantically gathering nuts on the last day before winter. For them it is always the last day before winter. There is always another nut they have to have."

"Yeah, Professor, and they always run out of time before they run out of nuts," I add.

"Well," says Pappy, "I's made some compromises, but I still tinks a kind of spiritual sponging takes place. And in de process, de best impulses in de human mind gets lost, often-times for good."

"Probably," we are pleased to hear the Professor agree. "No doubt you are right, Albert, my dear friend. But we must help whom we can if we hope to salvage some good opinion of us in the judgement of history. Gloria, this is something you can do. Persuade them that all they need to do — and I cannot emphasize this too strongly — is refuse to take part."

"Golly, Professor, you mean break away from the dum-mies?"

"Yes, my dear. They must have the courage to make a break from the great confraternity of idiots. They must dare to set standards. They must want to live in a sane world. The first step is to get their brains back. The rest is easy."

Pappy's nodding. He agrees. And so do Gloria and I. There is no other way things will change. They must want to turn themselves back into decent folk, like the kind we were when we lived off the land or the ocean, only a short while ago in time. And we drank our water from a well and watched the brine on the kraut rise in the full of the moon. We knew less, but in many ways were wiser.

Everybody is smiling now. No more rift in the Party. I am fully persuaded of the correctness of our position. I never really believed that Triffids had to be shot from overpasses. Nor do I think they should be nailed to crosses like the poor lost souls hanging in the Valley of the Shadow of Death.

I can only hope, when the Terror ends, as soon it has to, we will all know what to do to keep and foster the Spirit of Humankind, and to guard the soul of True North, so that we can all be proud men and women again, instead of spineless counterfeits.

"And now, my good friends, I feel like flying," the Professor tells us jubilantly. "We have done our best; it is all anyone can do. In due time all will be known, and we will be at home in the universe. But until then – what do you say we sneak over to the university and do something civilized? I will prepare tea and chutney. Then I will show you the light and harmony of yogic flying."

"In due time," we all say, or something equally non-committal. And we have a good laugh. We shake the Doctor's hand. Gloria kisses him on the cheek.

We give each other a parting caution: Be careful. Do not open if you get a knock in the middle of the night.

On a clear night, when you can see a good piece of forever, and if the venomous street flies have droned off to some other quarter, Pappy and I go up on the roof with the telescope and take turns peering out into the Great Peace, the maelstrom that is our galaxy. There is where our destiny lies.

Are the other stars also stars of misery? Do we flourish and die for a purpose? If our star went, would it make any difference? Odd that we can ask the questions long before the answers are ready.

There is a sign in our window that says: "Out of town, serving the Revolution." Pa and I have tired of playing demagogue. There will be no more harangues.

Pappy continues to commune with Tau and the sealers. After the latest conference in Chevy, he solemnly proclaimed that each Triffid had an id which yearned to fire at trucks on the highway. That was the same night we stayed up to see *The Forbidden Planet*.

The idea is too dangerous to let pass. Gloria and I lay down the law. We forbid Pappy ever again to say, think, write, or dream anything about ids.

It was a shame, really, that we declined the Professor's invitation. And Pa is sorry now for not having treated the great man more like a friend and less like a rival. Because as the months pass, it becomes clear to us that we will not see him again.

Pappy's first notion was to consider him murdered by some Triffid goon. But lately he's had the temerity to suggest that Radshak may have returned whence he came – not Asia, but Tau Ceti!

Gloria and I refuse to respond to that.

At the University, witnesses are not lacking who say the Doctor's yoga at last attained perfect enlightenment. They claim to have seen him achieve the long-sought levitation while bouncing on his mattress. And though they think it took him by surprise, he drifted the full length of the gym, waved to them as he passed through an open window, and rose into the heavens until he was no longer visible.

We must keep an open mind on the nature of his fate. After all, Doctor Abedni was the genius who empirically demonstrated that nine drivers out of ten do what they do without any use of the upper cortex whatsoever. And together with Pappy, he showed us how these miserable shadows could conquer their meanness and reclaim the stature granted them by destiny.

Pa has the last word: "Frog-floppin' and mattress-hoppin' aside, he were a bye to be reckoned with. Such a yarry wizard might well find a way to his far star, or even into paradise."

But the black cat and the white cat are gone, and so is the Harley.

What was it Abedni said? "If sanity ever returns to the road, that is where I will be. On my beautiful bike."

W. MESSER was born in St. John's, Newfoundland, and has Lunenburg as well as Newfoundland roots. He attended school in Halifax and Toronto. After earning a B.A. at the University of Gothenburg, Sweden, and a B.Ed. at the University of Toronto, he taught English as a Second Language and Driver Education.

Mr. Messer is firmly committed to a revolution in the way Canadians drive. In car, on a one-to-one basis with students, he has taught 1000 people of all ages to drive "with their brains turned on." At present he lives in a mobile home near Gravenhurst, Ontario.

The author welcomes and encourages comments on the book and can be reached at *wmesser@thesink.ca*, or through the mail, care of: Breller Books, Box 789, Gravenhurst, Ontario, Canada P1P 1V1.

For more information about *The Sink*, please visit the web site: *www.thesink.ca*.

To order additional copies of
The Sink: The Last Days of Driving

Please try your local bookstore,
or order direct from:

Breller Books
Box 789
Gravenhurst, Ontario, P1P 1V1
Canada

An order form is available on the web site
www.thesink.ca

Canadian orders

Please send $19.95 plus $6.00 shipping, handling,
and GST. For each additional book in the same order,
send $19.95 plus $2.50 shipping, handling, and GST.

U.S. and elsewhere

Please send US$15.95 plus US$5.00 shipping and
handling. For each additional book in the same
order, send US$15.95 plus US$1.00 shipping and
handling.

Payable by cheque or money order, in Canadian or
U.S. funds only. Allow four weeks for delivery in
Canada and the U.S., up to six weeks elsewhere.